CW01261784

THE SHOW WOMAN

About the Author

Emma Cowing is an award-winning journalist and writer. She has written for a wide number of publications including the *Sunday Times*, *Scottish Daily Mail*, *Guardian Weekend Magazine*, *Spectator* and *Scotsman*.

Emma is a former Feature Writer of the Year at the Scottish Press Awards, and two-time Interviewer of the Year. She holds an Ochberg Fellowship in Journalism and Trauma at Columbia Journalism School in New York for her work covering the war in Afghanistan and its aftermath.

Emma was shortlisted for the 2023 Cheshire Novel Prize and longlisted for the 2023 Bath Novel Award and Blue Pencil First Novel Award. She lives in Glasgow with her husband Jonathan and their cat, Moses.

The Show Woman is her first novel.

EMMA COWING

THE SHOW WOMAN

HODDER & STOUGHTON

First published in Great Britain in 2025 by Hodder & Stoughton Limited
An Hachette UK company

1

Copyright © Emma Cowing 2025

The authorised representative in the EEA is Hachette Ireland, 8 Castlecourt Centre, Dublin 15, D15 XTP3, Ireland (email: info@hbgi.ie)

The right of Emma Cowing to be identified as the Author of the Work has been asserted by her in accordance with the Copyright, Designs and Patents Act 1988.

All rights reserved. No part of this publication may be reproduced, stored in a retrieval system, or transmitted, in any form or by any means without the prior written permission of the publisher, nor be otherwise circulated in any form of binding or cover other than that in which it is published and without a similar condition being imposed on the subsequent purchaser.

All characters in this publication are fictitious and any resemblance to real persons, living or dead, is purely coincidental.

A CIP catalogue record for this title is available from the British Library

Hardback ISBN 978 1 399 73739 5
Trade Paperback ISBN 978 1 399 73740 1
ebook ISBN 978 1 399 73741 8

Typeset in Plantin Light by Manipal Technologies Limited

Printed and bound in Great Britain by Clays Ltd, Elcograf S.p.A.

Hodder & Stoughton policy is to use papers that are natural, renewable and recyclable products and made from wood grown in sustainable forests. The logging and manufacturing processes are expected to conform to the environmental regulations of the country of origin.

Hodder & Stoughton Limited
Carmelite House
50 Victoria Embankment
London EC4Y 0DZ

www.hodder.co.uk

For my mum, the original show woman

'She stepped away from me and she moved through the fair, And fondly I watched her move here and move there. And then she went onward with one star awake, As the swan in the evening moves over the lake, I smiled as she passed with her goods and her gear, And that was the last that I saw of my dear. Last night she came to me, my lost love came in, So softly she came that her feet made no din. And she laid her hand on me and this she did say, 'It will not be long, love, 'til our happy day.''

She Moves Through The Fair,
Traditional Celtic folk song

Ayr, Scotland
September 1910

Prologue

The fall

Showtime.

High above the tent, Violet glistens like a sleekit fish. Stock-still, toes pointed, head bowed as though in prayer. The crowd below twist their necks as Lena the ringmistress flits among them, her words seductive as a hypnotist's. Do they know that Violet is the greatest trapeze artist who ever lived? That some believe she may actually have wings?

The throng shifts with restless excitement. They suck loudly on boiled peppermints and lumpen caramels. Sweat rises above the ring in steamy clouds. They have heard about this circus of ladies that travels the land, thrilling the towns and villages with their flying girls, daredevil horse-riders and the mysterious, tail-coated ringmistress with the velvet voice. It brings glamour and danger, and the hint of something darker, teetering on the edge of illicit. They have queued at the ticket booth and paid their pennies. It is their turn to be dazzled.

'Look up,' says Lena. 'Can you see her? Right at the top of the tent. Look up, ladies and gentlemen, because this young woman is about to fly.'

Taut as piano wire, Violet swings forward and grabs the bar. For a single, perfect moment she is flying. Soaring through the tent, light as the air that carries her.

And then, as if it were planned, as if it were the most graceful of movements, Violet's hands slip from the bar as though it were spun from silk. Or coated in grease. She falls, her body like an arrow shooting for the ground.

The tent glitters. Lena runs. But not even the tail-coated ringmistress can stop gravity.

Violet, heavy as the moon, lands on the sawdust with a toneless thud. The crowd begins to howl. The greatest trapeze artist who ever lived is lying flat on the floor of the tent. Her toes are still pointed. But only she is looking up.

PART ONE

She Moves Through The Fair

Six months earlier

Vinegarhill Showground, Glasgow
March 1910

I

Carousel

It is past six o'clock when the old man finally dies. Outside the wagons women crouch over smouldering fires, prod hopefully at reluctant flames. Men are downing tools for the day, loud and brash, in need of hot tea and a plate of soup. Children are told to shush now and away to bed. Woodsmoke coils over the showground. High above, a lone gull circles a tender pink sky.

Lena has been sitting with him for three days now. Three days in which Joseph Loveridge has stubbornly refused to die. Three days of taking rags to his hot forehead, dribbling water and whisky on his dry, chapped lips, singing soft, childish lullabies in his ear. She looks down at the thin, papery hand in hers, fingers twisted like the worn roots of a tree.

'Daddy,' she says.

A slight fluttering of the eyelids. His lashes, long and dark, flare in the gloom, but the old man's eyes remain closed. Through the caravan window a span of draught horses pull her father's carousel to the far side of the ground, their wooden counterparts bobbing serenely. She wonders if the blood has dried.

It is early March, plump with cherry blossom and harebells, and they are on the cusp of a new season. In berths across the ground they have been painting up wagons and stalls, rehearsing acts, tinkering with their rides, preparing to get back on the road. There is a crackle of anticipation in the damp air. They do not like to be tethered, these acrobats and jugglers, boxers and tarot-readers, trapeze artists and cinematographers and menagerie-owners and horse-riders. They are show people, men and women of the road. They have no business with life on a hill at the edge of this vast, blackened city.

Everyone on Vinegarhill knows what is happening at the Loveridge wagon. They heard the shouts when Joe fell. Saw the bloody, mangled aftermath, a leg sliced clean open, like a ham. A doctor has been fetched, brought poultices and rubbing alcohol, and was sent swiftly away. There will only be one ending to this story. They leave hot ginger cakes on the steps of the caravan, kettles of strong tea, mutton stew, a bottle of cheap, watered-down whisky. She has left it all, except the whisky.

Lena marvels at their misfortune. There is a whole fair season ahead, so close she thought she could touch it. Through the barren city winter she has dreamt of spring mornings out on the road, watching the dawn canvas above soften from lilac to blue. There is a smell on the roads at that time of day, earthy and primal, as though the world has been washed clean. It rises up from the hedgerows and the fields, filters through the dense pine forests of the Highlands, fuses with the salty swell of the coast.

It was there, perched high above the road at the front of the caravan as they headed to the next town, the next fair, that Daddy taught her to train a horse from a foal so it would work steadily with the wagons. How to punt your stall at the shows, whether you were selling mouldy plums or rides on a Wurlitzer. Once, he told her of the time he had seen a real mermaid at a fair in faraway Cumbria, who had swished water at him with her shimmering tail and called him her darling. Sometimes he spoke of his own father, a long-dead bareknuckle boxer who could knock a man out with a single punch. In all those mornings, there was only one thing Lena was forbidden to talk about.

Then, the nights. The fairground lit up and sparkling like a jewel box, the heave of the crowds and the noise, the bold brass bands and the finicky barrel organs, pickpockets racing through the swell in search of a loose shilling or a stray button, sweetie wives touting their edible gems, cries of 'birds of paradise!' and 'penny gaff!' and 'now, ladies and gentlemen'. There is a smell there too, deep in the heart of the fair. It reeks of sour bodies and piss, burnt sugar and lust, a dank redolence that seeps from the earth. To Lena, it smells like home.

'Never forget,' her father told her once, 'that for the flatties this is a treat. This is the most exciting day of their summer. But this is our life. Our everyday. Aren't we lucky, hen?'

A movement from the bed. Slowly her father's eyes open, roll back into his head, exposing the yellowing whites. A showman to the end. One last, spectacular performance.

'Maggie,' he says. His voice is brittle.

'Can you see her, Daddy?'

His hand scrabbles at the sheet. 'Maggie,' he repeats.

'She's not here,' says Lena. 'She's gone. Don't you remember?'

'Find her,' he says, and his voice cracks, as if his gullet has been stuffed with ashes from the fire. 'Sell the carousel. And find your mother.'

Lena grips his hand. It is years since he has mentioned her mammy. That apple-cheeked face. Her sweet lavender smell. The way she smiled at Lena, swathed in her favourite blue shawl, as she vanished into the crowd that very last time.

'How do I find her, Daddy? Where did she go?'

But her father shakes his head, gasping with the effort, falls still on the damp sheets.

'Daddy? Where is she?'

His dry lips move, but no sound comes out. There is a soft pop, and her father's face shutters like a seashell. The air in the caravan lightens. She smoothes out his hair, still thick and black, and opens the window. She wants to set his spirit free, into the air, the old tradition. He will sail across this rumbling city, over the darkening river and the shrouded houses, past clattering trams and the crumbling drinking dens, out into the wide, gaping night.

A dram of whisky now. There is not much left. It is probably for the best. She sits in her chair, hands folded, eyes dry as corn husks. Oh, Daddy, she thinks. Why have you done this to me?

'Lena? Lena?'

The knocking at the door is sturdy and loud. Lena wakes with a start from distant dreams of wooden horses cantering over hills, her father being pulled behind in a rough coal merchant's cart. Someone is tapping at the caravan door and she rises stiffly to open it.

'Ach, Lena. When?'

'Last night. I'm not sure what time. I should have come but . . .'

'You did the right thing, hen. Have a bit of time to yourself with him.'

Mary Weaver climbs into the wagon, her stout frame filling the room. Lena's father lies on the furthest berth, silent and impassive. Tenderly, Mary touches his cheek.

'He was a good man, your da,' she says, fussing with the sheet round his chin, pulling it up over his head. 'Now come on over and I'll make you a cup of tea.'

Outside one of the Weaver family wagons, an enormous tea kettle bubbles over a low fire. Exhaustion washes over Lena. She is twenty-one years old and an orphan. She rolls the word around in her mouth: *orphan*. It is a word that swells to fit the space, expands like the huge air balloon she had once seen at a fairground near Edinburgh. She remembers the thick flames that licked at the base of it, the basket where the people stood in wonderment as they were lifted high into the air. She starts to cry.

Mary drops the tin mugs she is carrying and wraps her thick arms around her. She is a large, comforting woman who smells of greasy scalps and warm milk.

'It's alright, lassie,' she soothes. 'It's going to be alright.'

'Is it?' Lena asks her soft, bulky shoulder. 'I've hardly any money. The season's about to start. And Daddy told me to sell the carousel.'

The carousel had been her father's pride and joy. He'd started out a boxer like his father, a face that was always blooming purple with bruises and knuckles worn down to the quick, but had always aspired to own a ride. When he'd married Lena's mother, Maggie, they'd scrimped and saved to buy their own, a basic platform with a hidden mechanism inside that made it spin. He'd built the rest of it himself, carving the horses during the winter months and painting their glossy coats, adding gleaming jewels for eyes. Mr Loveridge's Cantering Carousel, he'd called it. Pride of the Scottish fairs.

Lena had loved it as a child, was always proud that her father's ride was one of the smartest on the showground, but as she got older she'd tired of its sameness. And it had become shabby over the years, particularly after her mother vanished and her father seemed to no longer care.

And now, it had become a killer.

'Selling it is the right thing to do,' Mary says, pulling back to pour the tea. 'It's too much work for one lassie like you. You'd need to hire a few hands, and if you've not got the money . . .' She passes Lena a steaming cup. 'I know it's probably too soon to be thinking of these things, but, well, you could always join us. You've got a good voice on you, and we always need women to do some of the smaller parts in the theatre.'

'Maybe,' she says. 'I'll need to think on it. My daddy's not even cold yet.'

Lena's family had always known the Weavers – a brash, noisy tribe whose wagons followed the same roads they did, year after unpredictable year. William, the eldest of the four siblings, now running the family show with his own wife and bairns. Harry, who is trying to make it as a singer. Violet, away performing with the famous Linden's Circus for the past few years. And Belle, the youngest, a pale, baleful-looking child whom Lena finds difficult to talk to. Their daddy, Billy senior, a jovial man who always looked as though he needed a good feeding up, had died several years before.

But it was Mary who ran the show, had done even when old Billy was alive. The Weavers had their own travelling theatre, performing the same three shows every year. As a child Lena had occasionally appeared alongside Violet playing the part of a flower or an angel. It was Mary who looked after the takings and hustled the punters in, who would take a drink afterwards with the rest of the showmen out on the ground while Billy saw to the horses. She was hard-headed, even harsh at times. She had a curious, unsentimental relationship with her children, more forewoman than mother, as though they were all performing bit parts not just in the theatre, but in her life, too.

The Show Woman

Lena had a sneaking jealousy for their boisterous ways, for she should not have been an only child. Three times her mammy had given birth after her, and three times the cold, lifeless bairn had been wrapped in newspaper and buried in a far corner of a showground. Lena remembers her mammy's hot, salty tears, her father's face, grim and set. How each year when they returned to the grounds they would lay flowers the first night, and by the end of the second find them trampled into the ground by fairgoers.

'If only I'd had a few brothers and sisters, eh?' she says now, gazing wistfully at the Weaver wagons.

Mary is suddenly brisk. 'Well, we've all got to be content with our lot. Now shall I ask some of the Codona boys to come and deal with your daddy? You don't want flies.'

Later, after they've taken the old man's body away and she's eaten the remnants of the cold mutton stew, Lena sits on the steps of the caravan and considers her options. Mary is right. She does not have enough money to hire someone to operate the carousel for her, so if she keeps it she will have to run it herself. That means carting it across the country, from one town to the next, with no one to help her.

Or, she could sell it, and start her own show. Her mother always said that show women could do anything. They weren't like the fancy, puffed-up ladies who came to the fairs in their frilled dresses, who seemed carved from porcelain, who might shatter into a thousand pieces at the slightest jolt. Show women were strong and hard. They were built like the steamships on the Clyde. They did not break.

And yet her mother had broken, hadn't she? Or rather, she had disappeared, which amounted to the same thing. It was eleven years now, near enough. They had been at a fair at Galston, in Ayrshire. A funny wee town, her daddy always called it, with a coal mine nearby, men walking the streets still blackened with soot, falling about with the drink they'd already spent their pay packets on before the light drained from the sky.

A wind had been getting up that day. The carousel busy, whirling with excited children, and the scent of toffee apples on the air. Lena was playing hide and seek with Violet and another girl, Betsy, crouched behind a fortune-teller's stall, hands gripping her knees, eyes shut tight. When she'd felt the hand on her shoulder she had assumed it was Violet, ahead of the game as always, but when she looked up it was her mammy standing there, gazing down with her familiar affectionate gaze. Lena had pressed her finger to her lips, mouthed 'hide and seek', and her mammy had smiled, touched Lena on the cheek, and whispered that she was just going to get some apples for her father. And then, wrapped in her beloved blue shawl, with its intricate pattern of white birds and flowers, a gift from her father one long-ago birthday, she disappeared into the crowd.

Lena had watched her go and felt nothing. She was absorbed in the game, fearful of discovery, thought only that she, too, would like an apple when her mother returned.

But her mother did not return. When Violet and Betsy found Lena, when they had played two more rounds of hide and seek, their hair sheened with sweat, heads drooping with tiredness, when she had returned, finally, to the carousel, thinking of the sweetness of that first bite of her apple – only then had she realised that her mother had vanished.

The carousel had stopped. Her father was standing on its platform, shouting her mother's name. Lena had turned to run, her shoes sinking into the muddy ground, jostled and shoved by noisy fairgoers, plaintively calling out,

'Mammy! Mammy!' until her daddy grabbed her, lifted her bodily off the ground, and said roughly that he was not going to lose his wee girl today too, and she must stay put.

Before long, other men joined the search, the whole fairground echoing with the cries of 'Maggie, Maggie'. But Maggie was gone. A policeman was fetched, a tall man in a stiff dark uniform and a worn, unsympathetic face. 'Probably run off with a lad whose house isn't on wheels, son,' he told her father.

That first night without her was unbearable. Her father out searching most of the night, Lena shoved into a corner of the Weaver wagon, Violet's pale, worried face telling her everything she needed to know but could not yet face.

Two days later, after the rest of the fair packed up and left, they had searched in coal sheds, down streams, even knocking on doors, and the policeman had returned and moved them on. They were causing a nuisance, he told them. And he couldn't be responsible for what happened next if they stayed.

And so they had gone. To the next show, the next fairground. Her father always asking, always searching. But they never found her. Eventually, he just stopped asking, and Lena feared, deep within, that they might never see her mammy again.

Across the showground plumes of smoke spiral upwards from family fires. It is one of those mild March nights that signal the start of spring. Daffodils are blooming, their sunny heads nodding in the evening breeze. She falls into a deep, uneasy sleep, right there on the steps.

Over the next few days, grief clings to the world wherever Lena looks. It is as though everything is too bright, infused with a harsh white light. She sees her father's face in the men at his funeral, distant Loveridge relatives from other

Glasgow showgrounds in threadbare suits with similar noses and jowly, hangdog faces.

It is a hedge burial, in the portion of the showground quietly reserved for such matters, her daddy's body dressed in his good suit, clutching a small spray of snowdrops Lena has gathered that morning, the dew on their drooping white petals still fresh. She is watching the earth being shovelled over his flimsy coffin, trying not to imagine how quickly the petals will wither, when a man approaches her, introduces himself as Uncle Jimmy, and says he will buy the carousel for eight guineas.

'It's a beat-up old thing but the towns we tour, they'll never know the difference,' he tells her. He has small, ferrety eyes and teeth as sharp as tacks. She wants to kick his heels. Instead she thanks him and pockets the money in her thick black mourning dress. She never wants to see the carousel again.

Around Vinegarhill Lena sometimes thinks she hears her daddy's voice, the grunt he made when heaving himself up on to the carousel. She catches the scent of his cheap, tart tobacco. People are kind, respectful. They keep their distance, tip their hats. She cannot stand it. She wants to scream that this should never have happened, that life without her father is unimaginable, that she simply cannot go on. At nights she sits on the steps, holding the little ivory box her mother used to keep her precious things.

In there is a postcard. It is creased now, but when Lena holds it up to the fire she can see the faces clearly. There is her mother, young and bonny, a shawl wrapped round her shoulders and cradling a baby: Lena. Her face is a chubby round blur, in contrast to her mother's, which looks severe, almost sad. Then there is her father, standing straight and tall, holding his horse and with a pipe in his mouth. *A show family, 1890, Ayrshire* read the words underneath.

The Show Woman

Her mother told her the story many times. The man with the strange box who appeared at the showground one day and stood, snuggled under a big black blanket, shouting at them to stay still. Weeks later when they were up in the Highlands he reappeared, holding postcards with their faces on them. They would be sent across the world, he said. They would be famous.

Her mother was so proud, kept the postcard propped up by the bedside for years. When she disappeared her father put it away, couldn't bear seeing her young, shining face, full of promise and hope, every time he opened his eyes. Now, she realises, it is the only record of their faces left. Everything else is inside, tucked away in a memory.

There are other things in the box, too. She has made it her own since her mammy left, stored the few things in her life that remain precious, touchable and immediate. Things she can look at when all else feels as though it is lost.

And so there is a bunch of lavender, her mother's favourite. *If you lay them under your pillow,* she often told Lena, *they will give you the sweetest dreams.* The buds are dry and dusty, so fragile now that Lena is scared that if she touches them they will crumble to dust.

She brings out a ticket stub for Linden's Circus, crumpled, the lettering faded, and pictures the glitter of the big top, her mother's hand clasped firmly in her own, the elephant that came trotting round the ring with a sparkly headdress, the largest beast she had ever seen in her life. Cowering, she had hidden her head under Mammy's arm, but her mother told her not to be silly, elephants were friendly really, all you needed to do was give them a sugar lump and they'd be your friend forever. How clever her mammy was. How much she knew about the world.

Carefully, Lena reaches down to the bottom of the box. There is her mammy's pendant, silver and cool to the touch. A pebble, kept safe for reasons long lost. And the letter she was given three years after her mother vanished, that told her exactly why she left.

2

At Linden's Circus

Serena Linden's bones pop and crackle like firewood as she heaves herself out of the velvet day bed. She is fifty-seven years old and has carried eight children, six of whom had the audacity to leave her before taking their first breath. Her muscles ache as though they have been squeezed up like an accordion. And she does play the accordion sometimes, on warm nights when the circus performers linger outside after a show, with a drop of whisky to oil her stiff fingers, acrobats flinging themselves across the scorched grass like graceful, bony birds.

But Serena has troubles. That's how it is when your husband ups and dies on you, leaving you with a circus to carry on your back. She leans heavily on a carved, ivory-handled cane as she rummages in the old teak cabinet at the back of the caravan. Brandy tonight. She needs it for the shock.

Serena was making her late rounds when she heard them, out by the small hay wagon kept for the animals. A deep groaning, thick and guttural, yet curiously and improbably feminine. She stopped, her cane sinking into the soft earth below, and listened.

'Shh,' came a voice, followed by soft, suppressed laughter. She rounded the corner and saw the glow of a lantern up ahead, two shadowy figures pressed up against each other by the side of the hay wagon.

'You there!' she shouted. The two sprang apart, and Serena saw that the figure against the wagon was little Elsie Donald, one of the new stilt-walkers. She took a step forward, and Violet Weaver emerged from the dark. Red hair loose and unruly, face slicked with sweat, a languid smile on her lips.

'We were just out for a late walk, Miss Linden,' she said. She picked up a strand of her hair, twirled it lazily round her finger.

Serena sits down on the day bed, her bulk causing the entire wagon to shake. Once again fury kindles as she recalls the girl's insouciance, her damp-faced cheek. She feels an excitable rage that mingles with something deeper. An undefinable stirring she has not felt in many a long year. Humiliated, she swigs deeply from her brandy. It is rough on her parched gullet, burnishes her shame.

It's disgusting, she thinks. Two lassies. Ungodly. Serena's relationship with her God is tenuous at best. It is years since she has stepped inside a church, bowed her head in solemn prayer and dropped to her knees to praise her Lord. But O Father who art in heaven, she knows the difference between right and wrong. And the Weaver girl is wrong, through and through.

Violet Weaver was always going to be difficult. Serena knew it the moment she clapped eyes on her: that tangle of long copper hair, those fat, berry lips and green eyes. Far too sharp for a bairn's. Violet was a wee skelf of a thing when she came to Linden's, with a body that was soft and pliable, like oil. But the things she could do on a trapeze . . . Serena Linden has been in the circus her whole life. She knows talent. Exciting talent that can bring in the punters, slack-faced flatties who will pay to see her again and again, who will bring their friends and tell their families and shout from the rooftops about the girl in the silver costume with the mass of red hair who flies through the air.

It was her pa who taught her what to look for in a performer. How the trapeze artists should have a stretch in their body, like warm bread dough, ripe for the oven. How the equestrians and the lion-tamers and the elephant-handlers must show no fear, but look their charges straight in the eye. That it was the man at the centre of it all – or woman, he said once, dispensing a wink in her direction – who must control them all.

As a child Serena drank it all in; listened, eyes bright, as her father led her through every wagon and tent in their circus, reminding her that one day this would all be hers, that she had a legacy, a responsibility, that she could not let him down.

Serena sighs, takes another sip from the bottle. Sometimes she wonders if she has failed her father. Made bad decisions, hired the wrong acts. Because after five years at Linden's, cosseted and admired, the star turn in every performance, Violet has become arrogant and smug. She thinks she is invincible. Serena has seen it again and again in the younger performers, the ones who supposed their bodies were made of rubber, that the ground was covered in feathers, that they really had sprouted wings. They believed they could do anything, even acts that went against God.

Violet needs to be taught that the ground is as hard for her as it is for the rest of the world. Serena sips her brandy, feels its amber warmth spread down to her toes. Perhaps the girl can work in the yard for a bit. Learn what it's like to have her wings clipped. The other girl is dispensable. Serena will have one of the McCracken boys take her into town and leave her there the next morning. But Violet Weaver, well. That lassie needs to be taught a lesson.

Serena is in the big top. A bareback horse-rider trots dolefully around the ring on a plumed pony, balancing on one leg, watching nervously as Serena shrieks that he needs to stand up straighter. 'You're not riding a cart to the cattle market, lad,' she shouts, and the boy does his best to straighten his leg before wobbling, flinging his arms out and finally toppling into a heap on the ground. Serena raps her cane on the thick sawdust. 'Useless,' she says.

She limps over to an upturned bale of hay, scrabbles in a pocket for her pipe. It is made of cherry wood, its bowl battered and worn, and as she puffs away at the stem like a lamprey the air fills with the cloying scent of her tobacco. Three Nuns. Her favourite.

The bareback rider scuttles out of the tent, muttering apologies and promising to try again in the afternoon. Serena grunts. Once upon a time she could have shown him herself. She was a dab hand on a pony as a girl, could do cartwheels and handstands, her body as bendable as an eel's. She had what her pa called 'the flourish': that indefinable something that kept the audience watching, mouths open, caught in her spell. All in the past. The peaceful, painful past.

Violet enters the tent, that maddening smile still on her lips. 'Good morning, Miss Linden,' she says. Serena's eyesight isn't as good as it once was, but the girl appears tired, and impudent.

'Come away over here,' she says, and Violet approaches, her thin leotard emphasising her tiny ribcage. 'Have you ever scrubbed a pot, lassie?'

Violet looks uncertain. 'For my mammy, aye,' she says.

'Well, you're going to do it here now. A wee bit of time off the bar.'

'Scrub pots? But why? 'Cause I took a wee stroll with my pal?'

Serena sits back and regards the girl. She looks appalled. Furious.

'I'm not a maid,' says Violet. 'I'm the best trapeze artist you've ever had.'

Serena laughs. 'No, Violet, you *think* you're the best trapeze artist I've ever had. Believe me, lassie, I've seen far better than you.'

Violet knows this is untrue. Gianni the Italian juggler told her Serena said it once, a few months after she'd joined Linden's, one of those late nights out on the grass last summer when there had been whisky in the mugs and hope on the air. She'd even put it on a poster, brought a man in to sketch her, trace the lines of her body as she flung herself over the bar. They'd been slapped up all over the country. Violet Weaver. The Greatest Trapeze Artist Who Ever Lived.

Serena deposits a globule of spit on the ground and coughs. 'You'll wash pots and that's the end of it. Nobody is better than Linden's.'

For once, Violet is stunned into silence. Her usual nonchalance is gone. She looks, Serena notices with some satisfaction, like a frightened wee girl. And so she pushes it. Presses down on the bruise.

'I should have known never to hire a Weaver,' she says. 'You're a bad lot, always have been. The things I could tell you about your mammy would make your hair stand on end.'

But what exactly it is that would have made her hair stand on end Violet never finds out, because she knocks Serena out cold.

Dear Lena,
Tell yer daddy not to look for me in Galston. I am done with that life. I have a new man and a bairn. I am happy now. Sorry.
Mammy

3

Walnut

A watery sun washes over the showground. It is early morning and wagons gleam with fresh, gaily coloured paint. On the far side of Vinegarhill Lena can make out the tinny sound of a barrel organ, its staccato notes comfortingly familiar. A boy flits past with a cage of yellow birds, shouting that the little one has got away and has anyone got a net?

Lena has dreamt again of the wooden horses carrying her father over the hill. Except this time they are headed for Galston, sweat on their manes like sea foam, and she is in the coal merchant's cart with her daddy's dead body. The corpse is a bright, bony white yet she is covered in soot, her blackened hands throbbing with a deep, crackling heat. And somewhere ahead of them her mother, her blue shawl in the distance like a fading beacon.

Lena pounds at sodden sheets in a tin bucket. She has been slack with the laundry and the wagon has taken on a sour, tainted smell. It is about time she got a hold of herself. Made things nice. Just like she did when Daddy was alive. Perhaps it is time to take off her black mourning dress, its hem ringed in mud, the cuffs frayed and ragged. It had been her mother's once, although whom she had mourned, and for how long, Lena can no longer remember.

She never told the old man about the letter. It would have broken his thin, delicate heart, sliced it neatly in two. She was still a bairn herself back then, but she knew that hope had to be kindled in order for it to burn. That her father must believe that Mammy was trying to return to them, that she would find them again, somehow.

The boy who tapped her arm that day in Galston was young and wolfish. Black holes where his front teeth should be and a cap that sagged over his eyes like a bluebell. It had been one of those times when her daddy had been asking around for Maggie Loveridge, a show woman with yellow hair and a shawl the colour of cornflowers. Last seen in this town, at this very fairground, three years before. There had been shakings of heads, hands in pockets, rough shrugs of shoulders. And then this boy, creeping up to the carousel while her father was away seeing to the horses, tugging at her sleeves, thrusting the letter in her hand and then scuttling off without a single word. She opened it that night by the fire when Daddy was asleep, tears running down her face as she read the short, callous note again and again. Her mother had left them. Her words were crude, cruel, and final as a sunset. She knew she must carry this secret alone.

'I'm sorry about your daddy.'

The voice, thin and high, is one she recognises. She turns around.

Violet stands before her, thinner and more bird-like than ever. Her sky-blue poplin dress hangs off her bony frame, her hair roped into a long and unruly plait. She is barefoot. Violet, whom she has known her whole life, who has always unsettled her with her high-cheeked temper, the drama she drags around like a sack of marbles. As children they were often flung together, in Weaver family plays, in wagons packed with bairns from different families, and during their itinerant and sporadic school days. Violet, her sort of sister. Whose tempestuousness, stubborn arrogance and, as they grew older, audacious beauty, rubbed Lena's sturdiness up the wrong way.

The Show Woman

'Violet thinks she's special,' Lena had remarked to her father once.

'Well, maybe she is,' he'd replied, and Lena had seethed with quiet, jealous fury.

'If you're here for the funeral you're too late,' she says now, wringing out a final sheet. Her hands are red raw from the water and she clasps them together, embarrassed. She has never seen Violet wash as much as a rag.

'I know,' says Violet. 'It's you I came to see. Come and have a smoke.'

Lena wipes her hands on her dress and reluctantly follows Violet over to the Weaver wagons.

'How long are you going to wear that?' Violet says, gesturing at the dress as she brings out a box of tobacco, its lid covered in gold lettering so fine it looks like thread. Lena raises an eyebrow. 'Turkish. Got it from a lion-tamer,' Violet says.

Lena feels her hackles rise at her showy ways. 'I'll wear it as long as I wear it,' she says. 'And how was he? The lion-tamer, I mean. Worth the bother?'

Violet delicately rolls the tobacco in thin paper and lets out a dry laugh. 'It wasnae like that,' she says.

Lena smirks. 'I've heard it never is.'

Violet ignores her and licks the paper, then hands her the roll-up and leans over to strike a match. Lena inhales deeply. She has always loved a smoke, but this last year money has been so tight she and her daddy had been ekeing out the cheap baccy, rough shag that tasted like toasted tar. Violet's tobacco is sweet and soft, like inhaling a rich, musky cloud of toffee.

'Good, isn't it?'

'Aye,' Lena says. She blows a smoke ring, then slashes it through the air with her finger.

'Quite the show woman, eh?' says Violet.

'What do you want?'

'I was coming to that. It seems that you and I are in a similar situation. You've lost your daddy; I've lost the circus.'

Lena looks up. 'What did you do?'

'Never mind that. I'm well out of it. But here's the thing. You and me, we're more similar than you think.'

Lena opens her mouth to protest but Violet shushes her.

'I've been thinking about it, and as I see it we've both got three choices. Join my mammy and my brother and spend the rest of our lives performing the same three plays until we die. Marry the first dafty that comes along and squeeze out a few noisy bairns. Or, we start our own show.'

Lena looks at her. 'With you? Start a show with you?'

'Aye,' Violet says. 'I'm the greatest trapeze artist who ever lived. Haven't you heard?'

Despite herself, Lena smiles. Mary Weaver had been so proud when Serena Linden had put the line on her posters, edged in green and gold, with a drawing in full colour of Violet leaping from the bar, red hair trailing behind her, lips unnaturally red.

'You might be, but you're hardly the whole show by yourself,' says Lena.

'Well, I know that. But that's where you come in. Get a few more acts. Something to take on the road. As I say, you're more show woman than you think. I knew your mammy, don't forget.'

Lena bristles at the mention of her mother. 'Why don't you just join another circus? I hear Pinders-Ord is coming to Glasgow in the summer.'

Violet blows out a cloud of smoke. 'The Linden woman has turned my name into muck. Doubt I'd get a job shovelling their elephant shit. Besides, wouldn't it be fun to do it ourselves?'

The Show Woman

Lena is softening. Violet's plan excites her. The thought of being back on the road, of having purpose in her life, bringing magic to people, makes her heart sing. But with Violet?

'What makes you think it's what I want?' she asks.

'Well, I know you can afford it. I heard you sold the carousel. And what else are you going to do? Get a job in a factory? I can't see it, hen.'

Lena remembers a night, one summer season long ago and far away, up in the forests of the Highlands. Violet and Lena had been put to bed, a small box fitted with straw and blankets on the floor of a wagon. It was light out, too bright for sleep, the fair still clattering in the background, hen harriers noisily circling the sky. Violet had nudged her, produced something hard and mottled from her pocket.

'What is it?' Lena had asked, cupping it in her hands. It was brown and oval-shaped, the sides puckered like a scar. She enjoyed running her thumb over the ridges, and when she shook it she could hear something soft rattling inside.

'My pa says it's a walnut,' Violet said.

'Do you think we can crack it?' Lena had picked it up, dug her nail into the hard seam that ran around the sides. It was hard, stiff, and she could feel her nail bend and weaken as she worked at the nut's shell. Then Violet leant forward, cupped her hands and blew on it. The shell split miraculously in two, exposing the halves of nut inside, like opposing sides of a tiny brain.

'One for you and one for me,' Violet said. They had eaten slowly, savouring the bitter flavour, crunching the ridges in companionable silence.

'Look, there's another thing,' Violet says now, as she flattens a cigarette paper and starts rolling Lena another smoke. Her face is calm. Impassive. 'Don't you want to get to Galston?'

Lena stares at her.

'I read the letter. Years ago. I was rootling around in your daddy's caravan for baccy, found your precious wee box. Couldnae help but read it. Don't you want to go and find her?'

Lena cannot speak. She is outraged. Fizzing with fury. She has been sucked into the drama again, except this time it is her own personal business. Violet had no right.

'I never told a soul. I promise.'

Lena looks at her. 'Really?'

'Really. But . . .' She hands Lena another cigarette, waits while she sparks it up. 'I did remember something.'

The blood pulsates through Lena's ears. It is as though she is standing at a cliff edge, can hear nothing but the roll and crash of the waves.

'My mammy said once that your mother couldnae read or write. Her people, they weren't that type. She probably hid it from you but I always remember my mammy saying that, for Maggie, words all looked like dead spiders on the page.'

Lena is stunned. Her father was never good with writing, would ask her to help him sometimes, but now that she thinks about it, she never saw her mammy read a sign, or write a letter, or sign her name.

'Whoever wrote that letter, Lena, it wasn't your mammy,' says Violet. 'Don't you want to find out who did?'

WANTED!

Daring performers!
Ladies of all ages!
Sensational new venture!
Apply at Vinegarhill Showground, Gallowgate, Glasgow
Ask for Lena and Violet

4

Rosie

Darkness steals around Rosie like a blanket. Surely it must be midnight? She listens for the chime of the clock on the landing but the house keeps a heavy, watchful silence.

She shifts under the coverlet, careful not to wake her sister, mouth open, breath fluttering, limbs curled up around her knees. This is how it has always been. Jennifer deep inside her padded, cosy dreams, Rosie awake, waiting for the yawning creak of the loose floorboard outside their bedroom door.

He always comes after midnight. When the farm has laid down its tools for the day, when her mother is safe behind her own bedroom door, when there is no one around to hear her muffled protests. It started the day before her twelfth birthday. She was small enough then that he could still lift her, carry her out into the corridor like a ragdoll to the large linen cupboard at the top of the stairs. The first time she was so shocked, so disbelieving that her father, her pa, could have done such a terrible thing to her, his breath soured with alcohol, thick hands pulling at her long plait, that she had not spoken for three days, not even when her mother produced a plump round honey cake from the larder and sang *happy birthday* in her thin, wavering soprano.

She bled afterwards and her mother gave her napkins, thinking she had started her monthlies. She did not demur. She loved her mother, and, just as importantly, her mother loved her father, despite his sharp fists. To tell seemed unimaginable. The deep, painful fissure that had cracked open inside her body that first night would surely rip through the whole family, break them apart.

She wondered why he had not chosen Jennifer, a year older than her, sensible and forthright. Was she special? Or was it Rosie who was special? That was what he whispered as he clutched her nightgown, did unspeakable things with his calloused, pitted fingers.

It had started two months after his own father died. Grandpa, a hard man with a nose as red as a hawthorn berry, who frightened both sisters and whom her father loathed. He'd ruled the farm with a whip that seemed forged from iron, right until the very end. Something about his death had changed Pa for good. It was as though he had been handed a gift he did not want, a freedom he was not ready for. And Rosie had borne the brunt of it.

She shifts again, the coverlet scratchy at her throat. Perhaps he will not come tonight. He only comes after he has been drinking, at the pub with his farm hands or alone in the front parlour. Sometimes when he comes to her his face is wet, and she hears him sob as he buries his head on her shoulder. Afterwards he is kind, tosses her a sixpence or an extra hunk of bread when nobody is looking, lets her help him with the horses.

Rosie loves the horses, Clydesdales with flanks taller than Rosie herself, whose flared nostrils emit great clouds of steam on frosty mornings. They nuzzle her, let her pat their white noses, soft as sage. She likes to watch their fringed hooves drift across the fields like hems on a lady's dress, muscles glistening as they pull the ploughs.

And then there is Tommy Pony. Tommy is barely half the size of the Clydesdales that work the land, a joke of a horse really, but he is Rosie's favourite, because he belongs to her. Her father brought him home for her thirteenth birthday after another of those horrific, interminable nights in the cupboard, his face a repulsive mixture of guilt and pride. Tommy Pony was not so much a gift as a bribe, a reward even, for not talking, for compliance. But one look at that long grey snout, the little tuft of hair between his eyes and those long, lustrous eyelashes, and she was in love. She did not care that her father was buying her silence. Finally, after a lifetime of sharing everything from a hairbrush to a bed with her sister, she had something of her own.

Five years on her father comes less often now, although she is always careful to monitor his drinking nights. Occasionally she props something up against the door, and sometimes he gives up, stumbles back to bed. Other times though he appears in the doorway, edged by moonlight, and she gets meekly out of bed and follows him to the cupboard, burning with shame. He is rougher now, leaves red marks on her back and her inner thighs, and when she washes she has to be careful that Jennifer does not catch sight of her bruises.

No more. It ends tonight.

Rosie is short and lean. Her muscles ripple under her skin like water in a whirlpool. Her right leg is particularly developed, the sinew sticking out as though it has been carved from marble. That's what happens when you spend so much time standing on a horse.

The first time she tried it, her mother, hawk-eyed at the kitchen window, screamed in fright, came running out into the field, apron flapping, shrieking at her daughter. Rosie leant down, smoothly pulled on Tommy's reins and brought him to a stop. It was as though she and Tommy Pony were one, a single organism that could move anywhere they wished.

As a little girl she had been taken to the circus just once and watched, spellbound, as the bareback riders performed tricks on their elegant white horses. They stood on one leg, jumped from one horse to the next, tumbled and danced and pirouetted while the horses kept trotting, seemingly oblivious to the chaos on their backs. *That's what I want to do*, she thought, and when Tommy Pony became hers she knew she had found a way to turn her dream into something real, something she could grab hold of.

Beside her, Jennifer coos quietly. She looks down at her sister's plain, sensible face. She is due to be married in three weeks to Richard Wright, a big-eared boy from the village who works in the local mine. Jennifer will be sad that Rosie isn't there, particularly as they have already found her the material for a bridesmaid's dress, a floaty peach linen which hangs unhemmed in the front parlour, where her mother, a gifted seamstress, will work on it, giving her fingers a rest from edging the fine lace of Jennifer's veil.

She will be sad, too, that Rosie will not be there for the move into the village cottage already earmarked for them, the inevitable first baby, and the second, and the third. But Jennifer will be fine. She has a good heart, and she is happy. It strikes Rosie that to be oblivious, particularly to all that is bad in the world, might mean happiness.

But Rosie is not oblivious. She knows evil. She has lived with it, eaten bread and soup beside it, bid it good morning each day. For her, happiness will be different. Slowly, silently, she mouths the words on the poster she'd spied down in the village one last time. *Daring performers! Ladies of all ages! Sensational new venture!* Then, silent as the night, she creeps out of bed. It is past midnight. Her father is not coming. She will fetch Tommy Pony and she will leave this place, for good.

5
Circus of ladies

Spring arrives. Across the city they feel it: in the dense, clanking shipyards where huge hulls are constructed from sheet metal and men's sweat; in the elegant west where ladies take tea in chintz-papered parlours and waft tiny fans against smoothly buffed faces. In the packed, stench-ridden Gorbals where families live ten to a room, children run barefoot over jagged cobbles and the whole place reeks of piss and despair. The air is coming closer, needling its way through brick walls, under doors, and on to skin. Soon, a damp warmth will rise over the city. The showmen and women are already streaming away from its cloying grasp, out into the countryside where the air is clear, soft patches of grass await them among the tall, swaying lupins and moonlit nights beckon, fresh and alluring as a young lover.

At Vinegarhill, under a threadbare awning that stretches over the front of the wagon, Lena clutches her mother's pendant to her throat, enjoying its metallic coolness. It is mid-afternoon and auditions are under way. A young lassie with no shoes and an oversized pinafore is show-casing an uninspiring flea circus. Her fleas are limp and lethargic, and, despite repeated prods by the girl, the little paper steam engine she has built for them refuses to move. Lena suspects at least two of the insects are dead.

'Can't you make them do something?' asks Violet. She looks hot and irritated, a bead of sweat rolling slowly down her cheek like a tear.

The girl flushes. 'I'm trying, miss,' she says. 'I think it's too hot for them.'

Gently she picks up a single flea and places it on top of a tiny miniature horse next to the steam train. It immediately hops off.

'I think we'll leave it there, hen,' says Lena. The girl dispiritedly packs up her circus and trudges off. Lena turns to Violet, who is rolling her eyes. 'Do you think that's it?'

So far they have seen an old tarot-reader named Mavis who her father always said spent more time with the bottle than her cards, and Violet's sister Belle, who at thirteen can perform an excellent cartwheel but little else, and anyway, her mammy has strictly forbidden her from getting involved in Violet's latest hare-brained venture.

Then came a large woman with a peculiar flat nose and wide, flared nostrils. She was the pig lady, she said. Would they like her to dance? They said no.

The year her mammy vanished Lena had been separated from her father at one of the large Edinburgh grounds, stranded amid a throng of loud, excitable fairgoers. A crowd of men, beery and shouting, had jostled her, and she'd fallen through a curtain into a dark, acrid-smelling tent. An oil lamp flickered in the corner next to a vast bed. On it sprawled a woman. She was naked save for a bolt of ruby-red silk draped over the vast folds of her body. She stared at Lena, as surprised to see the little girl as she was to have encountered her.

'Hello,' the woman said. 'What's your name?' The flesh on her arms hung down by her sides like a set of folded wings.

'Lena,' she said. She turned her head away, suddenly ashamed to be staring at the woman, and to her surprise the lady laughed.

'You're not embarrassed to be looking at me, are you?' she asked. Her voice was high and unusual, and her laugh had a tinkling quality. Lena wondered if she might be foreign.

There had been more and more Europeans at the shows in the last few years, her father said they had changed things, brought new acts and curious languages and a breath of strangeness that hung over the showgrounds. 'Everyone looks at me, young girl. That is what I am for.'

Lena turned her head back. The woman was beautiful. She had a rosebud mouth, and long black hair that tumbled in messy curls. The layers of flesh around her middle pillowed out in soft white rings. Lena thought she could fall asleep on her, that she would be warm and comforting, a mother of sorts. Her eyes pricked with tears.

'Do you like to be looked at?' she asked.

The woman smiled again. 'That, little girl, is not the point. It is what I am for,' she repeated.

Lena took a step towards her and the woman stretched out a round, pale hand. But just as Lena reached her a man appeared at the door, shouted at the woman in a sharp, staccato language. Lena could not understand what he was saying but knew he was angry. He shooed her out of the tent like a troublesome dog and she ran as fast she could, out into the crowds, back towards the sunlight and away from the strange, beautiful fat lady. But she had never forgotten that woman, or what she said. *It is what I am for.* It made her unbearably sad. Lena knew that freaks were popular, but she could not bring herself to hire one.

'I'm starting to think this is the worst idea I've ever had,' says Violet, lighting a cigarette. 'And I once slapped Serena Linden.'

Lena looks out on to the vast ground, strangely empty now. Vinegarhill has lost some of its usual hum since the shows went back on the road. The shouts of drunken men falling into wagons at midnight have gone, replaced by the cackle of foxes. Where Hammond organs piped all day next to Wurlitzers and carousels, now the thwack of women from the tenements across the way beating their washing carries on the air.

They have bought a large tent with gay pink stripes down the side from a friend of Billy Weaver, Violet's brother. It is big enough for Violet's trapeze, and if they can hire another three acts they can catch up the shows already on the road by May, make enough money to get through the winter. But that will only be possible if they have acts to show.

'Lena?'

A sharp voice cuts across the showground. Lena shades her eyes from the sun, sees Mary Weaver standing staunch, arms folded, outside her caravan.

'Lena, come over here, will you? I'm needing a word.'

'Uh-oh,' says Violet.

'What does she want?' whispers Lena, rising from her seat. 'I've already told her we won't be taking Belle on the road with us.'

'I imagine,' says Violet, a small smile playing on her lips, 'she'll be wanting to give you a wee bit of advice.'

Lena trudges across the ground. The earth is hard and dry, tufts of moss nudging through the cracks. Mary was always trying to give Lena's mother advice when Lena was little. She'd materialise in their wagon, sometimes late at night, or early in the morning when her daddy was still asleep, hustling Maggie to one side, talking in a low, urgent voice about takings and money and other things too, matters that Lena could never quite grasp. She knew her mother only endured it because her daddy had such respect for old Billy. That Maggie found the older woman oppressive, stifling.

'Oh, she doesn't even let me breathe, that woman,' she said once, after a particularly long session at the Rood Fair down in Dumfries. Lena's father had been minding the carousel, and it was just her and Mammy in the caravan when Mary came calling.

'Tell her to go away, then,' said Lena, and her mother's face had hardened.

'It doesn't work like that, hen,' she'd said. 'Not any more.'

Mary is wearing an apron now, her face red from the flames of the open fire. Flour has streaked her grey hair white, and she looks old and tired. 'Just been baking some bread,' she says, motioning for Lena to step inside. 'I've been wanting a word with you, seeing as you're hell bent on this circus idea,' she says, shutting the caravan door. 'Are you sure you know what you're doing? You're still a wee lass.'

Lena prickles at the remark. She is twenty-one years old. She has been running the takings for her daddy since she was a bairn of ten. She might not be a married woman with a brood of her own, but she knows how to run a show.

'I think I know what's best,' she says. 'It'll take time, I know that. But once we get a few acts . . .'

'Acts?' Mary interrupts her. 'You've got that wayward daughter of mine on the trapeze and that's it. You won't last five minutes on the road, the pair of you.'

Lena has never quite understood Mary and Violet's relationship. As a child Violet was always out on the ground, hanging around Lena's daddy's carousel, begging other families for a go on their rides, flitting into the nearby town – anything really, so as not to be back at the wagon with her mammy. And yet, although she knew Mary could be stern, Lena has always thought her a good mother, fierce and protective. When her own mammy disappeared it was Mary who gave her cuddles, soothed her when she cried, when some of her other friends' parents had retreated, backed away, as though Lena were somehow tainted.

Perhaps Violet and Mary, both stubborn and equally unpredictable, were just too much alike.

'We'll get some acts, I'm sure of it,' Lena says.

'And what about money? You won't get far without it. Have you enough to feed your horses, pay your fees for the pitches on the fairgrounds? How will you feed yourselves, for that matter?'

'I've got money,' Lena says shortly. And she does. The carousel was a good sale. There's enough for a few months on the road. But her mother used to drill it into her that you did not talk about money to outsiders. It was a private affair, not to be discussed. As far as Lena was aware, Mary was the only person outside the family that Maggie had ever talked to about it. But that didn't mean Lena had to.

'Your mammy wasn't always good with the takings, did you know that?' Mary says now, and Lena flinches. 'Ach, she could talk a good game, but she was a little light-fingered at times. Don't know what she did with it all.' Mary laughs, showing yellowing teeth.

Lena shakes her head. 'I don't think that's true. My mammy ran a tight ship.'

Mary regards her, one eyebrow raised. 'As I say, she could talk a good game.'

Lena looks around. The caravan is dark, not as cosy as she might have expected. There are few drapes, and the day bed is threadbare. Only one window ledge is decorated, an array of shells, stones, and forgotten fairground knick-knacks. The glass eye of a carousel horse. An old ticket stub. A penny with the old Queen's head, polished to a bright copper. That'll be Belle's, thinks Lena. What a curious little child she is.

Lena stands up. 'Is there anything else?' She doesn't want to hear anything more about her mother. Not from Mary.

The Show Woman

'Well, I can't stop you,' Mary says, brushing flour from her apron. 'But just you keep an eye on Violet. She can be a menace at times. She needs a firm grip. Not even the Linden woman could control her in the end.'

Lena snorts. 'I don't even plan to try.'

She steps outside the wagon, Mary at her heels.

'Here,' says Mary. 'Dinner's on me.' She hands her a loaf of bread, still warm.

Back under the awning Violet sees the loaf and rolls her eyes. 'Been bribing you, has she? Telling you to keep an eye on me?'

'Something like that. Anyone else been?'

'Nope. Quiet as the grave. We might as well pack up. It's not going to happen. Not today, anyway.'

'Let's give it another few minutes,' says Lena.

They sit in companionable silence, watching a group of boys at the far side of the ground playing marbles, the soft clack cutting through the silence.

'Look,' says Violet. 'Do you think she's for us?'

At the far end of the showground near the tall front gates, a figure on a horse is trotting towards them. The girl is riding a bedraggled grey pony that looks as though it needs a good feed. The girl is thin and wiry with long brown hair. She is barely five feet tall.

'Are you Lena?' she asks shyly, as she approaches. Lena nods.

'Are you here for the audition?' she asks her. The lassie looks exhausted.

'Yes. My name is Rosie. Am I too late?'

'Not at all, but are you sure you don't want a wee rest?'

The girl shakes her head vehemently. 'I've been practising my routine in my head all the way here. I'd like to do it now, please.'

Lena turns to Violet.

'She says she'd like to do it now, please,' Violet repeats, in a lazily mocking tone.

'What are you going to do for us?' asks Lena.

Rosie pulls a whip and some pins out of the small bag secured round her tiny waist, and fastens her smock up above her knees. She removes the pony's saddle and affixes a small cone of feathers on to his head. The pony tosses his head disdainfully. Then Rosie leaps on to his back and carefully stands up.

'Ah,' Violet whispers. 'We've got a bareback rider.'

Rosie cracks the whip lightly over his side and the pony trots elegantly in a circle. Rosie is ramrod-straight, her spine rigid. Then, slowly, as though her joints have been oiled, she lifts one leg and turns her head to the side. Tommy speeds up and Rosie jumps, landing on her other leg. The pony continues his circular trot, and this time Rosie moves backwards, until her tiny feet are almost dangling off the side of the pony's rump. She raises her arms, spins slightly to the left before turning a cartwheel on his back.

Violet raises an eyebrow. 'Well, well, well,' she says.

Rosie slows the horse down to a stop, dismounts, and performs a little curtsey.

'Was I any good?'

She is flushed, two high spots of colour on her cheeks. Despite the purple shadows under her eyes she is clearly excited.

'It's just that I taught myself. I've only been to the circus once. But it's all I've ever wanted to do.'

'*Brava*,' says Violet. 'You'll need a few more bells and whistles to your act but you've got the technique, at least.'

The tiny girl bobs on the balls of her feet, and Lena relaxes. Life will be much easier if Violet gets on with the

The Show Woman

other acts. She sits Rosie down and gives her a cup of tea. The girl's arms are covered in old, dirty bruises.

'Where have you come from today?' she asks. 'Not Glasgow, surely?'

The girl shakes her head, suddenly shy again. 'I came down from Ayrshire,' she says. And then, in a smaller voice, she adds, 'I didn't tell my family. But I doubt they'll miss me.'

'So you've never been on the road before? What age are you?' Violet asks. She looks sour again.

'I'm eighteen,' says Rosie. 'But I turn nineteen in May. Oh, look. Do you think that's someone else coming to audition?'

A woman is heading for them, colourful ribbons streaming from every part of her body. She looks like a walking rainbow. As she approaches, Lena can see that she is tall, with dark hair and large hoops in her ears.

'Lena? Violet?' she asks. Her voice is deep, heavily accented.

'Aye, that's us,' says Violet.'

'I am the rainbow girl. Let me show you what I can do.'

Later, as the city quietens and the night sky spreads out a blanket of stars above them, the four women sit around the campfire smoking and talking. The rainbow girl, who turns out to be called Carmen, is an acrobat, and she is from Spain. She turns cartwheels and spins and twirls and rolls. It is as though she, Carmen, is a ribbon too, as flexible and airy as a reed in the wind. She can do her act on the ground or in the air, and has also worked as a catcher on the trapeze, which pleases Violet. And she is funny. Standing next to little Rosie, she says drolly, 'Look at us. I am a tree and you are a little bush.'

She has changed out of her ribbon costume now and seems suddenly older, more mature. Lena notes that she is wearing rouge on her lips, has put on a pair of black leather shoes with heels. There is an air of glamour about her, and something else, too, something she can't quite place.

Lena wonders how Carmen and Rosie will cope with life on the road. Rosie is a flattie, has never lived anywhere other than a house. Will she revel in a home that is constantly moving, with a different view each week, horses to maintain, all the noise and danger of the fairs? Or will she be away home to her mammy and a nice warm bed within the week?

There is only one way to find out.

She gazes into the flames, dying now, the firewood torched to black. The last recurring image of her mother returns, her vibrant blue shawl, that toffee apple smell, her father's face twisted in fear and panic. She slams it back into the furthest recesses of her mind.

She has a new family now. Her show. Her circus of ladies.

6

Birthmarks

There is only one lamp left burning in the showground at Kirkcudbright. Its low flame lures moths to the window of the wagon, their wings crumbling as they crash against the grimy glass. Serena watches them impassively. At night she prefers to be alone. By then she has had enough of the circus and its hullabaloo, the deadened laughter of the crowds. Silence, and the inevitable bottle of brandy, are what she craves.

Here she can brood. Ruminate over her past mistakes, her triumphs, fulminate over those who have crossed her.

Tonight, though, is different.

'Go on,' she says, taking a swig from the bottle. The bruise on her cheek where the Weaver girl took a swing at her is still purple and angry, the furious eye half-closed. 'I haven't got all night.'

Benjamin hangs his head. He is twenty-nine, a tall man with large, meaty hands and a loose sprinkling of freckles across his nose. Serena has always told him he looks like his father, and this half-mocking, half-pitying remark has made him awkward, ungainly. Despite his size he prefers to fade into the background, fold himself up like a pen-knife. Serena despises him for it.

'It's Lucy—' he starts, but she is already interrupting him.

'Lucy? Who's Lucy? I don't know a Lucy.'

'You do; she came on tour with us last year. She was one of the animal-handlers. She looked after the lion.'

Serena's cross, confused face clears slightly. 'That wee slip of a thing with the strawberry on her face?'

She is referring to Lucy's birthmark, a small bloom under her right eye that Serena considers an unsightly blemish. She does not know that Benjamin is thinking of it now, how it felt when he laid his lips against it for the first time, its exquisite softness, like the skin of a ripe blaeberry. She does not know that he thinks it the most beautiful part of her.

He nods, runs his hands through his hair. 'Aye, well. We're married.'

Serena puts the bottle down and regards her eldest son. He has always been a disappointment. A puny boy, weak as watered-down milk, with too much of his father in him. Had she not tried her best? Taught him the trade, shown him the ropes, and smacked him hard in the gullet when he'd botched a job? And now he had gone and married a silly English lassie, and hadn't even had the grace to tell his own mother.

She shakes her head and fumbles in her skirt pocket for her pipe.

'You daft laddie.' Her voice is almost a whisper.

'I'm not a daft laddie, I'm a twenty-nine-year-old man. I'm married to a wonderful woman. And I love her.'

Serena reaches for the brandy again and then stops, hand in mid-air, like a moth which has suddenly sensed the deadly heat of a seductive flame. This is not over, she realises. There is more to come. She places her hand back in her lap. There will be time with the bottle later.

'And?' she says.

Benjamin takes a deep breath. 'And we're away. Lucy's father has a circus down south, near Stafford. He says I can help with the general running of the show.'

Serena laughs coldly. 'Oh, so you'll be running the man's show for him, will you? God help him.'

Benjamin shakes his head. 'They're good people,' he says. 'Which is a damned sight more than I can say about you.'

The Show Woman

So there it is. He is leaving her. The ungrateful bastard is abandoning his mammy, just like all the rest. She lights her pipe and scrabbles at her wrist for the bracelet Davey made her, all those years ago. He had been a pearl-fisher when he met her, up on the Spey, made his living on the river bank prising open the mouths of coy, sodden mussels. A good-for-nothing, her pa said, and she should have listened to him, but oh, how she had liked the pearls. How smooth they were, hard as glass, the sheen of them, a strange coolness which warmed in your hand, like oil.

Davey made her a bracelet, a pearl for each baby, the moment her belly began to bloom, the string becoming longer, the pearls duller, as the bairns kept coming, tearing at her insides, ripping her flesh. Six had died inside her, or on their way out, their limp bodies spirited away before she could even take a look at their soft, senseless faces. Of the two who had made it, screaming and bloody, there had been nothing but disappointment. Simon, a quiet, moody boy who high-tailed it into the Navy the minute he turned sixteen, never to be heard from again. And Benjamin. Lumbering, gangly, a failure.

Who is to help her run Linden's Circus now? There are the lads, of course, the rough McCracken boys whose father had been hired by Davey years ago, and who stayed with the circus through thick and thin, sorted out a few problems for her when the need arose. But the idea of handing the circus over to them? Good God, no. Dirty thieves, the lot of them. They'd sell off every last piece of the show before she was cold in her grave. It is unthinkable. Her pa is long dead, and she has no siblings to speak of. The wraiths who have threatened her circus over the years, slipped under the corners of the big top, wound their way round her gleaming trapeze bars and shiny animal cages, she has long since chased away.

A kernel of doubt sprouts in the back of her mind. Perhaps she was too hasty, too intent on having things her own way. She blots it out. It is too late for all that now.

'Am I not good enough for you any more? Does being a Linden mean nothing to you? Surely you'd prefer to run your own show than work for some English fly-by-night?'

Benjamin shakes his head, and she can see in his refusal a hint of pride, a final defiance. It turns her stomach.

'I've never wanted to inherit this place,' he says. 'Not even when I was a wee boy. You run it on fear. Your performers are terrified of you, and your henchmen. Everything in this place has been built on lies, on breaking the rules. You've turned us all into criminals. Lucy saw it the moment she came here. She'd have left if it wasn't for me. The way you give backhanders to the McCrackens. The pickpockets you have running through the audience . . .'

Serena tries to interrupt but he talks over her.

'Anything for a quick ha'penny, and bugger the poor souls who've paid their honest wages to see the show. You're a fraud. My father would be turning in his grave.'

'Don't you bring that lazy, good-for-nothing old man into this!' Serena is shouting now, hot with fury. She, Serena Linden, has built this place from the ground up. Davey would have wasted it all; he knew nothing about being a showman. After she plucked him from the riverbank he had been happy with his pathetic little show, his three clowns and his unicycle and that feeble wee stage act with the bowler hats. It was she who had taken her own father's circus and brought it kicking and screaming into the twentieth century, made them money, real money that they could use for better wagons, decent horses, lions and elephants, and a wee nip of brandy whenever the mood takes her. How does he not realise that?

The Show Woman

'He was a good man, my father. And I'd rather be like him than you.' Benjamin stands up. 'I've to meet Lucy in Stafford at the end of the week. I'll leave my caravan, and take my belongings. I want no part of it. Any of it.'

Serena raps her cane on the floor. 'How dare you!' she shouts. 'Lazy. Useless. No backbone.' Her head is fizzing with anger.

The door to the caravan opens. It is Dougie McCracken, the oldest and meanest of the brothers.

'Everything alright, Miss Linden?'

Serena's chest rises and falls wildly and she coughs, a deep, rasping wheeze. 'My son here was just leaving,' she says through ragged breaths. She looks past Benjamin at Dougie. She will not look her son in the eye again.

'Aye,' says Benjamin. He puts his cap on his head and pushes his way out of the wagon past Dougie, who regards him narrowly.

'Thank you, Dougie,' says Serena. 'That will be all.'

'Need me to deal with him?' he asks.

She shakes her head. 'No, thank you. Away to bed now.'

He pulls the wagon door shut and she hears his soft footsteps walking over the grass.

Serena slumps back on her day bed, cradling the bottle as though it were one of her tiny, lifeless bairns. They were never coming back, and neither was Benjamin. She battles the sting in her eyes with a long, gulping swig. She will not weep for her lost sons. She lights her pipe, unsteady hands striking the match. To hell with them all.

7

Loosening

The sun hangs suspended in the sky, waiting to drop like a stone. Lena's hands are red raw from the thin leather reins as the caravan pulls into Linlithgow showground, and her hair is damp and sticky. Violet sits placidly next to her at the front of the wagon and with a flicker of irritation Lena sees that her neat bun still rests perfectly at the nape of her neck.

It has clearly been a busy day on the rides. Wrappers and bottles litter the grass, along with a forest of cigarette butts. One carousel in the distance is still lazily turning, wooden gondolas creaking up and down with a loud *hrruuuk hrruuuk* now that its barrel organ has stopped playing. The air is sweet and cloying, smells of tobacco and burnt sugar and sweat. Shrugging away her exhaustion, Lena inhales the scent as she draws the horses up. Home, she thinks. I'm home.

Violet nudges her hard in the ribs. A man wearing a cap and a smart jacket is heading purposefully towards them, sheaves of paper in his hand.

'*Vedere*,' whispers Violet, and Lena's heart lifts at her use of Parlyaree, the old language of the shows. 'There's a flattie if ever I saw one.'

'No room,' he shouts before Lena can speak. He is short, with polished brown shoes and a beetling black moustache that looks as though it must permanently tickle his upper lip. 'You'll have to go elsewhere, we've no more space here.'

He looks down at his papers before peering up again at Lena. 'Who's in charge here, miss?'

'I am,' says Lena, surprising herself. 'I'm a show woman, and this is a showground, is it not?'

'And I've just told you, young lassie, that there's no room here. Now where's your man?'

Violet leans over and gives him a huge, beaming smile.

'What did you say your name was, sir?' she asks. She narrows her large green eyes, cat-like and feral.

The man puts his hand to his forehead, looks down at his papers again. 'I'm Mr Robert McAllister, but that's not the point—'

'We're just four wee lassies, you see, Mr Robert McAllister. Four wee lassies and a couple of horses. And we won't take up much room here. Look – tiny, we are.'

She clears her throat and Carmen appears from the back of the wagon, stooping her tall frame as much as she can.

'Hello, sir,' she says haltingly. 'It is so very nice to be here.'

Rosie, now walking an exhausted Tommy Pony on his reins alongside them, sidles forward too.

'I mean, that's not even really a horse, now, is it, Mr McAllister? Show him what you can do, Rosie Posy.'

Rosie looks at Violet, aghast. She is so exhausted she might just drop down asleep at Tommy Pony's feet, right where she is standing.

'Go on, Rosie,' Violet says again, more gently this time. 'Just a wee jump.'

Rosie unfastens Tommy Pony's saddle. The little horse whinnies softly. He knows what this means.

'Now, ladies, the thing is, I'm sure this is all very interesting but we just haven't any room. I run this showground for Mr Robertson and he's asked me very firmly to make sure—'

'Oh, Mr *Robertson*!' says Violet, clapping her hands in recognition. 'We know him, don't we, Lena?'

The Show Woman

Lena nods vigorously. She is starting to enjoy this, the game of it all. Mr McAllister has a single bead of sweat running down the bridge of his not inconsiderable nose. He must be roasting in that tweed jacket and his high, fancy collar.

'There'll be no bother if it's Mr Robertson. No bother at all.'

Rosie is now standing on top of Tommy Pony, her neck erect, her tiny, tired body a perfect line. She looks Mr McAllister straight in the eye, and executes a star jump. Tommy does not shift an inch.

'Now you see, Mr McAllister, this is a very high-end show we have here. Four lassies, all of us with our own special and very clever skills, a ladies' circus if you will. And I happen to know that if you turn us away, Mr Robertson will be very displeased.'

Mr McAllister droops. 'A ladies' circus, eh?' He shakes his head. 'Just when you think you've seen everything. Well, then, you'll need to go right at the back, up by the stables. You can pay your fee in the morning.'

'Oh, thank you, sir, I promise we'll be no bother,' Lena bursts out, to a furious look from Violet.

That night Lena dreams of a deep, wide river, and no matter how hard she tries, she cannot get her feet on the bottom. Instead she kicks out, flails her arms, but finds herself borne away on a thick, strong tide. Up in the sky, just out of her field of vision, a storm is coming, dark, angry clouds, thunder that will wake up the gods.

But when she opens her eyes it is to a silent wagon, Violet snuffling into her pillow on the bunk beside her, Rosie curled up in a ball next to Carmen, who sleeps with one long, gangling arm hanging down until it almost touches the floor. But there *are* noises. Lots of them, coming from outside. It sounds like a crowd at a shooting gallery, whoops and shouts and excitable cries. She sits up and wonders if they have slept late, so exhausted from the journey they have failed to stir as dawn crept in through the thin muslin curtains on either side of the wagon. Perhaps the day's fair has already started. Perhaps it is late morning, the crowds are already surging through the grounds and they have missed half a day's takings.

Admonishing herself, she puts her bare feet on the floor and creeps towards the little window where the sound is loudest, peers through the crack in the middle. There is a crowd out there, alright. Showmen mostly, the odd woman, standing around smoking and laughing.

'What is it?' says Violet from across the wagon. She is sitting up, her hair a huge crimson halo fluffed out around her head, and Lena hears from outside the words 'Ladies' circus, eh? That'll be right.'

'I think,' says Lena, 'we have attracted some attention.'

Violet swings down from the bunk with a whoop. 'In that case,' she says, 'let's go and have some fun.'

They emerge several minutes later, blinking in the hard glare of the sun.

'Ooh,' shouts a man in a bunnet who is, at most, five feet tall. 'La-di-dah. Here comes the ladies' circus. Look a bit loose if you ask me.'

Violet fusses at her midriff, where her corset should be, then decides to ignore him and instead performs a small pirouette. The men laugh and elbow each other.

Lena feels the heat rise in her face. This is what she has quietly feared, but not had the courage to say out loud. That they are a laughing stock. A prank. Wee lassies, not to be taken seriously.

'Is that the best you can do?' shouts another man, taller this time and older, his jowls bobbing up and down like gills on a fish.

'You want any more you'll have to pay for it,' shouts Violet.

The men laugh harder and this time it feels charged. Nasty. 'Where have I heard that before?' shouts a short man with a tweed bunnet, and another replies, 'Down the Leith docks on a Friday night, no doubt.'

'You'll see,' Violet says, but her voice is subdued, as though she realises she has been caught out.

Lena is scanning the crowd for faces she knows, friends of her daddy perhaps, old hands from Vinegarhill. But they gape back, anonymous. A group of unknowns. Perhaps they're down from the Highlands, or even from faraway England.

'Give us another twirl,' shouts the first man, the short one, and Lena realises his accent is lilting, unfamiliar. Not her daddy's lot, then. She feels a little puff of relief leave her chest. She doesn't think she could face it if her own people turned on her, even if she is just a silly wee lassie. She puts a hand on Violet's arm and they turn away. The crowd are losing interest, talking about setting their stalls up, readying for the day.

'Bastards,' Violet mutters under her breath.

Back in the wagon Rosie is huddled in her bunk, dirty knees pulled up to her head. Her eyes are pink and wet.

'It's alright, *dona*,' says Lena gently, and sits with one arm round her tiny, trembling form. 'They're away now, eh? No more of this.'

Rosie shakes her head but says nothing. Lena and Violet exchange a look. They have both noticed the girl's reticence around men, how the confidence she displays on Tommy Pony vanishes into meek fear whenever they are around others.

'You don't like the lads much, do you, chicken?' says Violet.

She doesn't say it harshly, but Rosie baulks at the remark, sticks her fists in her eyes. Lena touches her shoulder but Rosie pulls back.

'I'm sorry,' she says eventually, and her voice is thin and reedy. 'I'll be fine in a wee minute.'

There is a smart rap on the door of the wagon. They freeze.

'Vi?' comes a deep voice. 'Vi, is that you in there?'

'Harry!' cries Violet, and is at the door in one leap. She throws herself into his arms.

The man who enters the wagon is so tall he has to stoop. He is angular, but not thin, the white shirt he is wearing accentuating his sinewy frame. The stubble on his chin is the same colour as the hair on his head: a vivid strawberry blond.

Lena is astonished. She has not seen Violet's older brother for years. He is a singer, a jolly good one too by all accounts, and, while he has been working the fairs in recent times, it is in the music halls, where there is good money to be made and fame to be had, that he has set his heart.

'What in God's name are you doing here?' Violet asks into his chest.

'A charming welcome, as ever,' he says. 'Change of plan. I was going to spend the summer in Glasgow, trying the music halls for the odd concert, but Jimmy Moore gave me an offer I couldn't refuse.'

Violet narrows her eyes. 'Which was?'

Lena suppresses a smile. Jimmy Moore is notorious on the fair circuit, has been for years. Each year he turns up with a different ride, or a fancy new stall. One infamous summer it was a dancing bear. By the time they got back to Vinegarhill Jimmy had inevitably lost any money he'd made, and quite often his ride too, lamenting that the crowds just weren't as good as they used to be, and it wasn't his fault the damned ride packed up. Whatever happened to the bear, Lena didn't like to think.

'He's got himself a big dipper, would you believe,' says Harry. 'Needs a couple of men to shift it from place to place. It's grunt work but it's not for the whole season, and the money's good. It'll give me the chance to put a bit by for when I do start on the singing. I might be able to do a wee tour of my own.'

Violet rolls her eyes at the end of this speech, and Harry turns his attention to the rest of the women. Rosie has stopped crying. Carmen shrinks into her bunk. But it is to Lena that Harry speaks.

'I hear there's a new show woman in town,' he says. And with a theatrical sweep he lifts his cap and doffs it elegantly. Violet cracks up laughing.

Harry spends the morning with them. It is still early, and after a swift breakfast of bannocks warmed on the fire served with a thick, sweet syrup that Carmen produces, he helps them put the tent up.

It is hot, thankless work. Twice, despite Carmen and Harry's best efforts with the thick wooden poles, the stripy pink canvas collapses into an undignified heap on the ground. Then Lena realises there isn't nearly enough sawdust to cover the ground inside, and worries that the mud will churn up under the crowd's feet. It dawns on her too that they should have invested in chairs, stools even, although they have no room to move them from place to place. Everyone will be standing. If it's busy the audience will be packed in like tinned sardines.

As they work, Lena feels Harry's eyes rest upon her. She is aware that he is looking at her intently, as though searching, really searching, for something within her. This silent attention makes her shy and unsure of herself.

She is unused to it. Normally it is Violet, with her insouciant charm and those big eyes of hers, who commands the male gaze.

Violet is softer than usual thanks to the presence of her big brother – her favourite, she told Lena once, after a few nips of whisky – and spends her time stretching. She leans her arms forward and up, pulling each muscle and sinew until they ripple under the skin. She arches her foot, lifts her leg into a right angle, her eyes closed as though she were communing with a higher spirit. Around her the rest of them puff and sweat as they hammer in the final poles, tuck in the canvas.

Carmen ventures a quick eye-roll towards Lena, and Lena catches it and gives her a smile.

'She is very dramatic,' says Carmen quietly.

'Yes,' says Lena. 'She certainly is.' The tall rainbow girl is getting the measure of Violet already, it would seem. Good, thinks Lena. It is better that she knows that Violet can be bloody hard work. She could be an ally, and a useful one.

She notes that Carmen has been avoiding Harry, has barely spoken to him. Perhaps it is because he is Violet's brother, and she is wary. Or perhaps she too, like Rosie, dislikes men.

'Have you a sign?' asks Harry. He has rolled his sleeves up. The hairs on his arms are strawberry blond too, glinting merrily with tiny beads of sweat.

The question stumps Lena. 'A sign?'

'Aye, you know, to put outside the tent. To tell people who you are. Surely you want everyone to know that you've got the greatest trapeze artist who ever lived in there.'

Lena shakes her head as Violet stops stretching to raise an eyebrow at her brother. Another thing she has forgotten.

The Show Woman

How on earth will anyone know what's inside the tent? They might not even come in at all.

'Right,' says Harry. 'Well, you'll need one. For today, though, I can get one of the wee lads who works with us to come and hawk for you. He can stroll up and down outside and shout out prices and show times.'

Prices and show times. It is another thing Lena has forgotten about. She has been so wrapped up in the show itself, in presenting something that looks beautiful and different, which would glisten somehow, a tiny pearl in the vast, shifting ocean that is a summer fair, that it never occurred to her she would need to sell it. That people would need to be persuaded to push past the soft canvas flap in order to see what was inside.

She stares back at Harry, silent.

'Come and have a smoke,' he says, and leads her over to a bale of hay by the door of the stables.

Violet is still stretching and Rosie and Carmen have disappeared. It is warm now, and the stables are almost empty, most of their occupants dispersed into a nearby field while their owners get their shows and stalls set up for the day.

He brings out a packet of cigarettes in a gold-edged case, and a fancy matchbox with foreign writing on it. There is a picture of a ship on the front.

'Where did you get these?' she asks as he lights her cigarette. It is long and white, with a proper filter on the end.

'Tobacco shop in Glasgow, just off George Square,' he says. 'Violet's always saying I'm a fancy dan, but I like a wee bit of sophistication in life. Makes it worth living.'

He gives her a lopsided grin and she feels something inside her flip like a fish on a line. She inhales the cigarette to steady herself. It is rich and smoky, quite different from the rough, loose tobacco her father smoked, and from the smooth, toffee-sweet one that Violet had offered her. It reminds her of the scent of burning peat. She has seen men on the hills in the Highlands set it alight when spring is aloft, releasing a rasping earthiness that smells as though it has come from deep within the ground.

'So you've not worked out any prices, then,' says Harry.

Lena shakes her head and takes another puff.

'Well, that's easily done. A penny should do to start with, and Violet's got a reputation so that should help. You start out cheap, let word spread, bring the crowds in, get them excited, and then you can start hiking your prices. You'll know that from the way your father did things.'

She feels a flash of irritation. How dare he bring up her father now? Tell her what to do, when he knows so little about their show, their plans?

She quells her annoyance and flashes a smile. 'Actually I thought I'd start at tuppence. And it'll be two shows an hour. It was just all a bit much back there with the tent; I think it's too hot. But I know what I'm doing. You'll see.'

Harry looks down at the ground. A large clump of straw has detached itself from the bale and he puts his foot down on it until it crunches, like spun sugar.

'Well, good for you,' he says shortly. 'I'll send a lad over soon to help you with the hawking. *Bonne chance.*'

He walks away, leaving Lena with the feeling that she has just let something precious slip through her fingers.

8

Cascade

Later, when she thinks back on it, Lena realises it could never have been any other way. She had thought their wide-eyed naivety, the thrum of excitement and bluster, the tingle of opportunity and newness which carried them all the way from Glasgow to the smart town of Linlithgow, would be enough to sustain them. That, having created the bread, the butter would magically appear.

It did not. They were not prepared. They had done nothing. And their first show is a disaster.

It starts with the hawker, a feral-looking child with bare feet and large, ruby-red ears. He tells Lena his name is Tam. She thanks him for coming and asks if he will walk around the area near the tent and shout: 'Ladies' circus. Tuppence a show. Come this way, please.'

'But why, miss?' he asks.

She studies his face. 'Why what?'

'Why would you have lassies in a circus?'

'It's ladies, Tam. And why not?'

He rocks back on his heels and whistles, as though he could never have imagined such an extraordinary thing. 'And what's in it for me?'

'Tuppence, and a meat piece for your tea.'

'I'll have the pennies now, then,' he says. He smiles. He has gaps in his mouth where the baby teeth have fallen out, pink gums waiting patiently for the new ones to grow in.

'Alright,' she says. 'But you get your piece later on.'

He snatches the money and scuttles off into the sparse crowd that is starting to gather, shouting, 'Lassies' circus, lassies' circus.' Lena feels her irritation rise as she heads into the tent.

At the bar, Violet is panicking. 'Are you sure this is safe?' she's asking Harry, who looks unflappable and unhurried.

'Of course it's bloody safe, you silly wee girl. You think this is my first time at the circus?'

'Well, it doesn't look it. And don't swear. Lena doesn't like it, do you, Lena?'

Lena ignores her. 'Where's Rosie?' she asks.

Violet shrugs. 'At the stable, I suppose, getting Tommy Pony ready.'

At that moment there is a commotion at the door of the tent. It as though a great horde is pushing to get in, and Lena worries that the hawker has done his job too well, too quickly, that there is a crowd of excited fairgoers already, until a muzzle appears through the tent. 'Lena,' Rosie shouts, and her voice is muffled behind the canvas. 'I don't think Tommy will fit.'

Finally, it is showtime. Rosie has gone back to the stable, heartbroken, unable to perform, leading a morose and confused Tommy Pony through the crowd. Harry says they can work on the tent, make it bigger, but it does not stop Rosie from sobbing, great heaving hiccups that turn her normally grey eyes a clear, watery blue.

But now there are people, real people, shuffling into the tent, faces confused but expectant. Their clothing is hand-stitched and smart: sturdy boots, long, sensible dresses, overalls made of thick workman's canvas. Children cling to their mothers' skirts or pull faces at each other. Men mutter quietly to each other. There are occasional digs in the ribs. Their expressions are familiar. Lena knows what they want, what they expect to see, because she has seen it every summer since she was a bairn. They want a cheap thrill, and it is up to her to give it to them.

There are maybe fifteen folk in the tent. Lena wonders if Tam has brought them in, but when she peeks outside he has, predictably, vanished. She gives a small nod and Carmen dances into the small ring they have created with the sparse sawdust. Her streamers fly in all directions, a blur of colour, and there is the odd murmur from the audience as they watch this rainbow confection. It is a beautiful sight, until a child darts suddenly forward, entranced by the whirl of colours, and grasps one of her ribbons. It is like pulling a loose thread. All the streamers cascade from her costume and on to the floor and Carmen, her face panicked, freezes. The child darts backs and Carmen recovers herself, does her best to cover her body with her hands. A deep, rumbling laugh ripples through the crowd.

'Stopped by a wean!'

'Off with ye!'

'Give us a striptease instead, hen!'

Lena, standing at the back, is aghast. Something as simple as a nosy child has railroaded the whole show. She looks up at the rafters where Violet hides, unseen by the crowd, ready to swing down on her trapeze, and nods at her, furiously.

Violet swings, and the crowd looks up in shock. Their faces lighten. They had not expected *this*. Violet sways slightly, then pulls herself up on to the bar and performs a somersault before catching the next bar, which has been pushed forward by Harry, hiding on the other side.

There is a collective gasp. While the first swing is still moving she does it again, and there is another gasp as the bar bobs and weaves dangerously, the top of the tent flapping precariously. But then Violet looks at Harry and shakes her head.

'Not strong enough,' she shouts at him. 'I can't risk it.'

She hauls herself up on to the platform and looks down at the crowd, furious.

The throng sag. Is this it? Is there no more to see? Is this the whole show? A man turns to go, and a handful more, seeing the real world emerge briefly from behind the flap, hearing the sound of a hawker promising toffee apples, follow him. Within minutes the tent is empty. It is over.

Lena slumps to the ground, defeated. She balls her fists into her eyes to stop herself from crying. She will not let them see her weep. But then Violet is there, all bony angles and cooling sweat, wrapping Lena into her, and she allows herself to lean in and sob. She thinks of her father, how disappointed he would be that she sold his beloved carousel for this. She feels a hot, prickling shame and, beneath that, a deep fear. She has let everyone down. She has failed. It is over.

'Come on, now,' says Violet softly. 'It wasn't that bad.'

Lena hiccups into her angular shoulder. 'It was bloody awful and you know it. We're finished. It was a stupid idea. What the hell was I thinking?'

She takes a deep heaving breath, tries to steady herself. All she can hear is the galloping of Violet's heart.

'Well, if it was a stupid idea, then it was my stupid idea too,' Violet says.

Lena shakes her head. 'I let you talk me into it. I spent all that money on the tent. It was me who wrote up the posters, dragged Rosie and Carmen away from their lives . . .'

'Rosie and Carmen *wanted* to get away from their lives – surely you can see that.' Violet sits back and produces a clean cotton handkerchief. Lena dabs at her eyes and looks at her. 'Those girls are desperate for an adventure,' Violet continues. 'And so are we. What else are we going to do?

Sit around Vinegarhill shouting at the crows and poking our noses into other people's business like my mammy?'

Lena giggles. It turns into a small sob. She looks around at the tent, empty now. 'I don't know where to start,' she says.

'You already have,' says Violet. 'We've started. And now we'll get better. I promise. We're in this together.'

Lena's eyes fill with tears again. 'Thank you,' she says, wrapping her arms around her friend once more.

'Anyway,' says Violet, '*bloody awful*? I thought you didn't like swearing.'

'Shut the hell up,' says Lena into her shoulder, and they rock, and cry and laugh together while, outside the tent, the fair whirls on.

9

Rosie realises

Night time. A sky of distant stars. Rosie sits on the steps of the caravan twirling a single daisy, worrying at the stalk until it disintegrates, sticky and green, in her hands. She was in the stables while the show went on, trapped in her own despair, but knows, now, what happened. A disaster. The end of things.

She tosses the tiny flower into the dark. Rosie does not think it is the end of things, even if Lena does. She is convinced, deep down, that had she been able to perform she would have blown them all away. That Violet is talented, as is Carmen. That Lena has talent too, she just doesn't know it yet.

Rosie may be small, and young, but a fierce heart beats inside her tiny chest. She has not come this far to give up now. She has not cantered away from her life, left its remains in rotting tatters, stoked her father's fury and her mother's despair, for it to fall apart because of a few sniggering men.

She remembers her mother, cowering one night by the fire, vinegar-soaked poultice at her blossoming purple eye, hand trembling next to the flames. How she had gone to her, gently taken the poultice and held it for her, wrapping her other hand in hers, stroking the rough skin of her thumb, tracing over the ragged nail. Her mother was a broken woman, and Rosie knew that she was trapped. She wondered who she might have become, this shell of a person, had she been allowed to sing openly, instead of living in abject fear.

Rosie realised she did not know who her mother really was, and that was because her mother did not know who she was either. Her sharp edges had been smoothed out into a blank white sheet. She knew that her mother liked plum jam, which she made herself each autumn as the leaves fell outside in golden clumps, smeared on a slice of warm bread straight from the stove. She knew that her favourite dress was the blue calico, even though it had been ripped once, years ago, when her father stood on the hem. That she liked to wear her hair pinned to the side, and that she would sing sometimes, old songs about ploughing and lost loves, as she fluttered around the kitchen.

But she knew nothing of her mother's desires and needs, what she dreamt of at night when her tormentor had finally fallen into deep sleep, what made her laugh. She knew only what made her cry.

Rosie gets up and walks softly away from the wagon. The rest of the girls are asleep. There has been brandy and tears, and now Rosie can hear soft snores from the back. She picks her way through the litter that a day at the fair has left, her soft footprints trailing into the dark.

'Violet, wake up.'

Violet snaps her eyes open in fear.

'Sshh,' says Rosie. 'It's just me.'

She jumps down from the bunk. She is still wearing her dress from the day before, even though light streams into the wagon.

'Get dressed. I want to show you something.'

Outside the air is fresh, and a low mist hangs across the showground. It has rained during the night, and the wetness seeps into her boots as they walk.

'Well?' says Violet, yawning, expectant. 'What's so important you had to tear me away from my sleep?'

The Show Woman

They round a corner and the whole showground opens up to them. There are caravans as far as the eye can see, some with little puffs of smoke chugging out from the flume in their roofs. Early risers are already pottering about, hanging up washing, starting fires, heating kettles for hot tea.

'This,' says Rosie. She points at the scene in front of them, and Violet shrugs.

'So? It's a bunch of show folk getting up in the morning. Hardly exciting, Rosie.'

'It is to me,' she says. She stops, crossing her thin arms over her dress. 'I think you've forgotten who I am. I'm a flattie, as you call them. A farmer's daughter. I've never seen anything like this before – this world.'

'OK, well, congratulations. Now you have.'

Violet turns to go and Rosie shoots out an arm to stop her.

'You're missing the point. This is what we need. I'm what we need. You and Lena, you grew up with all of this. The shows, the fair, living in these wagons. And now it's all got a bit . . .' she casts around looking for the right word '. . . stale. You're like that heel of bread Lena's been carting around with her since Vinegarhill. You've gone all crusty and hard.'

Violet gives her a small, languid smile. 'Go on.'

'If you want to put on a show, a good show, you need to see what the other folk are doing. Get a few ideas. Pretend you've never seen any of it before and it's just as amazing as the first time you ever saw it. See what's not being done, too, and who's getting it wrong. That's the only way we're going to do this between us, with what we've got. That, and figure out how to fit Tommy into the tent.'

Her lips twitch and Violet laughs. 'Aye, well. Right enough. You might be on to something, Miss Rosie.'

On impulse, Violet, still soft with sleep, leans in and hugs her. Rosie turns pink and hugs her back.

'So what you're saying is you want a wee day out at the fair?'

Rosie nods into Violet's hair, damp now from the early morning air.

'I really do.'

10

They move through the fair

It is a magical day, rich and endless. Threads of happiness spool through the hours like spun gold. They start, at Rosie's behest, with the big dipper, a swing boat as huge, she imagines, as any that must surely cast off from the Clyde. When Carmen hears this she laughs and says she should see the size of some of the men who come off those hulking great boats. They sit on its prow as it swings back and forth with a rollicking force, as though a giant hand is pushing it each time, and with a thrill Rosie feels her heart bounce into her stomach.

They ride on two different carousels, Lena remarking on how strange they are compared to her father's. One has a variety of farm animals: sheep, horses, cows, and improbably large chickens. The other has more traditional horses, bobbing up and down, and when Violet says they will look like silly wee bairns riding on them, Rosie knows that she doesn't care, really.

They follow the sounds of the brass bands and the barrel organs, as the mid-morning throng starts to swell. They stop to admire some birds of paradise, small, vibrantly coloured birds the colour of jewels that will hop on to your hand for a nibble of seed if you stand still. Rosie spots a small canvas tent advertising 'the world's larg'st lady'. There is a painting outside of a woman who looks like a cross between a pig and a toad, and a man beside it shouting for all and sundry to 'roll up and see them rolls'. Rosie is intrigued, takes off towards it, but Lena pulls her back. 'Come away,' she says quietly.

Down among the hawkers and the food stalls, the scent of chestnuts roasting over sputtering wooden fires, apples dipped in rich, hot toffee, is irresistible. Carmen buys a ha'penneth of round boiled sweets, vibrant red and rich grass green, and they suck them greedily as they alight upon another tent, its canvas an ancient, faded brown and torn in patches. Inside, a family – it must be; they all have the same thin lips and high, wide foreheads – are performing a melodrama. A young woman in a white nightgown flings herself to the floor of the tiny mounted stage while another, her hair standing up on end, weeps and cries, 'Dead! All dead! And no one to call me mother!' The audience roars approval while a man near the front with a cigarette sticking out of his mouth shouts, 'We can see your maidenhood in that nightgown, hen,' and the girl scuttles off the stage, her thin pale face turning bright puce.

But in among the coconut shies and the menageries, the whirling rides and the dark, mysterious tents, it is the crowd which fascinates Rosie the most. Gaggles of dirty-nosed children, some with no shoes on, who weave in and out playing elaborate games of chase. The young lad who shadows an elegant lady in a large hat, waiting for his opportunity to snatch her smart silk bag. She cries out as he does so, but he is so quick that by the time she turns round he is gone, swallowed up by the throng.

There are groups of farm girls, pink-cheeked with excitement at a day away from the constant grind of milking, washing and sweeping, and Rosie wonders idly why it was that her own parents never thought to bring her to the local fair; why there had instead been endless nights at home, her father seeking solace in the bottle, her mother sewing meek threads by the fire. There had just been that one trip to the circus, all those years ago. Linden's, she thinks it was called, where her pa sneered at the horses and her ma whispered to Rosie that she thought the acrobats were beautiful.

Because there are families here, great hordes of them, wives cautiously taking their lead from their men while marshalling squadrons of bairns in knickerbockers and sailor suits, wearing good dresses probably meant for church, and soon turned filthy amid the churned-up ground beneath them. Groups of men too, wearing their best jackets and bunnets – handsome, she can see that, but with something wild about them too, as though an invisible leash has been snapped, just for one day, and they can let out their full gregarious selves. One man grabs the bottom of a particularly fulsome farm girl, and Rosie is gratified to see that she turns round and swiftly slaps him on the cheek.

Suddenly Violet is beside her, squeezing her arm, her face flushed with something that looks like excitement but has an urgency to it, as though there are a million things she needs to say to Rosie right now, this minute, but somehow cannot find the words.

Instead, Rosie simply asks, 'Yes?'

Violet nods. 'Yes,' she says. 'Yes to all of it. Yes.'

11

Ringmistress

For Lena, the days that follow are swift and heady. Carmen and Rosie work on a double act, with Carmen and her elaborate ribbons, now sewn on twice as tightly by Lena, always a dab hand with a needle, providing both an entrance and a foil to Rosie's horse tricks. Lena engages the services of Tam again, who turns out to be a hard worker as long as he does not get paid until the end of the day, and he helps expand the width of the canvas entrance for Tommy Pony and cuts another one in the back, so that Carmen can enter at the last minute, surprising the audience.

Violet tweaks her act too, after haranguing Harry into securing the platform and the bar, bringing in some workies to affix the bar to the top of the tent just to make sure, and Tam is hired to push the bar to her when needed. With the wider tent she introduces some of her flashier moves, including one with her legs pushed out like a perfect triangle as she swings by one hand, the other nonchalantly resting on her hip.

One day, as she is watching Violet from the floor of the tent, marvelling at the ease with which she can swing from side to side, Carmen materialises beside Lena. She is holding a small black case.

'I have something to show you,' she says, bending down to open it, revealing something in three separate pieces that glints silver in the gloom. She hastily screws it together, and Lena sees it is a flute.

'You play? Carmen, why didn't you say?'

'I am shy. I did not know if you would want me.'

Lena studies her open, honest face. 'Play something for us.'

Up in the rafters Violet swings lazily from one arm, watching.

Carmen lifts the flute to her lips and plays, at first haltingly, her eyes on Lena's, and then, with more confidence. It is a haunting, elegant melody, one that just catches the fringes of Lena's memory. Carmen's long, bony fingers trill the keys in the silence.

When she finishes, Violet gives a whoop from above.

'That was wonderful,' says Lena. 'Do I know the song?'

'It is Irish, I think,' says Carmen. 'Something about moving through fairs.'

'We must work it into the show,' says Lena, and they spend the rest of the afternoon weaving her tunes into the performance.

And then there is Lena herself. Wandering the fair that day, she realises that she must be in charge, must present the show. She can no longer hide in the shadows, even though that is, and has always been, her instinct. She must take control, introduce her acts – for they are her acts, she realises – and take pride in them too.

The night before their first proper show, she sits alone by the wagon, watching bedsheets on a makeshift line flutter in the spring breeze, breathing in the mild country air. She has constructed an outfit – an old pair of her father's trousers carefully hemmed and pulled up to her waist, one of his white shirts, tucked in and with the sleeves rolled up, a black silk tie at her throat, her hair scraped back in a low bun, and a bowler hat which Tam found on the ground by the stables. Her lips have been reddened with Carmen's rouge.

'Ladies and gentlemen,' she whispers.

The Show Woman

She fiddles with the tight, starched white collar, her father's best shirt, worn on the rare occasions they went to church. She stands up and tries again.

'Ladies and gentlemen, boys and girls,' she says loudly. 'May I present to you, the ladies' circus.'

Silence. She bows low to the ground, sweeping the bowler off her head. High above, a lone kestrel circles the sky, searching for rabbits in the tall grass. And then, from behind her, the sound of a steady clap.

'Bravo,' says Harry, emerging from the side of the wagon. 'What time does the show start?'

Lena colours at his words, fusses at the neck of her shirt. She had not meant to be caught like this, for someone to witness this makeshift performance. She puts her hand to her cheek. 'I didn't see you.'

He hangs his head slightly. 'I'm sorry. I know you didn't.'

She looks at his handsome face, wonders if it is a twinkle of amusement she can see in his eyes, or pity.

'It was good,' he says. 'In fact, I'd go so far as to say that Scotland has never seen anything quite like it. A woman in the ring, in a bowler hat; you're going to cause quite the stir.'

'We need to,' she says. She heads back over to the wagon steps and sits down, aware of Harry's eyes on her as she does so, that she walks differently in trousers, more confident, assured. 'We can't afford to have two disasters.'

Harry puts his hands in his pockets. 'You'll be fine. Perhaps you needed a fright to get you on the right track.'

Lena laughs. 'It was certainly a fright alright. I've never been so ashamed.'

Harry shakes his head, steps closer to her. 'Don't be silly. Everyone has a bad show sometimes. Just ask Jimmy Moore. He's had more bad shows than you could shake a dancing bear at.'

'How are you getting on with him?'

'Ach, he's alright,' says Harry. 'He's good company, that's the main thing. And as long as he pays me I'm happy to stay. Speaking of which, I better get back and help him pack up the ride for the day.'

He bends down and picks up the bowler hat resting at Lena's feet, and places it on her head.

'Your daddy would be proud of you,' he says, and walks away, into the long grass.

12

Presence

They are ready. Lena fizzes with anticipation, her body taut with nerves, as she stands in the centre of the little tent. Tam and Rosie have pasted posters up around the fairground, introducing the ladies' circus. There have been raised eyebrows, catty remarks, wolf-whistles and sneers. Talk of moving the fair on early, up to Stirling and then on to Perthshire, in an attempt to deny them an audience. For who would visit a showground with just one lone, tiny tent? It is a notion that has, she understands, caused much mirth.

'They're running scared,' is Violet's only remark on the subject, shouted down from the bar, where she now spends much of her time. She reminds Lena of a bird in a nest up there, utterly at home and content, luxuriating in her natural habitat. She wishes she herself felt half as comfortable down here on the ground.

Carmen, meanwhile, spends every spare moment practising her flute. She has widened her repertoire and, while most of the songs mean little to Lena, she can appreciate her talent, the craft she has honed.

'Where did you learn to play?' she asks her one afternoon, finding her practising round the back of the wagons, away from the main drag of the fair.

'At home,' she says. 'Back in Spain my father was a fisherman. He did well on the boats and we lived a nice life. He wanted all his children to have a skill, particularly the girls. He said we should not just laze around waiting for our husbands to arrive.'

She stifles a laugh at the memory.

'For my big sister Consuelo it was the piano. My younger sister played the violin – the fiddle, as you say. And for me, the flute. I had a teacher, who lived in a house by the olive grove. He worked me hard, but I enjoyed it. But then my father died; he went out to the sea and he did not come back. And there was no more money for flute lessons.'

Lena is taken aback. It is the longest speech she has heard from Carmen, who is often quiet and meek, keeps her own private counsel.

'I am so sorry about your father,' she says.

Carmen bows her head. 'Thank you,' she says. 'Yours too. It is something we have in common, is it not? Our sorrow, I mean.'

'It is,' says Lena. 'You can always talk to me if you are feeling sad. We can be sad together.'

Despite their threats, the fair has not moved on, the various cynical showmen who pepper the ground opting instead for quiet disapproval. A group of wee lassies is no threat to them. Let them have their fun and they'll be away with their mammies in a week. Tam, earnest and trying to be helpful, relates this news, and Lena is surprised at how much it stings. If only they knew. That she has no mammy to return to, that she is instead searching for her, trying desperately to find some trace of her. The casual cruelty cuts her deeply.

She wonders if her mammy came to Linlithgow. Probably. The route the fairs follow each summer is as old as the hills they traverse to get to them. It has been walked by thousands of show women before, will likely be walked by thousands more. Their footsteps have worn grooves into the earth. Now, it is her time. A stop on the road that will eventually take her to Galston. And possibly, the truth.

The Show Woman

Lena walks to the back of the tent as she hears Tam pull open the canvas. A trickle of fairgoers walk in, young women in their best dresses, the colour high on their cheeks. There are still no chairs, simply a circle drawn around the ring in the sawdust, and they walk shyly up to it, gazing around them. They are followed by a gang of young men, showmen who have come to gawp. Then a swarm of children, barefoot and noisy, a few older ladies from the town, their faces showing a hint of disapproval.

Hidden in the shadows, Lena watches them, her heart fluttering in her chest. Beside her, Carmen clutches her hand, ribbons fluttering gently in the breeze.

'It is going to be good,' Carmen says to her, squeezing her wrist. 'Just you wait.'

Tam comes through the canvas and signals that there appear to be no more. This is it, then. Showtime, again. At last.

'Ladies and gentlemen,' Lena booms, striding into the middle of the ring. Her voice is louder than she expected, steadier too, and the small, shuffling crowd gapes at her. 'Welcome to the ladies' circus. What you will see today will thrill and amaze you. You will see women fly. Tumble. Throw themselves from animals and emerge intact. What you will see is no less than a miracle.'

She is striding around the ring, the only sound her own voice. The crowd stares back at her, curious, expectant.

'Are you ready to see miracles? Are you ready to see a woman fly?'

'I saw one fly last week down at the Black Dog,' says one young man. 'In fact she flew straight into a puddle. Landed on her face.'

His friends crow with laughter.

Lena rounds on him. 'And you didn't catch her, sir? Why, I would have thought a young, strong man like you . . .' She lets the comment hang in the air as his friends' laughter turns on him.

'Ooh, feisty, that one,' a man shouts. Lena ignores him.

'Without further ado, ladies and gentlemen – those among us tonight who are gentlemen, that is – I present, the ladies' circus!'

From a dark corner of the tent, music rises. It is Carmen, playing her flute. She trills furiously while Lena, with a theatrical flourish, lifts her hat and stretches her arm towards the top of the tent. The crowd's eyes follow, as Violet swings down on the bar.

She is holding on with both hands, swinging almost lazily, as though she were just an inch off the ground. Then, unseen, Tam throws the second bar on the other side to her and she leaps to catch it.

The crowd gasps with surprise, but before they can process what she is doing, Violet leaps again, back on to the first bar. Carmen trills her flute, an almost melancholy tune. It is strange and beautiful. And then Rosie emerges, standing on one leg, as Tommy Pony races round the ring while, above, Violet continues to swing.

Lena, back in the shadows, breathes a sigh of relief. It has worked. They have a show.

They do three performances that first day. Each time the crowd is bigger, and Lena's voice, her very presence, seems to swell too. She feeds off their energy and excitement, even their scepticism. She bats away the catty remarks, mocks the doubters, showers praise on those who throw themselves into the swing of things. At the end of the final show she brings several small, eager children into the ring

The Show Woman

to pet Tommy Pony. He obliges by snuffling at them, and Rosie even lifts one small child on to his back and trots around the ring with him.

Lena, standing back to watch Rosie, a natural with children, cannot quite believe that they have been a success. The shouts and applause ring in her ears. She wonders how much money they have made. Enough to take them on to the next fair at least.

'Well done,' says a deep voice behind her. Harry emerges from the crowd, his face a mixture of confusion and possibly, pride.

'What did you think?' she asks. After the elation of their performance she feels suddenly shy, unsure of herself.

Harry puts his hands in his pockets.

'You've got a good show here. Violet was fabulous but you were . . .' He pauses, searching for the right words. 'You've got a knack for the stage. A real presence.'

She looks up at his open face. 'Really?'

'Yes, really. I had an inkling you might be able to address the crowd the other night but I didn't expect all this. You're talented. I had no idea.'

'I honestly had no idea myself. My daddy always said I could be a show woman but I thought he meant operating a ride, a stall. The idea that I could come out into the ring like that . . . I didn't know I had it in me.'

Harry looks at her. 'You do. Trust me.'

He lights a cigarette. The crowd is dissipating now, back out into the warm evening.

'We're away tomorrow. Falkirk route, then on up to Stirling. Are you going?'

Lena nods. 'A couple more days here, I think. Scare up a few more pennies so we can make the journey. But yes. I think we might have a proper show here. Something that will keep us going all summer.'

'So do I,' says Harry. He takes a cigarette out of his box and tucks it behind Lena's ear. 'See you in Stirling.'

Violet is on a high after the show. She flips her body backwards and forwards, cartwheeling her way past the wagons, shouting about flying ladies and rainbow girls and the finest circus in the land.

'Shut up, Vi,' says Lena, 'some folk are sleeping.'

It is a mark of Violet's jubilation that she does not admonish Lena for calling her Vi – a name she loathes, partly because at the grim Glasgow school they were forced to attend in winter, the city kids would chorus, 'Hi, Vi,' and then collapse into giggles.

'Let her be,' says Carmen, who is still wearing her ribbon costume, its long tendrils trailing lazily in the grass. 'Look at her, she is happy.'

Violet turns another cartwheel, and Lena softens. It is what her own heart is doing, after all, deep inside her chest.

13

Lioness

Vengeance is cold, and today is too hot for rage. Serena swats at the air with a delicate hand-painted fan, legs spread wide like the man she often wishes she could have been. Being a woman has rarely been to her benefit. From the aches and disappointments of motherhood to the sheer inconvenience of impudent youths who constantly disregard her, Serena's sex has become a burden, heavy as the sagging breasts that give her back such gyp.

She is watching the new lion-tamer, a boy from Spain who has brought with him a young, miserable cub. He assures her it will grow as large and ferocious as its father, who was wide and heavy as a motor car. He dangles some meat and the cub leaps for it, a tiny pathetic jump, and the boy lowers his hand so it can tear off some of the bloody, rancid steak. The animal looks more like a mangy barn cat, although its jaws are reassuringly wide, the teeth inside comfortingly sharp. Serena likes the danger of these big animals. It is one of the trademarks of Linden's Circus, her show, the one she moulded herself with these bare, calloused hands, which she made in her own image after she took it over from her long-dead pa.

She darts forward and smacks the lion cub sharply on its back with her fan. The animal yelps and looks up at her, its face a mixture of defiance and feral aggression. It is measuring her up, wondering if she is worth attacking. The cub's weight shifts on to its hind legs, as though it might pounce, and she thwacks it again, this time on the nose. It rears back and rushes to its master.

'Do you not know how to train these animals, boy?' she asks.

The young Spaniard, with English that is negligible at best, retorts, '*Sí, sí, señora.*'

'More of this,' she says, shaking her fan. 'And less of that.' She points at the meat.

'*Sí, señora,*' the boy repeats.

She walks away. Useless, she thinks. So many of her animal-tamers make the mistake of treating their charges like pets, like those pathetic dog-owners that coddle their animals, bring them into their homes, let them sit by the fire and sleep on their soft, downy beds. That is not what animals know, not what they need. You must treat them as though they are wild.

She recalls the large brown dog her father owned when she was a child, which followed him everywhere and was so slavishly devoted that it would have followed him towards certain death. That relationship fascinated her, even as a small girl. How the dog would listen only to his commands, push in front of her to get food at dinner, snap at her if she tried to give her father a hug. The dog was more than his shadow. It was as though it was a part of who he was, his core being.

And yet it was tied up outside their wagon on a chain, never fed more than scraps, thumped on the nose for the most minor of infractions. And that was the point. Her father treated it as a mean and nasty cur, because he knew all along that, given half a chance, that was exactly what it would be. It was a philosophy she followed as slavishly as that dog followed her father.

She plods slowly back to her wagon, wondering whether she needs to get rid of the Spaniard and look elsewhere. Lions are not easy to come by, even in this magical new age of steamships and international travel, the influx of

Europeans who have landed recently on these shores, some of them with designs on the fairs with their fancy cinematographs. Then there are the Americans with their Wild West shows. She remembers still the huge stir when Buffalo Bill came to Glasgow twenty years before: how the crowds swelled to see the famous man with his guns in his holsters shoot a strawberry off a tin can with pin-sharp accuracy. Linden's Circus was at Vinegarhill at the time and Serena had been delighted at the increase in business, at the sweaty Glasgow youths who came to see her shows riled up from the gunfights, many of them drunk, no doubt; even at the stupid boy who leapt up during the lion show, stuck his head in the beast's mouth and wound up losing an eye. It had all been good for business, in the end.

There was something else Serena's father had taught her, back in those sunlit days: the honeyed taste of revenge. If someone crossed you, you double-crossed them back. And if anyone was foolish enough to try putting one over on a Linden, they'd pay for it and then some. Old Saffo, a circus proprietor from England, had learnt this the hard way when he tried to steal one of Linden's prime pitches in Edinburgh for the Christmas season. Late one night Serena's pa had sent one of his lads to throw a brace of meat laced with arsenic into the lions' cages. The next day he'd watched, triumphantly, as the entire cavalcade left the city, the lions' carcasses dumped into the Water of Leith, where they rotted slowly in the late winter sun, pecked at by seagulls and oyster-catchers who had never encountered such bounty. 'That's how you deal with a rival,' he had told her. 'That's how you keep us on top.'

Serena lights her pipe, feels the long-dead itch for revenge creep across her skin. Because Serena has heard of another show that is stirring the hearts of the flatties. A ladies' circus no less, with rainbows and horses and, at the heart of it all, a copper-haired demon with berry-red lips.

She might have known Violet Weaver would be back on the bar. She did not understand Serena, her capacity to hold grudges. It was time to pull that lassie out of the sky once and for all.

She sucks on her pipe, looks out at the showground where her circus is packing up. It is time to move on. She will circle the wagons, and creep closer. A lioness, stalking her prey.

14

Caged birds

Rosie sits astride Tommy Pony, breathing in lungfuls of early morning air. Ahead of her on a fencepost sits a magpie, its black wings gleaming like oil in the sunshine.

'Good morning, Mr Magpie, how's your wife and bairns?'

It was her mother who taught her to say this, a talisman against the bad luck of seeing a single magpie without its companion. One for sorrow, two for joy, three for a girl and four for a boy.

'I never did see four magpies,' her mother said once, when Rosie was about ten. 'That must be why I ended up with you and your sister.'

Rosie chokes at the memory. She misses her mother; fears for her, given how her father will react to her disappearance. The man treated her as though she were a possession, a plaything, believed she was under his complete control. Whatever rage has been kindled in him as a result of her flight, her mother will bear the brunt.

She thinks of Jennifer, preparing for her wedding, gathering her meagre trousseau, hopeful for a new life, bairns of her own. Rosie's bridesmaid dress still in the parlour, newly sewn and unworn. She wonders if she has been monumentally selfish, leaving them to him. Then she remembers her father's thick, evil hands. The words he whispered, rough and guttural, into her ear. The way he touched her. Running away from him is the only selfish thing she has ever done in her life. She will not persecute herself for it. She grew up believing that control was something only others could have.

Her father, his father before him. The women who orbited around them were merely possessions, assets, like the chickens kept locked at night in a coop in the front yard. Ready to be used when necessary. But the day Tommy Pony arrived it had dawned on Rosie that it did not have to be like this. That if she were brave enough, she could wrest back control of her life, herself, and her body. Finally, she had. She would never let anyone, or anything, control her again.

She reaches down to pat Tommy. He has been nervous around the big Clydesdale horses, and is not used to performing either. Yet he has been brave. Held his own. Been there for her, too, good as gold.

'Morning.' Violet strides into the small paddock, eyes bleary, hair tied loosely in a bun. It has rained overnight and a light smirr hangs in the air. The ground is soft, squelches under her boots. 'How's Tommy boy today?'

Rosie jumps down. The magpie is still on the fence, its beady eyes resting on her.

'Not too bad,' she says. 'Thought I'd take him out for a quick trot this morning, away from the crowds. It's been a big change for him.'

Violet lights a cigarette and perches on the fence. The magpie flicks its head with annoyance, opens its wings and flies into a nearby tree. 'You too, I'd imagine.'

Rosie says nothing. She is still a little afraid of Violet, her worldly ways, her experiences and her stories. She has met lion-tamers, toured with the famous Linden's Circus, and been all the way to England. Until she left the farm Rosie hadn't even got as far as Ayr town. But there is something else about Violet which unnerves her. An undercurrent. A sense of something *other*. When Violet is around, the air crackles with electricity. Excitement. She is afraid of her, yes, yet she wants to be around her. Life feels vivid, more brightly coloured, when she is near.

The Show Woman

Finally Rosie nods.

'It's strange,' she says slowly. 'Not being at home. It's where I've always been. All I've ever really known. And this world . . .' She gestures out behind them to the showground, where tents huddle together, Wurlitzers are striking up their tinny tunes and a swirl of people, ready for a day at the fair, are starting to gather. 'It's still so different. And it's always changing. I like it, but it's scary, too.'

'Perhaps you need to change with it,' says Violet, taking a long drag on her cigarette and looking at her closely.

'Is that what you do?'

Violet snorts. 'I suppose so. When your home is the road, you keep moving. Your head is always racing on to the next thing, the next place. It becomes part of you. The road, the travel, the life. It's all I've ever known.'

Rosie smiles shyly at her.

'Do you think you could ever live in a house? As a . . .' the word sounds strange in her mouth '. . . flattie?'

Violet snorts again, reaches her hand round to the nape of her neck to tug on her bun. 'Not likely. I'd feel like one of those birds they sell on the penny shies, all caged up.'

She looks up at the magpie, still solitary, watching them from a branch of the tree.

'You imagine Mr Magpie up there.'

Rosie blushes. Violet must have heard her talking to the bird.

'If we put him in a cage, fed him worms through the bars, how long do you think it would take for all those lovely black and white feathers to fall out? Do you think he'd still be a handsome, fine-feathered chap in a month? Or even a week? Or do you think he'd turn into a bald little coot, shrivelled and miserable, refusing even the juiciest worms?'

Rosie looks up again at the magpie, at its taut, gleaming feathers. Then she looks at Violet, imagines for a moment how she would look without her magnificent long hair, or the sparkle in her eyes.

'It's the only life I've ever known, but it's the life for me,' says Violet, grinding out her cigarette.

'I was caged too,' says Rosie in a small voice. 'In my own way.'

Violet looks at her. 'Tell me,' she says. 'I know you've been holding something in. Keeping it close. You can trust me. I'm like Mr Magpie. I won't breathe a word.'

And so Rosie tells Violet about her father, about the unspeakable things he did to her, how she was suffocating with anger and grief in that farmhouse, how she had to get away before it burst out of her and broke everything.

'I can't tell you how much it meant when I saw that poster,' she says, looking at Violet, at her pale skin, almost translucent, her wide eyes. 'I knew it was my ticket out of there. It was the end and the start. A new life.'

Violet catches her wrist and squeezes it. Her hands are cold, the fingers soft.

'I think you're the bravest person I've ever met, Rosie Posy. I'm proud of you. And you should be proud of yourself. And don't you go thinking you're the only one around here starting a new life. We all are. Me, Lena, Carmen – we all needed to be here. That's why it's working so well.'

She lets Rosie's hand drop.

'Lena says we're off tomorrow, on to Falkirk. So if I were you I'd get Tommy Pony trussed up for his show this afternoon, and then come and help us get the tent up.'

She touches Rosie's cheek briefly, then turns towards the wagons.

Rosie leads Tommy back to the stable, feeling lighter than she has in years. When she looks up at the tree, the magpie has gone.

15

Carmen's secret

Rain beats down as they pull into Stirling, but little can dampen Lena's mood. For the past two weeks in Falkirk their shows have been a success. Their curious little circus with its famous trapeze artist, its lithe, beautiful rainbow girl, deft equestrian and mysterious ringmistress have captured imaginations. Word is starting to spread.

On the way out of Denny, the last fairground before Stirling, they are stopped twice, once by a flock of young farm workers wanting to take them out for the night, and then by an older couple, asking why they were leaving so soon.

'You better get yourselves back here before too long,' the older lady shouts as they trot down the lane and on to the main road. 'We'd all like a squint at ye.'

Stirling showground squats underneath the old castle. Its battlements hulk over the town, forbidding and ancient. Lena is setting the wagon up for the day when she realises they are running low on food, almost out of bread and cheese.

'Come on,' she says to Carmen. 'We'll away up the town and pick up a few bits. The other two can see to the horses.'

On the cobbles of the old town, hooves clatter through the long, winding streets. In a small square they see the remnants of the fruit and vegetable market packing up, crates of early blaeberries, their skins soft and cloudy, great sacks of potatoes, piles of unscrubbed neeps. As they walk round the edge of the square, Lena hears a shout.

'Hey! Hey! Wait up.'

They stop and turn. A large man is running towards them, wearing an apron. He has fat cheeks and jowls, and a cap on his head. He stops in front of them and looks at Carmen.

'You're a long way from home, hen,' he says, peering at her closely. Spittle has dried in the corners of his mouth. 'Finally got yourself out of the rat pit, did you?'

Carmen turns away hurriedly, begins running out of the square. Lena, mystified, follows her.

'Or have you just brought another of yer rats for a day out?' He laughs loudly as Lena runs to catch up with Carmen.

'What is he talking about?'

Carmen's face glistens with tears. She shakes her head. Says nothing.

'Come on. Tell me. Did you know that man?'

Carmen stops, fumbles in her skirts for a handkerchief and eventually produces a grubby one edged in fine, delicate lace. She mops at her eyes, nods slowly.

'I knew him once. Maybe a few times. In another life.'

'Another life?' Lena is still confused. 'Before you came to Glasgow? You knew him in Spain?' The whole thing seems incredible. What would a fruit-seller be doing in Spain? How could they have met here, like this?

Carmen shakes her head again. 'No. I knew him in Glasgow. I have not been . . .' She pauses. Cannot look Lena in the eye. 'I have not been completely honest with you. With all of you.'

Lena stays silent. She has grown to like this tall, beautiful woman with the gangly limbs, who can turn her body at will into any shape she desires, who can write words with the curve of her spine, who gets up and helps muck out the horses, does her share of the washing, and cooks

The Show Woman

stews with strong, pungent spices that make Lena picture warm places she has never been.

'I was on the streets, before.' Carmen looks up at Lena, her eyes burning with shame. 'I had been with a circus, a Spanish circus. We came to Britain, we toured, but then, I had an accident.'

'An accident? What happened? Were you hurt?'

'No,' she says. 'You do not understand. An accident with a man. He was . . .' She pauses, as though trying to recall a face. 'He was an acrobat, handsome. And then I was pregnant. They threw me out of the circus. I was alone. In this strange country. No money. No job. I could not go home. And then I found the rat pit.'

Lena flinches. She has heard of the rat pit, vaguely. Remembers Mary Weaver talking about it once. A home for women who had fallen on hard times. She doesn't know much about it, but she knows that you have to be desperate to go there. On your knees. Without love, or luck, or any chance of redemption.

'How long were you there?' she asks. 'And what happened to your baby?'

She motions for them to sit down on the kerb and a woman, dressed in a neat coat and dress, curls her lip at the sight of them. Carmen starts sobbing again.

'I was there for many months. It was the only place I could find to sleep. I lost the baby not long after I arrived. I bled between my legs, and then it was gone. But the women there, they have been through so many terrible things. They are without hope. Without God. I was too, for a while.'

Lena strokes her long chestnut hair, lets Carmen cry, softly. She cannot imagine how frightened she must have been, to lose her unborn bairn in such a place, with no one she knew or loved beside her.

Carmen looks up. 'And so that is why I did it.'

'What?' Lena says softly. 'What did you do?'

'I sold my body. To men. Rough, nasty men on street corners who hurt me. All for a few pennies.'

She buries her face in her hands again.

'Some of them were OK. There were a few who would buy me food, bring me fresh sheets. But most of them just wanted one thing.'

Lena understands now. Carmen's maturity, mingled with a hard-worn weariness, a quiet sadness. It had struck her from the moment they met. Now she realises that it comes from a place of pain. That Carmen has truly been to hell and back.

'I always knew you were strong, but I had no idea that you went through all that,' she says. 'How did you get out, my duck? How did you find us?'

Carmen chokes back another sob. Her nose is red, her eyes rimmed with tears, but she is still exquisitely beautiful.

'One day I decided to find a church. I am a Roman Catholic, and I knew I had sinned, and so I wanted to confess. There is a beautiful church in Glasgow, on Garnethill. It reminded me of the churches back home in Spain. I started going regularly, speaking to some of the women there. I told them about my life back in Spain; that I had been in the circus. And one day, after Mass, one of them brought me your poster.'

'Fate,' says Lena.

'Not God?' asks Carmen, and they laugh a little, there on the steps.

'We all believe in different things,' says Lena. 'My mammy taught me that. That those beliefs, no matter what they were, could be tested in the most awful ways. That's why I think you're so powerful. You've faced the worst in life, and yet you still believe. In yourself. In your god. And

The Show Woman

in us.' She looks sideways at Carmen. 'You do believe in us, don't you? Us four? The circus?'

Carmen nods her head. 'I have never believed in anything more.'

Lena squeezes her shoulder, and Carmen stands up. She seems calmer now. Talking of her faith has soothed her.

'Would you like to go to church now?' asks Lena. 'Shall we find one?'

And so the two women link arms, and walk through the winding streets to a little chapel, tucked away on a side wynd. Lena has so rarely been inside a church, only really in her school days, that she finds the dark, dusty pews, the high stained glass windows and the altar with its large gold cross intimidating. As Carmen kneels to pray, Lena gazes up at an icon of Jesus on the wall, the blood pouring from his crown of thorns, and wonders if everyone is put on earth simply to suffer.

By the time they leave the chapel the rain has stopped. The air is saturated with birdsong. In the still-blue sky an early moon hangs. A boy runs past, his bunnet askew, waving the evening paper. He is shouting.

'The King's deid! The King's deid! Do you think we'll get a holiday?'

16

Rememberings

The days shift, rich with light, the world struck silent by public mourning. Shops shutter. Schools close. Muffled church bells toll. Men wear black armbands and women their darkest, dowdiest dresses. At Stirling showground, a patch of green spread out like an underskirt beneath the towering castle, the fair shuts for three days, the entire weekend, as a mark of respect. Anxious showmen roam the grounds with bottles in their hands and money on their minds. A royal death, all this mourning and respect, will not be good for business.

Lena busies herself sprucing up costumes, adding real feathers to Rosie's headpiece that she has gathered from a nearby wood, wading up to her ankles through springy bluebells to find them. She likes to hold the feathers in her hand, feel the bony sharpness that softens into a bendable, wavy spine, the pillowy down that spans out in colours of grey and slate and deep, mossy green.

She keeps an eye on Carmen, who is quiet and occasionally morose, only leaving the wagon, and the small, battered Bible she now reads each day, to do her daily stretches and exercises. Lena wonders if she regrets having spilt her secret, and worries the woman might leave them. But where would she go? Back to the rat pit? Surely not. No one would willingly turn back down the road towards hell.

Violet, meanwhile, seems irritable and restless. She never could stand still. The travelling blood runs deep within her veins. She seems to take it personally that the

King has died. Her only remark on the matter, sitting on the steps of the caravan one night next to Rosie, a tatty tartan blanket round both of their shoulders, is to say, 'He's not my king.'

'It's hardly the King's fault he's died,' Lena says mildly.

'Isn't it?' asks Violet. 'I met this acrobat once who knew a showgirl, Emerald I think her name was, and she told him she'd danced for the King once, and apparently he was never away from the drink. Belly on him the size of Ireland.'

Later that night, when Carmen and Rosie are in bed, Lena talks to Violet about the prospect of a trip to Galston. Ayrshire has always been one of the last places in Scotland that the fairs visit on the old, well-worn routes that all show people follow each summer, a last hurrah after the biting cold of the northeast and the granite-grey city of Aberdeen. But perhaps now, with this unexpected break, they could take a quick trip? Ask about her mammy?

Violet is reluctant. 'It'll take too long,' she says, pulling a piece of tobacco from her teeth. 'By the time we get there the fair might be open again. And we can't leave those two on their own. They don't know which way is up, bless their wee flattie hearts.'

Lena senses there is more to Violet's resistance but decides to leave it. There is money to be made on the road right now. They'll make it to Galston soon enough.

On Monday the ground's owners make the decision to open, and the crowds flood in as never before. There is a pent-up energy, a charge in the air, and the reverential mourning gives way to something joyful, loose, and excitable. It lingers in the throng in the tent that first day, the faces that leer and twist, the gasps and shouts, particularly when Violet takes to the bar. Her act is now flawless. She

The Show Woman

flips and twists and bends and weaves, her body so pliable, it is as though she has turned to liquid. She hardly needs the bar at all, simply soars from one side of the tent to the other, as though she really can fly.

Perhaps, thinks Lena, I can play with that. Tease the crowd, suggest that Violet actually has wings. Didn't her daddy tell her about the mermaid with the tail? And didn't she always believe him?

That night, Lena wakes to the sound of whispering outside the wagon. Low, male, rough. Flatties, perhaps, keen with the drink and thinking they can noise up the ladies from the circus. She elbows Violet, who is deeply asleep beside her.

'Can you hear that?' she says in a low voice.

'*Mff*,' says Violet.

'What's the name of the one in the hat? Nice legs, but looks a wee bit hoity-toity,' says a voice from outside.

'Violet,' Lena says urgently. 'Wake up.'

Violet opens her eyes. Beyond her Rosie and Carmen are stirring too.

'Loony, isn't it?' says another disembodied voice, closer now, right under the wagon window.

'Aye, well, they'll be carting her off to the loony bin when I'm finished with her,' the first voice returns, to a low, guttural laugh.

Lena grips Violet's arm in fear, feels her huge green eyes staring at her in the dark. On the road with Daddy she so rarely had to worry about the men who, as her breasts grew large and full, her hips curved out and her waist went in, would eye her hungrily from a distance. Her daddy had a reputation, after all. Being a bareknuckle boxer had served him well. Nobody brought trouble to Joseph Loveridge's wagon, no matter how ripe his daughter looked, or ready for the picking.

'Evening, gents.'

Another voice, now. Different. Familiar. Lena sinks her nails into Violet's wrist and Violet snatches her arm back. 'Ouch,' she says.

'Shh,' responds Lena. 'Sorry.'

'Out for a wee stroll, are we? Nice night for it,' says the new voice, and Lena realises, with a soaring flood of relief, that it is Harry. All four of the women sit stock-still now, every sinew in their bodies straining to hear what will happen next.

'Bugger off,' says a gruff, nasty voice.

'I won't, actually,' says Harry, 'although I hear there's some lads down by the river who are into that sort of thing. It's you two who need to bugger off.'

Two of them. Dangerous. Harry's a big lad himself, but could he take on two drunk townies?

'Who the hell are you, ya ginger bastard?' says one of them, and he spits loudly on the ground.

'I'm a man with more pals on this ground than you, son,' says Harry. His voice is even-tempered, moderate, but there is a steely edge to his tone. 'Never seen either of you two before. You blow in from the town, did you? You should know you're not welcome here after hours.'

There is a commotion outside, as though one of the men has taken a run at Harry.

'Hey!' comes a shout.

A flash of white streaks through the caravan, the door flings open and Carmen hurls herself at one of the men, kicking him in the face, forcing his arm up his back and pinning him to the trunk of a tree with her foot. 'No!' she shrieks, her hair wild, as the man writhes under her grip, while Harry punches the other in the stomach, forcing him to double over, and the air is full of the sound of voices and cries.

The Show Woman

They all crowd down the steps of the wagon as several other men from the showground appear. The two men, rough-looking with no hats, threadbare suits and mucky boots, are swiftly pinned to the muddy ground. Before long they are dragged off into the dark.

'Where in the name of God did you learn to do that?' Violet says as Carmen pushes her way back into the caravan, pulling her nightgown down and shaking her hair out.

'Just something I learnt when I first joined my circus, in Spain. The men were hard, so I had to become hard, too. It is useful, is it not?'

'You're bloody right it is,' says Violet, sitting down on the bunk with surprising force and staring at Carmen in admiration. 'Can you teach me?'

'Teach all of us,' echoes Lena. 'We could do with a bit of protection on the road.'

Carmen grins. 'I will. We can have a little lesson if you like.'

There is a knock at the door.

'Only me, Vi,' says Harry.

She lets him in, and Lena pulls a blanket round herself. She is wearing only her nightgown. Rosie still in her bunk, pulls the covers up, while Carmen retreats into hers.

'When did you get so bold?' asks Violet.

'You're welcome, dear sister. It was a pleasure to save your life, and that of your fellow circus ladies.'

'You hardly did anything,' says Violet. 'It was Carmen who saved the day.'

'You're absolutely right. Thank you, Carmen.' He performs a little bow, but she stares back at him blankly.

'What were you doing round here anyway?' Violet asks. 'Isn't your wagon miles away on the other side of the ground?'

'A fellow can't go a wee stroll of an evening and take in the night air?'

Violet tuts, but Lena can see she is pleased and proud.

'Can I give you a wee nip of whisky for your trouble, Harry? It's the cheap shite but it's better than nothing.'

She colours immediately. Despite her recent, much-mocked blip, she rarely uses curse words; it was one of the few things Daddy used to give her the strap for as a bairn. Why had she used one now? In front of Harry, of all people?

Violet smirks. 'Aye,' she says. 'Join us. Drink our cheap shite. The finest in all the land. What an invite, Lena.'

'I'll not trouble you further,' says Harry, turning to go, but he twinkles in Lena's direction. Curled up in her bunk, Rosie smiles at him.

'Thank you, Harry. That was . . .' She stumbles for the right words. 'Very kind.'

He nods at her and smiles.

'Carmen,' he says, looking at the acrobat, huddled in her blankets now, despite the warm night. But she turns her face to the wall and says nothing.

For the rest of the night Lena lies awake, her index finger worrying at a loose flake of skin on her thumb. Every creak and rattle, each distant voice, makes her body tingle with fear, sends a shot of adrenaline coursing through her.

She'd known, when her daddy died, that it would be the end of their life together. Of everything she had known, come to it. But she had not contended with the fact that she would lose her safety, too.

Lena's father had been her compass, her map, constantly guiding her, showing her the way, and throwing an invisible ring of protection around her. She had taken it all for granted, clung to him so tightly after Mammy left that

The Show Woman

they'd formed a bond she'd believed was unbreakable. She had forgotten about death, somehow. Its infinite nature, its cruelty, the sudden blow of its scythe. How stupid she'd been. How childish.

And now, here, in a new town with a new show, a show she still can't quite believe is hers, in her daddy's old wagon, once so safe and secure, she has been caught unawares. Vulnerable. Easy prey.

For the first three years after her disappearance Lena had thought that was what had happened to her mammy, too. That she had been taken, forced goodness knows where by God knows who, to do unspeakable things.

Then, after the letter arrived, she had pictured her lying in a strange bed with a strange man, a bairn whose name Lena might never know held close to her solid, comforting form.

And now? She simply does not know.

The birds are singing by the time Lena falls into a shallow, uneasy sleep, her mother's name lying softly on her lips.

The next day Harry is back with a large metal bolt that he screws on to the inside of the wagon.

'Just in case,' he says to Lena. He rolls up his sleeves, sets happily to work.

'Do you think they'll come back?' she asks.

'Nah,' he says. 'They were drunk, for a start. So they'll have sore heids this morning. Probably have forgotten all about it. And we'll be moving on in a few days anyway. But I don't think they were townies. They didn't have that look. Looked more like travellers to me. Gypsies.'

Lena has known many gypsy families over the years, although some of their customs, their words even, remain strange and foreign to her.

'They're like us but they're no',' her daddy once said, by way of explanation, when they had shared a small camp with a smattering of gypsy families in a quiet town in Argyll, where a stream ran over battered rocks and the men sang plaintive, melancholy songs in a language she could not understand as the sun dipped in the sky. 'They travel, but they don't travel with their work like us show people do,' the old man had said. 'They travel *to* it instead. They might head to Perthshire for the tattie-howking, or up to the Tay for fruit-picking and pearl-fishing, but you won't find them pulling a carousel.'

'Gypsies,' Lena says now. 'I didn't think they'd be around Stirling this time of year.'

'Well, you never can tell,' says Harry, affixing a final screw to the bolt. 'Might not have been, after all. Maybe they were townies, with a bit of gypsy blood running through them.'

Showtime comes and goes, as do the punters. Lena recognises the same faces twice, even three times, and it dawns on her that people are so drawn to the ladies' circus, so fascinated by this little show they have put on, that they want to see them again and again.

One night, about three weeks later, Lena lights the fire and looks out the whisky. They have had a good day, one of their best yet. Rosie, who takes the drink a bit too easily – so much so Lena is not sure she's ever tried it before – is flushed and gabbling, clasping Violet's arm and telling her about the first time she went to the circus.

'There were acrobats doing somersaults, four of them together, and this huge tent, at least five times the size of ours. And then the bareback riders came out. Oh, what a sight. Those beautiful ponies, their sparkly costumes and headdresses; it was beautiful. I knew then,' she says. 'I knew it was all I ever wanted to do.'

'Sounds like Linden's,' says Violet, throwing her a dark look.

Rosie nods happily. 'I think it was, you know,' she says.

'I'll tell you about the first time I saw Linden's,' says Violet. 'It was when I ran away from home.'

Carmen and Rosie look at her, surprised. Lena, who has heard about Violet's first night at Linden's before, takes another sip of her whisky.

'You ran away from home?' asks Rosie.

'Aye. Which is quite a feat when you consider that in our world, your home can run after you.'

Rosie giggles. 'But why?'

'Wasn't getting on with my mammy,' says Violet simply. 'My pa had upped and died on us, and my mammy was . . . well, she wasn't coping with it.'

Lena looks up. She has rarely heard Violet talk about Mary like this. When it comes to family, she usually keeps her own counsel.

'Anyway that wagon wasn't a good place to be. Not for me, anyway. One day I saw a poster for Linden's, said they were looking for trapeze artists. Well, I've been on the bar since I was old enough to walk, and I thought, *That's it. That's the way I'll get out of here.* So I got on one of our old horses – my brother Billy was raging when he found out I'd taken him – and rode off.'

Carmen takes a stick, gives the fire a poke, and the four women watch as the flames sputter and dance.

'When I got to the town, somewhere up in Fife I think it was, maybe Kirkcaldy, it was night time, and the big top was up, and I thought it was the most beautiful thing I'd ever seen,' says Violet. 'Really classy. Magical. All these flags fluttering, and music, sounded like a brass band, coming from inside.

'So I sneaked in one of the side doors and watched the show. There was an elephant, acrobats, like you said, Rosie, a huge lion that looked as though it could snap your neck in its jaws, bareback riders, and then the trapeze artists. They looked so beautiful, swinging up there on the bar. It was higher than I'd ever been, but my God, I wanted to get up there and show them what I could do.

'As soon as the circus was over I went and found Serena Linden, begged her to let me show her my act.'

She starts rolling a cigarette, and Lena looks at her. Does Violet regret leaving Linden's? Think their little show is silly, inconsequential, in comparison? No. Violet is headstrong. And honest. And wasn't creating their own show, this ladies' circus, her idea anyway?

'What was your first show, Lena?' asks Violet, interrupting her thoughts.

'I don't really know,' she says, considering the question. She brushes her hands across the grass beneath her, feels the soft blades fold under her fingers. 'It's just always been there. There's always been a show to go to, a ride to sit on, a penny shy to have a go at. I've always lived alongside it. It's as though my whole life has been a show.'

Violet gives Lena a secret smile, just for her. She alone truly understands what she means.

'What about you, Carmen?' asks Lena. 'When was the first time you saw a show?'

'My parents, they were, as you say, flatties, and we lived in a village near the sea. The smell of fish all day long, cottages painted in white.'

Carmen closes her eyes, as though picturing her faraway home. Lena imagines houses like the tall buildings in Fife fishing towns, or the blacksmiths' cottages in Ayrshire.

The Show Woman

Did her mother end up living in a white-painted house, a line of clean washing blowing in the wind?

'The first time the circus came I was nine years old,' says Carmen. 'Big event. Huge. Whole town is there. And there was a lelaphant.'

'A lelaphant,' says Violet. 'Big trunk? Grey? Hooves the size of Tommy Pony?'

'Yes, yes, a lelaphant,' says Carmen impatiently. 'And he got out. Ran through the town. He gets to the church and he cannot get up the steps. Too big. And the priest comes out and he blesses him, and the lelaphant just sits down and sleeps.'

Carmen is laughing now, and soon they are all laughing, and Lena looks at their faces round the fire and, with a surge of something like joy, is suffused by a warmth she has not felt since her daddy died.

Lena stands in front of the small, grubby-looking glass hung in the far corner of the wagon. She has wiped off the rouge, taken off her hat and her shirt and stands in only her stays, regarding herself. Her skin has taken on the sun, and a legion of freckles have broken out on her nose. There is a small mark on her neck where the high collar of the shirt, fixed at the back with hair pins, has dug into her throat.

She is alone. The other three have taken a drunken wander to the stables, because Rosie wants to say goodnight to Tommy Pony. Lena tries not to worry about their safety: three girls alone out on the showground when it's late, and they are full of the drink.

Lena is still getting used to her costume, this curious outfit that is supposed to make her resemble a man, yet somehow enhances her femininity. She is aware of the admiring glances from men in the crowd, the attention they pay her, the long, appraising looks. But it makes her uncomfortable, too. She has never really stood out before, and certainly not in Violet's company. She has become used to being the plain one, decently turned out but nothing special, little to write home about. Now she receives compliments, the occasional whistle. Like so many things in the past few weeks, it is a whole new world.

She mouths, 'Ladies and gentlemen,' into the glass, looks back to see what it is the audience see, how it is she is able to keep them under her spell. 'I present to you, the ladies'—'

'Lena!'

Carmen tears through the door of the wagon, her breath coming in ragged bursts.

'You must come to the stable. It's Tommy Pony.'

17

Small breaths

Rosie sits cross-legged on the stable floor, Tommy Pony's head laid gently on her lap. His breathing is laboured, flanks heaving with the effort, and there are wisps of foam around his sage-soft muzzle.

'Tommy,' she whispers into the white star-shaped mark on his head, and the pony gives the smallest of whickers.

He can't die on her. He just can't. In this strange, sparkling, dangerous new world, where every day brings challenges and unfamiliar faces, where Rosie has struggled to find her voice, Tommy has been her ballast. The part of her past she has brought into her present, a final breath of her old life.

When her father brought Tommy Pony home to the farm on her thirteenth birthday, pleased as punch in a way that made her stomach turn, Rosie did not know how to feel. She knew that Tommy was a bribe, a gift for keeping quiet, for letting his filthy hands do what they wished to her, but one stroke of the crest of his mane, a mottled grey streaked with white, and it all fell away. The dark, terrifying nights, the bruises that marked her inner thighs, the rough yanks of her hair. She knew, from that moment on, that Tommy would be her saviour, and that one day, together, they would leave that place and be free.

She rests her lips on his head. It is hot, wet with sweat. The crown that Lena made still sits on her head, its long feathers tickling the nape of Tommy's neck.

'Hold on, my boy,' she says. 'Don't go. Don't leave me.'

Lena slips into the stall beside her. Violet has squatted down on the floor, leans her head on Rosie's shoulder.

'How is he?' Lena asks, and Rosie looks into eyes filled with a deep, gentle concern. She cannot believe that it is mere weeks since she first met these women. She chokes back a sob.

'I don't know. It doesn't look good. The stable boy's gone to fetch a man in the town who knows about horses, a veterinarian.' Her heart flutters in her chest at the thought of it, what he might do, or not be able to do, for Tommy. 'I feel like I can't breathe,' she says, and Violet presses her hand to Rosie's heart.

'I'll breathe for you,' she says. 'In and out. Gently now. That's it. Small breaths.'

In Rosie's lap Tommy stirs a little, long lashes fluttering, his flank rising and falling in rhythm, or so it seems, with their breathing. For a moment the three of them sit there in perfect unison, in and out, in and out.

'What happened?' asks Lena. 'He seemed fine during the show. How can he have got so ill so quickly?'

Rosie takes another breath, gathering strength from the touch of Violet's cool palm, and rests her hand on Tommy's white star.

'I brought him back to the stable and he was hungry. He always is after a show. I took his bridle off, put him in the stall and let him have something from the feed tub. When I came back this evening he was shaking all over. Like a fit. His mouth foaming, snorting and stamping his hooves. I remember a lad at school once did the same thing, mouth foaming, jiggering all over. It was like that. And then Tommy fell, sort of collapsed on the floor, and I've been here ever since.'

Lena walks over to the feed tub, starts rootling through the hay. She picks out something small. It blooms purple, like a bruise. 'Deadly nightshade,' she says.

She roots further into the tub, picks out more and more of the bell-shaped flowers. They nod innocently in her palm, and she clenches her fist to crush them.

'Tommy's been poisoned,' she says, and Rosie collapses into tears.

18

Night shade

'I can't believe this,' says Violet, sucking vigorously on her tenth cigarette in an hour. 'Who would want to poison little Tommy? What has he ever done to anyone except trot round the ring like a fancy wee chicken?'

They are sitting round the fire, just the two of them. Carmen has gone to bed. Rosie is still in the stables. The man from the town has given Tommy a draught of something, told Rosie to keep him warm. Lena and Violet have fetched blankets from the wagon, old ones her mammy used to wrap round her when she was a bairn, and warmed a plate of soup for Rosie. When they left, she still hadn't touched it.

'Poor Rosie Posy,' says Violet.

Lena says nothing. She has noticed the way that Violet looks at Rosie, the tenderness in her voice, the softening of her face.

She knows that Violet is made differently, and that she has always been this way. She has never minded, never understood why others do. But she worries about little Rosie, so fragile and young, breakable, like ice-thin porcelain. Violet could cut Rosie with a dark look or a sharp word, could easily shatter her fierce little heart. And where would that leave the circus?

'You like her, don't you?'

Violet, who has been staring deep into the flames, looks up. 'What, you mean like you like Harry?'

Lena's face flares and her finger strays, once again, to the loose flap of skin on her thumb. 'No, I just meant . . .'

'I know what you meant. And aye, I do. What's it to you?'

'Nothing, it's just—'

'I'll tell you what, Lena. You keep your nose out of my affairs, and I'll keep my nose out of yours. I'd have thought you'd know better than to go chasing after Harry anyway.'

Lena lights a cigarette, her fingers fumbling with the match, and waits. If she keeps quiet, Violet will not be able to help herself.

Sure enough, Violet takes another puff, and continues. 'I know you think he's quite the gentleman, and don't get me wrong, he's a good lad, our Harry. But he's got his secrets, just like the rest of us. Don't you be getting worked up over him. Leave it be. That's all I'll say.'

Lena takes a long drag on her cigarette. 'I very much doubt that. You always have more to say.'

Violet stands up. 'I'm away to the stable to see Rosie. I probably won't be back until the morning.'

At daybreak, she hasn't returned. Lena wakes early, the dawn chorus springing to life in the trees around the wagon, but only she and Carmen are in their beds. She dresses quickly, hurries past caravans still veiled in sleep, to the stables at the far end of the ground.

When she pushes open the doors, she finds all three of them awake in Tommy's stall, Violet's thin frame wrapped protectively around Rosie's.

Rosie looks up at her, eyes red-rimmed with tiredness, but shining and happy.

'Just look at him,' she says, and Lena can see that Tommy is much improved. He is holding his head up, while Rosie scoops water from the tray into her palm for him to drink. The sweat on his back has dried, and his eyes are wide open.

The Show Woman

'Oh, thank goodness,' says Lena.

She collapses on a heap in the straw, leans in and gives Tommy a pat. The little pony looks round at her, benevolent, trusting, and it takes hold of her again, the cruelty of it. How could anyone hurt little Tommy? And why? Were they out to get Rosie? The circus? Her?

'We've got to find out who did this,' she says.

'Oh, we will,' says Violet. 'No mistake. 'We won't let them away with it, Rosie Posy.'

Violet strokes Rosie's hair and the girl lets her, her eyelids fluttering with drowsy pleasure as Violet's deft fingers run through her long brown locks.

'No,' says Lena. 'We won't.' And she leaves them to it.

She finds Harry loitering at the front gate to the showground, giving out handwritten flyers for the big dipper. Townies have started trickling in, farmhands and domestic servants from the surrounding villages, and already they are noising each other up, crackling with laughter, ready for a day out at the fair.

'Have you got a minute?' she asks, as he passes a flyer to a young woman with two long plaits roped down each side of her face, who flashes him a beaming smile.

'Of course,' he says. They wander out of the showground to a large bench, recently vacated by a swarm of young weavers from a local mill now heading back towards the fair. It faces a small stream and, as they sit, water trickles unhurriedly over the rocks, making slow, steady progress.

She tells Harry about Tommy Pony, and the deadly nightshade, that the pony nearly died, that both she and Violet believe someone has done this on purpose, that it could be connected to the men outside their wagon a few nights earlier.

Harry sucks the air in through his teeth.

'I mean, it's possible,' he says. 'You lassies, you stick out around here. A ladies' circus is quite a thing in our world. Nobody's ever seen anything quite like it.'

'That was sort of the point.'

'I know,' says Harry. 'I'm just saying that you girls are going to attract attention.'

'Do you think it could have been those lads from the other night?'

Harry shakes his head. 'Unlikely. If you'll not mind me being indelicate for a moment, I'm not sure it was your pony they were after.'

Lena colours and looks across at the stream again, waters implacably moving forward, sunlight bouncing off the surface in shards of pale light.

'You haven't upset anyone, have you?' asks Harry. 'I mean, I know my sister. She can be a right tearaway at times. She says what she thinks, and doesn't care who hears it.'

'Actually Violet's been behaving herself,' says Lena. 'For the most part.'

'Aye, well. Keep an eye on her,' he says. 'Not that you'll have much choice over what she does. Even her mammy couldn't control her. Not since she was a bairn. But then I'm not sure how much she really tried.'

'We've got another problem,' Lena says, and once again her finger is working over that loose flap of skin by her thumb. It flares out now over the nail, and there is a satisfying pinprick of pain every time she touches the raw skin underneath, the tiny spot of red. 'We can't do the show without Rosie. I mean, we could, but it'd be a bit spare. We've worked her act in with Carmen's and Violet's; they all have their own parts to play but it's all supposed to be one big show, and without her I'm worried the whole thing

The Show Woman

will collapse. I think Tommy's going to live, but it'll be a few days until he's able to get into the ring.'

'So you need a pony?' asks Harry. He strokes his chin, shorn from a recent shave. There is a tiny cut under his left ear where the blood has dried.

'I know it's a big ask. There can't be many around that can do the bareback stuff. But would you be able to ask around for us? I don't know many of the people here. They're not my daddy's folk at all.'

'I'll try,' says Harry. 'I might know someone.' He looks at her, a twinkle in his eyes. 'Anything else I can help you with, madam?'

Lena digs the nail of her index finger into the flesh of her thumb.

'No, thank you. Shouldn't you be getting back to your flyering?'

Harry appears at the wagon later that afternoon. They have made the decision to cancel the circus for the day, and every so often Tam comes tearing up to them, his face flushed, to say that dozens of folk have been asking around for the lassies' circus, are disappointed to hear it isn't running.

'One fellow said he'd be back every day until he saw you lassies and your circus,' reports Tam, a little breathless.

'It's *ladies*, Tam,' says Lena. 'We've had this conversation before.'

Harry, his forehead sheened with sweat, does not bring good news.

'There's a dray that apparently used to work with bareback riders,' he says. 'Used for carting a boat ride around the shows now, but his owner says he's competent. He'd be willing to rent him out to you a couple of times a day.'

Lena shakes her head. 'He wouldn't fit in the tent. In fact he'd probably rip right through it.'

'Aye, you're right,' says Harry. 'It was worth a shot, though, eh?'

Through the crowd, Lena spots Rosie and Violet heading towards them. They are holding hands, Rosie staggering under the weight of her tiredness. Violet looks as perky as ever.

'How is he?' asks Lena as they slump down by the front of the wagon, a damp tangled heap of matted hair, bits of straw and the raw tang of the horse stables.

'Much better,' says Rosie, yawning. 'He's had another draught, been on his feet, and even had a wobbly wee walk around the paddock. He's going to be fine. Violet says we should get going in a few days, head up through Perthshire, on to Blairgowrie.'

'Hello, Harry,' says Violet, looking at Lena. 'What brings you here?'

'Just seeing if I can help,' says Harry. 'But it sounds like you don't need me at all.'

The next day, Carmen gives them a self-defence lesson.

'Rosie,' she says, pinning stray tendrils of her long hair back with a hairpin. 'You are a little shrub, so come and stand here.'

Rosie, shy and unsure of herself, walks hesitantly towards her.

They are on a squat patch of land near the stables. Horses' hooves have worn away the grass and the ground is stubbly and flat. On the air they hear the rumble of the fair but here, with everyone out manning their rides and stalls, it is quiet.

'Now, what is the one place you should always aim for, if a man is coming for you?'

Rosie looks blank.

'Come on, Posy,' says Violet. 'Surely you know this one.'

A slow, dawning realisation comes over Rosie. She widens her eyes.

'Down . . . down there?'

'That is correct. Down there. I want you to use those strong legs of yours, and aim for that area.'

'What, on you?'

'Don't worry. I am quick.'

Rosie hoists up her long skirt, aims her powerful right leg towards Carmen and kicks. Carmen jumps out of the way, but not before Rosie almost loses her balance.

'Good! Well done, little shrub. Now you, Lena.'

For the next ten minutes they practise aiming kicks at each other's nether regions, amid a great deal of giggling and snorts. Violet nearly catches Lena with her boot, and when Lena aims a toe at her backside in return, she promptly falls over.

'What about that fancy thing you did to that fellow with your fists?' asks Violet as Lena dusts herself down. 'Can we try that?'

'We can,' says Carmen, and shows them how to turn their bodies to the side, lean in with a sharp elbow, and finally a fist.

Violet swipes at the air. 'God, this is great,' she says.

Carmen smiles, pleased. 'We are all strong, sí? We have powers we did not even know about. But now we do. And they can keep us safe if a man tries to come too near.'

'But what if there's more than one?' asks Lena, thinking of the swarms of men who sometimes fill up the tent, the keen look in their eyes, like hunters.

'Then,' says Carmen, 'you scream.'

From the Blairgowrie Advertiser

MISS S. LINDEN'S CIRCUS WILL VISIT BLAIRGOWRIE on MONDAY JUNE 6

Miss S. Linden, daughter of the late Benjamin Linden, has pleasure in announcing to the Public of this Town and surrounding District that the Company engaged for this year has been specially organised, and Patrons may rely on a Thorough, Clever, Refined and Amusing Entertainment being produced.

The only Circus 'specially commanded' (not granted permission, like others) to perform before the Queen and Royal Court at Balmoral.

Doors open at 7 Performance at 8 o'clock
ADMISSION, 2s, 1s, and 6d Children half-price

19

Rites of passage

And so the road rises up to meet them, curving and winding its way through shaded lanes and plump green hills that bulge like pillows. Late morning, their first day out of Stirling, they pass glowing fields of golden rape seed where farm workers, sweat thick and salty on their brows, till the land. Above them swifts and swallows circle, great masses of birds that darken the sky with swoops and dives, before the air clears once more to brilliant blue.

Lena breathes in the fresh, clean air and stretches her legs out before her. She wonders idly how much browner they will grow over the long summer months, now her face has sprouted its inevitable crop of pale, lazy freckles. It feels good to be back on the road again, with all its infinite possibilities stretching before them. When she was young her mother often sat her on her knee as they travelled the fairs, pointing out flocks of sheep on a hill, bushels of heather, the swollen curve of a loch side.

'Hands over eyes,' she'd say, and Lena would clamp her damp little palms to her forehead, leaving just enough of a gap between her fingers to peer out.

'No peeking,' her mother said, and Lena would reluctantly force her hand shut. 'Now, tell me everything we've just seen.'

Lena would list the sheep and the heather, the cow with the horns, the man stopping to have a smoke by the side of the road, conjuring up the images in her head while below, the wheels of their wagon turned beneath them.

'And . . . open!' When Lena took her hand away, there would be a new vista lying ahead of them, a fresh world to remember. Oh, how she misses her, the way she could make almost anything magical. I'm doing this for you, Mammy, she thinks. All for you.

She shifts in her seat. It is her turn to sit up front and drive the Clydesdale horses, while Rosie trots alongside on Tommy Pony, quite recovered now after those extra days in Stirling. He looks comical trotting next to the huge snorting beasts, like a toy horse, or one of the beauties that once sat astride Lena's daddy's carousel. The thought cuts through her like a shard of glass. Once upon a time, as a little girl, she had thought those horses huge, terrifying and exciting. Her daddy would lift her up on one when all the crowds had gone home and set the carousel to run just for Lena, and she would scream in delight as the horses bobbed up and down, her father watching on, satisfied and proud.

So long ago. Now she is the one with the show, and they are the ones in charge. There is no Daddy to tell her what to do, to lean on when things get hard. She misses him too, his bold shape, his comforting tobacco smell. But there is a heady freedom about it all. They can do exactly what they please, when and where they like.

'Alright, hen?' Violet pops her head out of the wagon and playfully tugs on Lena's long plait. Her face is flushed. They have made the wagon as homely as possible, with four bunks, each with their own blankets, and during those extra days in Stirling Lena pinned some of her mother's old silks on to the wall, their rich, deep colours rippling as the wagon moves. But it can get hot when it's sunny, particularly when they are thumping along the road courtesy of two enormous shire horses.

'Want a break yet?' asks Violet.

'Soon,' Lena says. They are reaching the brow of a hill, and the horses slow as they pull their heavy load.

Rosie slows too, her forehead glistening, and she leans down and pats Tommy Pony's flank. 'It's so hot,' she shouts up to them. She seems energised by the ride, her cheeks high with colour, but Lena can see by the curve of her thin shoulders that she is also tired.

'We'll stop in a minute,' Lena says. 'Get the horses some water and you can rest those sore thighs of yours.'

Violet cackles.

'Oh, shut up,' says Lena, her face twitching.

'I said nothing,' Violet replies. 'I am the perfect picture of innocence.'

They pull into a glade of tall lime trees, their wide green leaves shading them from the sun, tangles of wild strawberries hidden among the long grass. Carmen disappears into the trees and before long emerges with huge buckets of cool, glistening water. The horses drink as though they have never seen water before, the sweat slicked thick on their manes.

Lena produces bread and cheese, and a small bag of apples. She had gone to the big market in the town before they left Stirling and stocked up as much as possible. It could be feast or famine on the road. Sometimes you came across friendly farmers who'd give you eggs for free, or they might bring food to barter with to the shows. Many was the time her daddy had given a free ride to a man's bairns for six hen's eggs, or a wheel of fresh cheese.

Other places, though, they refused to even serve you. Lena remembers one occasion, when she was around seven years old in a town in the northeast, when a man, his red face mottled with deep acne scars that made Lena think of raw meat, insisted his child get a free ride on her father's carousel. The next day he refused to let them into his baker's shop, calling them dirty. He bent down and looked into her face and with breath that stank of rotting fish said, 'You're a filthy little tinker.'

Her father pulled her away, shaking his head, clutching her hand tightly while Lena tried to fight back tears. 'They're just flatties, Lena,' he said. 'They don't understand us. Pay them no mind.'

But the incident stayed with her. They had gone hungry that night all those years ago, Lena shoving her fist in her mouth to stop the pangs in her tiny stomach. She likes to stockpile food now, know where it is, and keep it safe. If they are running low she becomes anxious and fretful, counting out the pennies she keeps in a small velvet drawstring bag that belonged, long ago, to her mother. She is forever thinking ahead to the next town, the next farm, the next showground, and the next meal.

Rosie chews her bread thoughtfully. 'How long do you think, Lena?'

Her hair, down to her waist and a pale dusty brown, has been pulled into a low bun. A few tendrils have come loose and bob in her eyes. Violet reaches over and pushes them back for her.

'At this pace we'll be there by mid-morning tomorrow,' Lena says.

'Where is it we're headed again?' Carmen asks.

'Blairgowrie,' says Lena. 'Nice town. Start of the Highlands.'

The rest of them contemplate this as they eat. Violet pulls off her thick boots, lets her toes wiggle in the grass. 'I need to cool off,' she says, unbuttoning her blouse and loosening her corset.

Rosie blushes. She puts her hands to her cheeks, but it only makes the pinkish bloom worse.

'Come on, Rosie, there's a good lass,' says Violet as her corset comes off. She stands there in nothing but a pair

The Show Woman

of white bloomers that have seen better days. 'Time for a swim.'

Rosie is trying not to look at the bold Violet, at her small, milky-white breasts, the concave stomach speckled with bluish bruises from her time on the bar. At how much she appears like a boy without her clothes, except for her magnificent mane of orange hair, loose now and so bright in the sunshine that it shimmers like a bolt of cloth.

'You scared a wee laddie will steal your corsets, Rosie Posy?' she says. 'The wagon will keep us covered, don't you worry about that.'

Rosie shakes her head, puts her hands back up to her cheeks.

'Come on, Rosie,' says Lena, tugging off her blouse. 'It's a show woman's rite of passage, this: a dip in a stream. Give you a chance to wash that hair of yours.'

But the girl simply bites into her apple.

The stream is cool and slippery. As Lena eases her way in, her feet touch the slimy rocks below. How long had these stones lain in this secret, shaded place? Had her father once stood in this stream as a young man, stripped to the waist and cooling off on the way to the Blairgowrie fair, his hair slicked back with water as a pal dunked him under the ripples? What about her mother?

She tries to conjure her mammy's face but it remains blurry, out of reach. Her eyes, her lips, the colour of her hair, which her father always said was brown as a berry. For a moment the grief washes over her afresh, trickles its way into her pores, through her spine, all the way down to her toes. It is as though the pain pulses through her whole being, a great weight, heavy as a horse.

Should she have told her daddy about the letter? Would he have known, with great certainty, that her mammy had not written it? Had she shielded him from the truth, not knowing that the truth might have helped them find her?

She looks up, sees Rosie at the water's edge.

'Coming in?' she asks, but Rosie shakes her head.

Violet swims over and Rosie bends down on her haunches, grasps Violet's long wet hair, strung like weeds down her back, and pulls her gently over to the bank.

'I brought some soap. Thought your hair could do with washing.'

Violet says nothing, but, treading water, she closes her eyes and lets Rosie massage the soap into her scalp. Rosie's tiny fingers work quickly and methodically, small circles towards the base of her neck, larger ones up to the highest point of her forehead.

'I must look a sight,' says Violet. There is a languid quality to her voice Lena has rarely heard.

'You're perfect,' says Rosie. 'Just as you are.'

The two of them stay there a moment, Rosie's hands resting on the base of Violet's skull, Violet's head thrown back, suspended in time, completely still.

'Go on,' says Rosie eventually. 'You're done now.'

Violet swims away, dunks her head under the surface to get rid of the suds. Lena falls back in the water too, convinced she will sink to the bottom like a stone, is almost surprised to find herself floating, weightless, staring up at the gaping blue sky. She thinks, briefly, of Violet, the way she launches herself through the air each night, on nothing but invisible wings, and possibly a prayer. How brave she is. To take that leap of faith, straight into the unknown.

She gazes over to where Violet is splashing in the water with Carmen, her long red hair clean now, gleaming in the sun. Violet, whom she has known all her life. Who is difficult and obstinate, and lets little Rosie wash her hair. How she loves her, she realises, this infuriating, blazing flame of a woman, her dearest friend, her sort of sister.

But before she can follow the thought, turn it over in her mind like a stone in her palm, Violet splashes over and dunks her head under the water, and all thoughts other than the sunshine, and the day ahead, are lost.

20

Old Queens

Serena is coughing, a deep, guttural splutter. She produces something green and unmentionable, spits it into a tatty lace handkerchief, and glowers at Rory McCracken.

'Read it to me, lad,' she says. The boy, the youngest of the three brothers, waif-like and dingy-haired, looks down at the newspaper and mumbles.

'*Miss S. Linden . . .*'

'Louder,' she says. The grip on her cane is vice-like.

'*Miss S. Linden's circus will visit Blairgowrie on . . .*'

Serena leans back on the day bed to listen. Clever and refined, that was her grand show. Amusing, too. Even more amusing to remind the Perthshire folk that she, Serena Linden, is the only circus proprietor in the land to have been commanded by the late Queen, may God rest her soul.

What a day it had been, the first time they rode through the gates of that fine castle, its granite turrets glinting like silver blades, servants scurrying out on to the grass as though they were greeting royalty.

Linden's had been touring Deeside when the invitation came, delivered on thick creamy card by a fine footman in a wig and a rich red waistcoat, breeches immaculate. An invitation to Linden's Circus, to Miss Serena Linden in particular, to perform for Her Majesty the Queen. If only her father could have seen it.

It had been an overcast day at Balmoral, but nothing could dampen the high spirits of the royal household as they gathered on the grass. Grand ladies and gentlemen trussed up in stylish dresses and morning coats, among their number at least several princes and princesses, Serena was later told. Children from a local school, done out in their best bib and tucker, teachers in their good skirts, as shining-eyed and excited as their small charges.

And then the old Queen, who arrived on the grass in a carriage and remained there, opera glasses raised to her eyes, throughout the performance.

Serena's acts had done her proud that day. The elephant, Bostie, and the pony, Snookles, who did a wonderful turn with Bostie up on his hind legs and Snookles running rings around him. Her performing dogs who ran through rings of fire. That marvellous dancing donkey, a lion that reared up and roared, and her cowboy, resplendent in his Stetson, who thrilled the crowds on horseback with his pistols.

Afterwards, a footman had beckoned for her and young Benjamin to approach the carriage. The old Queen had leant down, trussed in the gloomy black of her widow's weeds, but with festive flowers like a crown adorning her hair.

Up close her face looked like melted wax, Serena thought, the rheumy eyes, tinged yellow, deeply hooded by folds of skin.

'You have amused me greatly, Miss Linden,' she said. 'I have very much enjoyed the day.'

And then she gestured at the footman, who darted forward and handed Serena a gift. A jewel box, studded with emeralds and with a pretty shell pattern on the front.

'Thank you, Your Majesty,' Serena said, performing a deep curtsey that to her great shame made her knees crack, and the Queen's eyes widen. 'I shall treasure this forever.'

That had been the first Balmoral visit. There had been two more after that, the old Queen looking frailer, less human each time, lavishing upon Serena greater and

The Show Woman

grander gifts. A hair slide of tortoiseshell and onyx. A gold brooch, set with diamonds and rubies.

And then, the Queen had up and died in the cold days of January, hundreds of miles from her beloved Balmoral on the rain-lashed Isle of Wight, and Serena, who had taken to calling her circus the Royal Linden's Circus, felt that something had withered away in her, too.

She thinks about the old Queen now, what she would have made of this modern new world. Would she have approved of the cinematographs, the Spaniards and the Italians who flooded the fairs . . . the all-female acts who threatened Serena's very existence? She was a lady of sophistication and taste. A breath of the old world. Serena had known it as soon as she saw her. She would not have put up with all this modernity.

Her son the King, a drinker by all accounts and a terrible philanderer, had not been a patch on his mother, and now he was dead too. Why, the more she thinks about it, they had a lot in common, Serena and the old Queen. Disappointing sons. A great inheritance. A grand fuss wherever they went. And when all was said and done, wasn't royalty a show, just like the circus?

The boy has finished reading. He sniffs loudly, wipes his nose on the newspaper. Serena is disgusted. 'Get yourself a kerchief, boy. Filthy animal.'

'Sorry, miss.' He stares down at his feet. His boots look as though they have never seen a lick of polish since the day he bought them. Or, more likely, stole them. He'd whip the coat off your back as soon as look at you, that one.

'When do the fairs get here?' she asks.

'Two days after we do. They won't be happy, miss.'

'Exactly,' says Serena, and she emits a cackle that soon turns into another hacking rasp. 'Teach those young lassies a lesson, won't we, lad? Aye. Well. Away with you. Long day tomorrow.'

When he has gone, she lights her oil lamp and sits down on the velvet day bed. It has been a good day. Hundreds of townspeople turning out to welcome the circus into Blairgowrie, the gaily coloured cavalcade that stops the flatties wherever it goes, its giant cages, a lion in one, a tiger in the other, the old elephant, the trail of horses, even her performing donkey – all take on a magical allure when they enter a new town, a new village.

It reminds Serena of the old days. When Davey was still at her side, when Benjamin and Simon were young and showed a wee bit of promise, not just disappointment. So much to remember. So much she wishes she could forget.

Well, she is here now, and there is work to be done. The queen of the shows has arrived.

21

Big top

It is Rosie who spots the big top first. It rises out of the morning mist, jewel-coloured flags strung from its huge awning quivering gently in the breeze. A great beast crouched, panther-like, among the rolling Perthshire hills.

'Look,' she says to the others from her perch astride Tommy Pony, giving the wagon a great thump on its side. Lena, who is up front with the horses, lifts her hand to her eyes, then looks back at the road.

'I can't see properly,' she says. 'Is it the rest of the fair?'

'I don't think so,' says Rosie. 'It looks different. Special. Like the circus that came to the village when I was a bairn.'

Violet's head snaps out of the wagon door. She looks up ahead, curses, and kicks the floor. Rosie does not like it when Violet swears, mucks up the air with her coarse slang.

'You have got to be kidding,' says Violet. 'Serena bloody Linden. Just what we need.'

Linden's Circus, Rosie realises, which visited their village fairground all those years ago. With the lions and the elephant, those flying acrobats and the horses that her pa had been so rude about.

'That's the woman who fired me, Rosie Posy,' says Violet. 'All because I gave her a bit of cheek.'

Lena gives Violet a withering look. 'There's rather more to it than that, isn't there?' she says.

'I've no idea what you mean,' says Violet. But she will not look her in the eye.

'What exactly did you do to that woman?' asks Lena, sounding like a prim schoolteacher.

'No more than she deserved,' says Violet.

Lena sighs and leans forward. 'It's quite the set-up,' she says, her eyes fixed on the majestic big top.

'Fancy yourself as the next Serena Linden, do you?' asks Violet, but Lena ignores her.

When they pull into the showground, squashed into a smaller space as the circus tent is taking up so much room, there is much consternation from the gathered show people. Rosie listens to their raised voices as she dismounts Tommy, prepares to tack him up in the stables. *Why, Linden's never take the same routes as the fairs. They always plough their own furrow. They perform in winter, isn't that when they do the Perthshire towns? What are they doing in Blairgowrie at this time of the year? It's a damned disgrace.*

'Why doesn't Linden's come on the road with the fairs?' asks Rosie once they have settled on a pitch, started hammering up the tent.

'Have you seen the size of that big top?' asks Lena. 'They're huge, a whole night's entertainment. It wouldn't be fair on the fairs.'

She smiles at her little joke and Rosie feels a surge of affection for her, this statuesque show woman with the sweet smile, who scooped her up that terrifying day in Glasgow and let her be a part of her show.

She wonders if Lena knows about her and Violet. About the things they have started to do in the dark. How Violet will stroke her hair until every nerve in her body feels as if it is jangling like a bell, sparks shooting across her skin. How sometimes Violet will brush the nape of her neck, lingering on the soft hairs there, and her head feels as though it is about to explode with pleasure.

The Show Woman

Deep inside her there is a hardened little pearl that strains for more, just like the way the round rosebuds on her breasts harden too. But she is terrified of her own desire, and even more so of Violet's.

For so long now, touch, for Rosie, has been ugly and brutal. She has had to swallow down the disgust at her father's meaty hands, his hot breath, the violent words. What she feels now with Violet is different. There is magic, a tenderness, things she has never before allowed herself to feel. But she senses danger, too. What would happen if Violet tried to kiss her? To press her lips to her own, soft and blooming? Would she respond, as her body might wish? Or cry out, ruin it all, with the fear that still runs heavy through her mind?

'You look concerned, little shrub.' Carmen's voice cuts through her dreamy thoughts. 'Is everything OK?'

Rosie nods hesitantly. 'It is. It's just . . .' She pauses, tries to find the right words. 'It's just that sometimes I feel a bit lost. Among all this. So far from home.'

Carmen smiles at her. 'You are not the only one. I am so many miles from home, and sometimes it feels as though I have always been lost. At least, it did. Until I found you, and Lena, and Violet. Until we became the ladies' circus. Now I feel as though, if we are lost, we are all lost together. You understand?'

Rosie smiles. 'I do. I like that. All lost together.'

'Now,' says Carmen, linking arms with her, 'shall we go and find the others?'

Their show that afternoon is half-empty, the one after that emptier again. Over the strains of Carmen's flute they hear not just the brass bands of the fair, but louder music, drums and trumpets, tambourines and cymbals, drifting over from Linden's Circus.

When they finish for the day Violet is cross, resentful.

'I bet the old witch has followed me here,' she says in the wagon, pulling off her silver costume and flinging it to the floor with an angry throw. It makes a sad little tinkle as it lands.

'Don't be ridiculous, you're not that important,' says Lena, placidly picking up her costume and hanging it by the window to air.

'Aren't I? Are you sure about that, Lena? I was her star act, the greatest trapeze artist who ever lived. Don't you think she might want me back?'

Lena wheels round. 'Do you want to go back?'

Violet flushes. 'No. No, I don't. I wouldn't work for that horrible old bitch of a woman if she paid me twice what she was paying me before. But you don't know what she's like, Lena. She's sour as vinegar, and I crossed her. I really did. I don't know how easily she'll let go.'

Rosie thinks it is probably a fuss over nothing. Her memories of that night all those years ago are tinged with excitement and revelation. The circus seemed magical, and it had changed her life. Surely this old show woman, the lady behind it all, could not be so awful, if she had created something so beautiful?

She looks at Carmen, but she is quiet as she takes off her ribbon costume, hangs it carefully in a corner, pulls on a drab brown dress.

An hour later and Violet, still highly strung and damp-faced, has procured some cheap brandy from a lad who runs a penny shy and plays on the black market. She swigs straight from the bottle, offers a little to Rosie, who sips meekly. Rosie is still getting used to alcohol, the way it warms first her stomach then her throat, before finally fanning out inside her head, as though someone is pouring warm oil into her ears.

The Show Woman

'I'm not in the mood for the drink tonight,' says Lena. She has worked hard for them since the show, been away into the town for cheese and bread, slices of cured pork, a bag of toffees, then boiled up tea in the great kettle. All while Violet has been gone, sniffing out brandy.

Rosie feels guilty, as though her friendship with Violet might somehow taint her in Lena's eyes, make her seem lazy.

'Sorry, Lena,' she says.

But Lena smiles at her kindly. 'You have your fun. I need my rest.'

For once, Carmen has not joined them for their tea but gone out alone for a wander round the fair. Rosie worries about her Spanish friend. She seems sad and secretive, but she can be kind, too, shares her bread, helps string Rosie's hair into a long, flat plait for each show. 'Your hair is so soft and long,' she says to her every night as she untangles it with a coarse, horsehair brush, separates the braids. 'Like reeds in a river.'

Violet takes another swig as Lena vanishes inside the caravan.

'You know what we should do?' she says to Rosie. Her eyes are glassy, like great green pools. 'We should go and have a nose about Linden's. See what the witch has been up to. Maybe say hello to a few of my old pals. You up for it, my little Posy?'

She slings her arm around Rosie's neck and Rosie feels the little hairs there stand up to attention. 'Wouldn't that be dangerous?' she asks.

'Nah. We'll be quiet. And it's always a bit slapdash after the circus finishes for the night. Everyone on the drink, all the animals thumping about. I just want to see how the land lies.'

Rosie shrugs. She won't win this battle. And besides, she is desperately curious to get inside that big top, see those wild animals up close, recapture the feeling that made her heart soar all those years ago. The drink has made her brave and bold. An adventure. Why not?

'Let's go,' says Rosie. And they do.

22

Someone

Lena sits on her bunk, waves of tiredness crashing over her. Her eyes feel dusty and dry, and she is glad the light glows low, just a flicker of orange from the embers outside to illuminate the inside of the wagon.

She wonders where Carmen is, hopes she has not simply wandered off into the night. The showground is a perilous place for women after dark, but for show women, particularly foreign ones as beautiful as Carmen, the town holds even more danger.

Earlier that day, before the night's show, Carmen had produced a set of knitting needles and, with bundles of wool pooling at her feet, embarked on what looked like a scarf.

'I didn't know you knitted,' Lena had said, intrigued.

'I learnt it as a child,' said Carmen. 'My town, it was by the sea, and in the winter the winds were very cold, particularly for the men who went out on the waves.'

'Your father was a fisherman?' Lena asked.

'*Sí*. That is how he died. The boat went down.' Her face had clouded, her beautiful features momentarily stunned into sadness, before she shrugged it off, composed herself.

'My *madre*, she said we should knit jumpers for the men on the boats. Thick wool, very warm. She taught me when I was very young. He was wearing one of mine when he died, I think.'

'I'm sorry,' said Lena. 'You really miss him, don't you?'

'Very much,' Carmen had replied. 'He was my favourite man in the world.'

Lena unbuttons her corset now, breathes out with relief. She is pleased that Carmen is opening up to her, even if she still likes to go off by herself sometimes. She is less concerned about Violet and Rosie. She can see that their friendship, or whatever it might be, is blossoming, like the flowers which bear their names, and that to meddle in any way would be, not just unfair, but an unwise course. Violet on the warpath is never to be taken lightly. Just ask Serena Linden.

She wonders why the old woman has brought her circus here, to Blairgowrie of all places, at the same time as the fairs. Is she going dotty? Or is it a threat? A warning sign? She has never met Serena, but it was a name that was talked about in hushed tones when she was a bairn. She recalls a time when Linden's was at Vinegarhill and she had craiked to her mammy to take her to see the elephants and the lions, the funny little donkey that her old friend Betsy, who had been twice, told her could walk on its hind legs.

And so they did. Just once, her mammy reluctant, slinking in at the back of the huge tent, Lena's hand clutched tightly in hers. She had been entranced by it, those huge animals, the hoops of fire that dogs and ponies jumped through, the way those acrobats hurtled around the ring.

It's a memory that had been obliterated by her mother's disappearance. But ever since she stumbled upon the old ticket stub in her box of precious things, since Violet first made her the proposal, since they took their ladies' circus on the road, it has fluttered around her head like a starling. Could she, too, one day, run a circus to rival Linden's? With magnificent beasts, a whole troupe of acrobats, a sparkling big top that glistened from miles away?

A feather-soft tap at the door. Lena bunches her corset around her, stiffens. She has not drawn the bolt.

The Show Woman

'Who is it?'

'Harry.'

'Oh,' she says, furiously buttoning her corset back up again, fingers fumbling with the tiny hooks. 'When did you blow in?' she says through the door.

'About twenty minutes ago. Time for a chat?'

When she emerges from the wagon a few minutes later, dressed once more and with a faded green shawl shrugged around her shoulders, Harry has stoked up the fire, and flames are licking gently at the stone circle.

'Cigarette?' he says, offering her one from the now-familiar gold-edged box.

She shakes her head. 'My voice is hoarse enough as it is. Got to look after it these days you know.'

Harry strikes a match and lights his own.

'Right enough. Should be doing the same really. My pa used to say that honey's good for your throat. There might be a farm round here, do you a pot or two. I'll ask around.'

'Thank you,' she says. She pulls the shawl tighter, surprised at the nip in the air. She wonders why he is here. Is he looking for Violet? Or is it her he has come to see? The thought makes her nerves tingle.

'Violet not here, then?' he says, as though reading her thoughts.

She shakes her head, feels the sparkle drain away. 'Away out with Rosie. Don't know where they've gone, but you know Violet. Shall I tell her you were asking for her?'

'Actually it was you I came to see.'

He takes a long, methodical draw on his cigarette and looks at her.

'Violet told me about your mammy. That you want to find her. About the letter and all that. And, well, I remembered something from back then.'

Now Lena is sitting bolt upright. Hears the familiar rushing sound inside her ears, the blood pulsating.

'What?' she says. 'Tell me.'

'Ach, it's probably nothing. I was a lad myself back then. Spent most of my time in the stables seeing to my pa's horses. But that day one of them, Buster, the biggest of our drays, was lame. Didn't know what it was but he was suffering, the poor old boy, so I'd brought him out to the yard to have a look at his hooves.'

Far away and over the field, Lena hears a great whooping and shouting, as though a large mass of people is slowly making its way towards them. The circus, it must be, letting the crowds out from the big top. A high old night, by the sounds of it. Lena shivers.

'I had one of Buster's hooves in my hands, was having a proper look-see, when suddenly there was your mammy in the yard with me.'

'You're joking,' says Lena, and Harry shakes his head.

'She'd been greetin',' he says. 'Great tearstains on her face. And when she saw me, well . . .' He pauses. 'She started greetin' some more. She came up to me and Buster and she gave Buster this great old pat and when I asked what was the matter she just shook her head and said, "You think you know someone." And when I asked what she was meaning she just turned round and left. Or at least I thought she'd gone.

'But when I walked out of the yard a couple of minutes later she was standing in front of this tree. It looked like she was stuffing something in there. After she'd gone I went and had a look but I couldn't feel anything. I thought maybe I'd imagined it.'

Lena is stunned. She has so often imagined where her mammy went that day, after she'd vanished into the crowd like air. Who had she seen? Had it been a faceless man with a knife? A handsome cad with a rose, and a promise? Yet all along she had gone to the stables, and someone had made her cry, and she'd been confused and upset. Lena swallows a sob. It is almost too much to bear. And yet in the tendrils of Harry's story there is hope. Even, possibly, a clue.

'Give me a smoke,' she says, and Harry places one between his lips, lights it, and hands it to her. The end glints and crackles.

'Why didn't you tell us back then?' She doesn't know whether to be angry with him for keeping quiet all these years, for not speaking up, for not helping, when he could.

'Lena,' he says. He looks at her across the fire, fluttering flames casting shadows across his face. 'I did. I told yer daddy. The next day, when it was all over the showground. Came and found him. Didn't tell no one else, just him. And he just said, "Aye, thank you, son." That was it. I didnae really know what else to do.'

Lena takes a long drag on her cigarette. The tip is slightly moist.

'Did my mammy say anything else to you?'

'No. That was all she said. But I felt I should tell you, now I know that you're looking for her, and that you've been thinking she's been shacked up with another man all these years. I can't imagine . . .' He tails off. He is probably considering his own mammy and daddy back then, solid as their drays, with their squadron of bairns and unbreakable family, no matter how scattered to the four winds they were come the summer season, with Mary back at Vinegarhill with the youngest, Harry and Violet up to God knew what.

'Thanks for telling me,' she says.

She feels no urge to cry, nor weep or wail. It is as though she is putting together an enormous puzzle, like the old wooden jigsaws they kept in the primary school she and Violet attended in winter. Harry has simply handed her another piece.

'Nae bother,' he says. He stands up, tips his cap at her formally. 'Looks like I have a few concerts lined up later in the summer. Glasgow, and in Ayrshire too. Might you like to come and hear me sing one night?'

The question is unexpected, and Lena lets it hang in the air, enjoying the sound of it, its musical quality, the stiff formality.

'Aye,' she says. 'I might.'

Harry grins. 'Goodnight, then.'

Lena finishes her cigarette, tosses it into the fire. It is dampening down again, will soon be no more than clinkers and ash.

She is getting up to go to bed, at last, when Carmen materialises, ghost-like, out of the darkness.

'You're alright?' asks Lena. 'I was starting to worry.'

'I went to Mass,' says Carmen. There is a chain of wooden beads in her hand, a silver cross looped at one end. She looks calmer than Lena has seen her for weeks and Lena remembers that time in the little church back in Stirling, the great Jesus on his cross, his crown of thorns, the strange air, both damp and dusty. 'There was a bishop there. I took Communion. It was nice. But the wafers tasted like an old shoe. I am tired now, though.'

She drifts past Lena into the wagon, and the thought strikes Lena that Carmen was probably waiting in the shadows for Harry to leave, could see she has been upset. How kind of her to do that, she thinks, and how thoughtful.

23

Tusks

From a distance, the big top glitters like a smattering of faded stars. Up close, though, and Rosie can see that it is lit by dozens of tiny gas lamps strung around its perimeter, each one encased in its own glass lantern, paraffin flickering and casting shadows over every creature who passes under the glare.

The circus has just let out for the night and a great hollering multitude is streaming away from its circle of light, back into the darkness, across the fields where silent, suddenly staid homes await them. Rosie and Violet work against the swell, hands gripped tightly, careful not to let the rough jostlers break them apart.

'We'll head up to the animal wagons,' Violet says to Rosie. 'Go and see what we can see.'

She has told Rosie that Serena will already be ensconced in her caravan, tucked up for the night and swigging from the bottle. Rosie feels a surge of dislike for this woman who treated Violet so cruelly, who must surely drink as much as her own pa, with his whetted tongue and mean fists.

The brandy lies heavy and warm in her belly, soothes the nerves that scratch at the inside of her head. Rosie has done many brave things since the day she left the farm, but this feels different somehow. An adventure, yes, but one that is laced with danger.

A sour, earthy smell hits her nostrils. They have left the hordes behind now, are in a quieter, darker part of the ground.

'Look,' says Violet, and points up ahead of them.

There, so large and hulking that it near obscures the dark sky, stands an elephant. His skin is a ruckled grey, his hooves the size of dinner plates. His ears, like oversized beech leaves, flap placidly back and forth, and he is wearing a jaunty headdress over his long trunk in colours of red and gold.

'Alright, Bosco,' says Violet, and to Rosie's horror she walks straight up to the beast, rubs her hand along his snaking trunk. The elephant obliges by lifting the tip of his trunk to her ear and snuffling at it, and she laughs. 'Stop it, Bosco,' she says. 'That tickles. Come and say hello, Rosie.'

Rosie sidles up and Bosco swings a huge, benevolent eye towards her.

'You see this,' says Violet, and she points at a dark, hardened crust, an old and painful wound, up beside the top third of the animal's trunk. 'Poor old Bosco had his tusks sawn off. Ivory, see. Very valuable. But also so he doesn't gore anyone to death. Still, it had to hurt. Poor old Bosco.'

She gives the elephant another pat and his mouth opens a fraction, as though he is expecting a treat.

'What do they use ivory for?' asks Rosie. She has never heard of it before, is distressed that this magnificent beast might be mutilated, even for something beautiful.

'All sorts of things,' says Violet. 'Piano keys, chess pieces, jewellery. There's money to be made in ivory, and if there's one thing Serena Linden knows how to do, it's make money.'

Leaving Bosco behind in his sparkling headdress, they move on, past a cage with a small lion in it. The beast is so scrawny that Rosie can see ribs poking through its yellow fur.

'Leo's gone,' says Violet. 'I wonder if that means Lucy has too.'

The Show Woman

'Who's Lucy?' asks Rosie.

'She was a lion-tamer. Never liked Linden's. Her daddy had a circus down south. I wonder if she's gone back down and taken Leo with her.'

They round a corner and a forest of wagons opens up. Performers, still in their glittering, sequinned costumes, sprawl on the grass, the soft beat of a drum somewhere, a juggler in stripes flinging a riot of colourful rings into the air, neatly catching them with one hand.

'Gianni,' says Violet.

The juggler stops so abruptly that his rings, doing another turn in the air, crash on to the ground. 'Violetta?' he says. He comes running towards them, flings his arms around Violet. 'My dear Violetta, where did you go? You gave Miss Linden a terrible bad eye, you know. Which gave her an even more terrible temper.'

'Has she mentioned me?' Violet asks, while Rosie hovers in the background, uncertain.

'Come with me,' says Gianni. He leads them to a small wagon, painted in blue and white, the same colours as his costume. Once inside, he motions for them to sit on the little day bed. There is a variety of outfits hung around the small space, one a rich red with embroidered gold thread, another in pale lavender with flecks of silver running through it.

Gianni sits on an upturned bucket and produces a small metal box. From inside he brings out cigarette papers, tobacco, and something else. It is green, like moss, and gives off a sharp smell, somewhere between that rich scent you get standing on a pine floor in a forest, and cat piss.

'Now, Miss Violetta, I want to hear everything,' he says, and begins rolling his cigarette.

Violet tells him about their circus, about touring with the fairs, and being back on the trapeze. He listens, interested, his eyes occasionally flicking over to Rosie, travelling up and down her body. She shrinks back in the day bed and Violet, sensing her fear, puts a gentle, protective hand on her knee.

'And this girl, she is with you?'

Violet nods. 'This is Rosie. She's an exceptionally talented bareback rider. You should see the tricks she can do.'

Gianni raises an eyebrow as he picks up the green moss and, to Rosie's amazement, lays it in his cigarette alongside the tobacco.

'What is that?' she asks. Her voice appears to have got stuck halfway down her throat and she coughs, hating herself for her shyness, wishing she could appear more grown up and worldly in front of Violet.

'Just a little extra something,' says Gianni. His voice is heavily accented, and she wonders where he has come from, this curious and strange man; how he has ended up here, in this small Scottish town, putting herbs into a cigarette in a blue and white costume.

'So how has she been, then, the auld witch?' asks Violet. 'Do you think she has it in for me?'

'Who can say?' says Gianni. He is now rolling his odd cigarette, licking at the paper to seal it. 'She is a vengeance bitch.'

Violet laughs. 'You mean vengeful, but, to be honest, vengeance works.'

Gianni lights the cigarette and the wagon fills with the same sharp smell, much stronger now, and muskier. He inhales deeply and passes the cigarette to Violet, who does the same thing, then offers it to Rosie.

'Go on, Posy,' she says. 'Something to calm your nerves.'

Rosie takes a cautious, shallow puff. Immediately she coughs, the thick, acrid smoke filling her lungs. 'Oh, God,' she says between splutters, handing it back to Violet.

The Show Woman

Violet bangs her on the back until she stops, hands it back to Gianni.

'It's just that I know what those McCracken lads are like, and Rosie here had her pony poisoned a week ago. Deadly nightshade put in his feed. I wouldn't put it past her to try and track me down. Just for the sheer devilry of it.'

'Oh, you're not wrong, missy,' says Gianni. He takes another long deep puff of his cigarette. 'Did you hear about Benjamin?'

Violet shakes her head.

'He's off. Away to Stafford with Lucy the lion-tamer. They got married. Serena says she never wants to hear his name spoken again, had all his belongings chucked in the river before he could pack them up. She did the same thing with her sister, I heard, years ago. Didn't fancy sharing the circus with her, wanted to run it on her own. So she chucked her off a wagon one night in the middle of nowhere one winter and left her there. Most folk think she probably didn't even survive the night.'

Rosie is trying to follow the conversation but her head is swimming. With thoughts of Violet and the way she strokes the soft tendrils of her hair, of Gianni and his costumes, how funny they seem now, how quaint and silly, so much so that, peering at the lavender and silver one on the wall, she has to stifle a giggle. A man! In purple! Suddenly it is too funny, too ridiculous, and she is laughing and laughing, and then Violet is laughing too, because the costume isn't purple, it's violet, and Violet is violet, and she slumps back on the day bed in hysterics, her stomach aching, and Violet is holding her hand.

When they leave the wagon an hour later Rosie is still giggling. A star-studded sky gazes down on them as they stumble past the circus wagons and the big top. Violet keeps a careful arm round her waist, and Rosie is suddenly overwhelmed at the gesture, Violet's protectiveness.

She stops and turns to her.

'I like you very much,' she says, looking into Violet's clear green eyes.

Violet smiles. 'I like you too.'

And then Violet's lips are on hers, soft and pillowy and warm, and she tastes of brandy and burnt sugar, and no one in the history of the world has ever experienced something so magical and special, Rosie is one of the lucky ones, the luckiest of all, right here in the showground on a warm Perthshire night under the twinkling lights of the big top, far, far from home.

Perhaps that is why neither of them notices that in the nearby trees, deep in the gloaming, someone is watching them.

24

Cream and honey

Lena rises early. The air in the wagon is stuffy and close, and she creeps past the three still-sleeping figures, huddled under blankets, to open the window.

Once dressed, she makes her way to a small stream that putters methodically over rocks that have been smoothed out like silk. For a moment as she crouches to fill her buckets with water for tea and porridge she is tempted to touch them, feel the slimy sheen for herself, but instead she stops to watch a mayfly, its wings glistening in the morning air. It hovers, dives towards the ripples, then disappears into the sky. She stands up, glances to see if anyone is around and, seeing that the bank is empty, crouches again to urinate.

Back at the wagon, she sets the fire with the collection of wood she and Rosie gathered the morning before, carefully arranging the kindling, just as her daddy taught her.

Lena has always loved the ritual of the early morning, when the day is still ripe with possibility, tingles with a languid, unspoken magic. When her mammy left them it had seemed natural for her to take on her chores, keep things running seamlessly. To sweep out the wagon, keep it neat as a pin, to cook the porridge and the stews and the soups, and, when her daddy gave her the pennies for it, to buy bread and apples, thick blocks of cheese from a nearby dairy.

At times she had begged, would go to a farm outside whatever town or village they were showing in, with an empty milk pail and a winning expression. Some would shoo her away like a troublesome flea, others take pity on her – 'You're only a bairn, fancy making you come and beg, where's your mammy anyway?' – and she was always left with the sour feeling that even when she was given something – a drop scone hot out the oven, a jar of pinkish raspberry jam, a pail heaving with ripe plums – somehow, she left poorer than she'd arrived.

She hangs the smaller cast-iron cooking pot, the one they always use for breakfast, over the fire, and fills it with oats, water, a wee dab of salt and, a surprise for the girls, some cream. Nothing begged or borrowed here. She bought these oats herself from one of the towns further down the road in Perthshire, and the cream yesterday, from a stall in the fair. A bit of luxury to start the day, kept cool overnight in the shallows of the river. And then, to swirl in at the final moment, another rare treat: honey. She had found the jar waiting for her on the doorstep this morning.

Once again she considers the words Harry said to her last night. She has been turning them over in her mind all night like small, precious beads. Her mother, obviously distressed, sounding as though someone had betrayed her. The possibility that she had hidden something in a tree, miles and miles away in an Ayrshire showground. What was it? And why would she have tucked it away like that? Or was Harry merely mistaken?

Then there was her daddy's reaction. Had he not believed Harry? Not taken him seriously? Or had he been to look himself and, like Harry, found nothing? How she wished she could ask him.

'Morning,' says Violet, emerging from the wagon, wrapped in a tatty blanket and yawning widely.

'How'd you sleep?' asks Lena. She is stirring the pot now with an old wooden spoon.

'Like a happy wee babby,' says Violet.

'Where did you go last night?'

'Nowhere exciting. Just a wee turn around the fair. Rosie wanted to see the fortune-teller.'

Lena knows she is lying, says nothing. The porridge is starting to thicken now, great creamy globules sputtering happily, and she feels in her dish bag for the dishes and spoons. 'Wake the others, will you?'

Violet, who has lit a cigarette, removes it from her mouth, bangs on the door of the wagon and shouts, 'Wakey wakey, sleeping beauties.'

'Such grace, such refined elegance,' says Lena, but she is smiling. Indulgent, in anticipation of her treat.

The other two emerge just as Lena is dishing up the porridge.

'Right, ladies, a wee bit of the good stuff for breakfast this morning. Porridge mixed with a dod of fresh cream, and some honey.'

Rosie, whose face – pale at the best of times – is a greenish colour, does her best to smile. Carmen merely says that it will be better than last night's wafer.

'I'll just finish this cig first,' says Violet.

Lena, deflated, starts eating. It does not, in her opinion, disappoint. The porridge is smooth, the cream rich, and the honey impossibly sweet.

'So what did the fortune-teller say, Rosie?' she asks between spoonfuls.

'The who?'

'The fortune-teller. Violet tells me you were away seeing her last night. It's that Madam Esmeralda, isn't it? My daddy always said she was an auld hack.'

Rosie blows on her porridge, looks at Violet for guidance. Violet, however, is studying a tiny ladybird crawling up her dress.

'Oh, just, you know, the usual?'

'The usual?' asks Lena.

But they are interrupted by a shout. Tam, their loyal hawker, is tearing towards them, barefoot and panting, his cap clutched in his hands.

'It's the tent,' he says, gasping for lungfuls of air like a fish on a river bank. 'Somebody's slashed a hole in it.'

They have the tent sewn back up by morning's end, and in Lena's humble opinion the four shows they perform that afternoon are better than ever. Violet seems energised, her leaps and twirls showing such flair and poise, while Carmen has taken to joining her on the bar for a final spectacular scene, which provokes much cooing and gasping from the crowd.

Rosie meanwhile, after a wobbly start, gives a masterclass in horsewomanship. She controls Tommy with a mere nudge of her foot, performs exacting jumps, and gives a proud little smile when she hops off at the end.

But the trouble with the tent has unsettled Lena. It was a crude slash, probably done in pitch dark and by someone who'd had a bit too much of the bottle, and it has not cut as long or as deep as they perhaps intended. But it *was* intended. By the same person who tried to poison Tommy Pony? Or another malevolent force?

That night they bring the tent back to the wagon, instead of leaving it sitting out on the showground. They are staying in Perthshire for three weeks, then they will be heading north, up towards the Highlands and the chilly northeast coast. The rest of the season is stretching ahead of them. She holds it close, like a secret, resting next to Harry's last words to her.

Montrose, Arbroath & Brechin Review
Saturday, 9 July 1910

LADIES' CIRCUS VISITS ARBROATH

Earlier this week a most unusual sight came to Arbroath during the annual visit of the fairs. Among the amusing delights of carousels and Wurlitzers, and the usual rigged penny shies, we were intrigued to come across a circus of ladies. Four young women, seemingly travelling unaccompanied, each with their own skill to share with their audience.

We were particularly impressed with Miss Rosie Carluke, a bareback horse-rider, whose tricks on the pony defy even the most fleet-footed of equestrians, and Miss Violet Weaver, formerly of the great Royal Linden's Circus, whose death-defying stunts on the trapeze left all who witnessed them gasping for more. Special mentions must also be made of the dazzlingly exotic 'rainbow girl', Miss Carmen Almeida, and the mysterious, tail-coated ring-mistress, Miss Lena Loveridge, who kept her crowd spellbound, and her performers in line.

We predict that these ladies – if they can hold on to their modesty among such rough company as the fairs regularly carry – will be the hit of the shows this summer, and we hope very much to catch them again in 1911, God willing.

25

Swells

Summer spins by like the slides in a zoetrope. Violet and Rosie steal kisses in darkened stables, behind whirling carousels, in fields thick with skeins of cottongrass. Lena acquires a top hat and tailcoat from a kind gentleman in a town near the sea, and their starched formality adds a rigour to her act, imbues her with a power she had no idea she possessed.

Kirriemuir. Forfar. Arbroath. Montrose. For the best part of two weeks they hug the coastline, the sea winds tangling their hair and threatening to blow the tent down. They eat stewed crab apples, bushels of wild blackberries, and Violet takes Rosie to dig for spoot clams on the beach, watching her delight as they shoot, jack-in-a-box-like, out of the sand. Later, Lena cooks the rubbery fish on an open flame, and their edges blacken and curl. They taste like fire and seaweed.

Brechin. St Cyrus. Johnshaven. Stonehaven. The accents are different here, flatter, more abrupt, and occasionally they hear Doric spoken, *fit like* and *foos yer doos*, as the shows fill up with fishermen straight off the boats, bringing the scent of the swell on their oilskin boots.

Inland briefly, to Ballater, where they catch a glimpse of the King's grey granite castle and Carmen goes foraging in the hills for mushrooms that taste like mud and give them all stomach aches. She is more confident now, calmer. She tells more stories of her childhood on the whitewashed Andalusian coast, where the sun baked the ground to a hard shell and the sound of locusts filled the air. If she understands the nature of Violet and Rosie's relationship she says nothing, but she is protective of Rosie. Tender. Like a sister.

Harry has vanished, back down to the Lowlands for shows in Edinburgh, Glasgow, a touring production performing in real theatres and music halls. Lena thinks of him sometimes when she's up front on the wagon, steering the horses towards the next town, the next show. Of those golden hairs on his arm, his lop-sided grin. Then Violet's stark words come back and she tries, instead, to banish him from her thoughts.

Aberdeen now. One of the biggest showgrounds on the trail. When they arrive, the flattie who owns the ground proudly leads them to one of the prime spots in the whole fair.

'So delighted to see the ladies' circus in town,' he says in brisk northern tones, lifting his hat, and Lena glows with pride. 'We've folk down fae Fraserburgh and Peterhead to see you tonight,' he says. 'They've heard about you girls, read about you in the papers. Had to come down to the toon to see you for themselves.'

By the time they open the canvas door the crowd outside is heaving, impatient, and Lena wonders if they will all fit. But they do. It is as though the tent herself has sighed, shrugged her shoulders and gracefully widened to accommodate every last soul. Once in, they gasp. Clap. Cheer. Clutch at each other. Upon Violet's final act they throw hats in the air. They leave in raptures.

That first night, after they have finished their shows, counted out their pennies – so many pennies, thinks Lena, and she is already planning what they will do in the winter, hire a new act, perhaps acquire a bigger tent, throw a grand party at Hogmanay – and all taken their share, Rosie decides to visit a fortune-teller.

The Show Woman

'I want to know how my ma and Jennifer are doing. If they're OK.'

She glances surreptitiously at Violet, who is engrossed in a back stretch that curves her spine in a letter U.

'And other things too. Will you come with me, Lena? I didn't understand the last lady.'

Lena links arms with her as they sway through the dying throng, decides to let it lie, Rosie's little fib. Shearwaters circle the sky, cawing plaintively. The days are that bit shorter now, even here in the bristling north, the light fading into the dark.

Rosie turns to her. She looks fraught, and a little sad.

'You alright?' Lena asks.

'Aye,' she says with a shrug. 'It's just – well, we're going to Ayr next. That's home for me, or near enough. Our farm's just a few miles down the road. I just thought that maybe . . . Well, my ma doesn't read too well. Perhaps she won't see anything in the paper. And my sister never read the paper at all. I just . . . I'm hoping that if they could get round my pa, perhaps they might come and see me. But maybe they're still angry.'

Lena takes her arm. 'A few months have passed. I'm sure they'd love to see you. We'll be there for a few days too, so you never know.'

In through a heavy velvet curtain they go, and there Miss Sibyl sits, a small headdress of golden coins roped around her skull. She motions for Rosie to sit down, waving her hands over the glowering crystal ball on the table before her while Lena hovers in the background.

'You are named after a flower,' she says. She does not look at Rosie but at the cloudy glass before her and Rosie nods, meekly.

'And you are very far from home.'

Lena snorts quietly in the background. This woman likely knows exactly who Rosie is, how far she has come. She's been in the paper. They are the talk of the fair.

Miss Sibyl ignores her.

'You nearly lost someone,' she says. 'Someone very dear to you. Tom.'

Despite herself, Lena's skin prickles, and Rosie's eyes fill with tears. 'Yes,' she says. 'I nearly did.'

'Tom is safe now,' says Miss Sibyl. She has parched lips, and the coral rouge she is wearing has dried to a flaky crust. She waves her hands again. 'Danger is coming,' she says, and this time she lifts her eyes, looks not at Rosie but at Lena. 'Danger is coming. For you in particular.'

Lena stares back at her, blank-faced.

'There will be great sadness. A terrible loss. You might never recover.'

'I think that's enough now, Rosie,' says Lena. And pulls her away.

One last performance. One final cheer. A rose, handed to each of the four women by a grateful fairground-owner who says he can't remember such crowds. It must be a miracle.

Now, they are finished with this clear, salty-aired, jagged part of the country. It is time to head back down the road, and go south. To Ayrshire.

They will stop first in Ayr and then on to Galston, where it all started. Or finished. Lena wishes she knew. She feels a tingle of excitement at the prospect, laced with something more sinister. She will find that tree, chop it down if she has to, in order to get to the truth.

They pull the wagon out of Aberdeen showground, away from the town, back across the well-worn grooves, chattering all the way. In the sky above, the sun bears down on them, impassive.

26

Names

Try as she might, Serena cannot get out of bed. Her chest feels heavy and sore, and each time she breathes in, it is as though a great clump of feathers and hay is squatting on her lungs, forcing the air back out.

Her legs are weak as a kitten's, and she has manoeuvred herself into a lumpen, awkward position, feet dangling pathetically over the covers, her bulk squashed painfully into the corner wall. She coughs, a hammering chorus that produces phlegm, blood, and something that looks curiously like tar, and feels her breath crackle.

This is how Rory McCracken finds her when he knocks on the door of her wagon and, upon receiving no answer, barrels straight in.

'Get out,' she says, seeing an infuriating combination of pity and amusement flit across his long, sly face.

'Sorry, Miss Linden,' he says. He looks down at his feet but does not move. 'Can I give yer a hand? You don't look too comfortable there.'

'I'm fine,' she says. With a heroic effort she twists her torso round to face him properly and, seeing that he is not leaving, relents. 'Well?' she says. 'Why are you here?'

'It's those lassies,' he says. 'Talk of the shows in Aberdeen, we hear. They're away over to Ayr now. Wondered if you wanted us to go and have a bit of fun, seeing as we're not far.'

Serena gazes out of the wagon window. It is smeared with grime, has not been cleaned for months. Outside, her equestrian riders are rehearsing their latest acts, which involve a complicated new jump with hoops. They are in Largs, a jaunty seaside town down the Clyde coast, and it is full of Glasgow day-trippers decked out in their Sunday best, fresh off the paddle steamer. They do good business here this time of year, always have.

Violet Weaver. The name still incites a rage in her, a fury that rumbles deep in her belly. Her eye has long since healed, the bruise fading into her puckered, milky skin, but the anger remains.

She wonders now about the other lassies alongside her. She has been so intent on getting to Violet, ruining her new show, bringing that jumped-up madam to heel, she has forgotten to enquire about the company she keeps.

'How many lassies are there in this show?' she asks.

'Four, I think. There's an acrobat, and a bareback rider. And then the lass who runs it all. Does a turn in the ring with a top hat.'

'And what does she go by?'

'It's Loveridge,' he says. 'Lena Loveridge.'

'Loveridge,' says Serena. She turns the word over in her mouth, forming the syllables, tasting the old name. 'No,' she says. 'No. It can't be.' She coughs again, gasping for air. 'God in heaven,' she says between gulps. 'Not a Loveridge.'

27

And on the night before

They are pulling into Ayr showground, near the racecourse on the edge of the town, when Lena spots him. That brawny frame. The cap pulled down low over his forehead. And, under it, the blossoming smile.

'Harry,' she says, and she draws up the wagon, steadies the horses, as he smiles and waves at them.

'Ladies,' he says and lifts his cap.

'Hello, big brother,' says Violet, from her perch on the box beside Lena at the front of the caravan. Beyond Harry Lena can see a small crowd forming at the gates of the ground, catches the excited shouts. *Is that the ladies' circus? Look, they're here!*

Violet ignores them, focuses her attention on Harry.

'What brings you to this part of the world?'

He pulls himself up so he is standing on the wagon step, so close to Lena she can see the flecks of gold in his eyes, the fresh stubble on his chin. 'Well, I've an invite for you. Special event.'

Lena clutches the reins in her hands, feels the leather work into the skin of her palms.

'I'll be singing tonight, at the Gaiety Theatre in the town. Thought you'd like to come along. I've four seats for you.'

He fumbles in his jacket pocket, produces tickets the colour of raspberries. Violet leans over and snatches them from him. 'Ooh, the stalls, too,' she says. 'Aren't you the fancy dan?'

'Thank you,' says Lena. Her heart is hammering in her chest. 'We'd love to come. What time is it?'

'Starts at eight o'clock,' says Harry. 'Figured you'd be finished for the day by then. See you tonight.'

He gives Lena a toothy grin and jumps back down off the wagon.

They do three shows that afternoon, each one as packed as the last. Their reputation has clearly spread. They are a curio, a must-see, and when Lena takes a bow at the end of their final performance she feels a warm glow in her chest: happiness. The season will be at an end soon, but before that there is Galston to get to. She imagines herself wandering the streets, knocking on doors, asking if anyone knew a Maggie Loveridge, and does she still live around here or has she moved? The thought terrifies her, makes her want to shove her fist in her mouth in fear, but there is a kernel of excitement there too. A hopeful tingle.

And then, when the season is over, they will return to Vinegarhill for the winter. There will be much to do. She has been careful with the takings, paying everyone each night and keeping some back to tide them over, make improvements while they're back in the ground. A new tent, perhaps. New shoes for the horses. Maybe she will hire another act, a lady boxer perhaps, or a clown. She has never seen a female clown, but surely there must be one, somewhere? The rest of the year stretches out before her, endless, exciting, ripe with possibility.

As they are packing up the tent Lena hears an excited squeal. She turns to see Rosie wrapped up in the embrace of two women. Lena sees the family resemblance immediately, in Rosie's mother, bird-like and delicate; in her sister's kind, open face.

'We're so proud of you,' her mother is saying. 'You and Tommy were wonderful, I just can't believe it.'

Violet nudges Lena and Carmen. 'Shall we say hello?'

The Show Woman

They approach the three women, still clutching arms, Rosie stifling tears, her face beaming.

'These are my fellow . . .' she hesitates over the word, and swallows. 'My fellow show women. This is Lena, and Carmen, and Violet.' She gives Violet a small, secret glance.

'You girls are quite something,' says Rosie's mother, her face flushed and excited. 'You were flying up there, Violet. It was beautiful.'

Violet smiles graciously. 'Your daughter's our star turn, really. Well, her and Tommy.'

'Yes, Tommy Pony,' says Jennifer. 'I never knew he had it in him. Always thought of him as a wee runt but he's doing a great job with you.'

Rosie's face suddenly clouds. 'Does Pa know you're here?'

Jennifer shakes her head. 'God, no. We kept the paper away from him – that's how we found out you would be coming here, Rosie – but he's been very angry. You know what he's like.'

Lena sees Rosie's ma's face darken too, streaked with something like pain.

'I don't want you worrying about it, though, hen,' she says. 'I can see it now. This is the right place for you. Don't you be coming back to the farm.'

The three women stroll away to buy some sweeties as Violet, Lena and Carmen finish taking the tent down for the day. Lena takes Tommy back to the stables, but, just as she's finished untacking him, Rosie appears beside her with a sugar lump for the pony.

'They came, they really came,' she says, her eyes shining and happy.

Lena slides an arm round her tiny waist. 'There now,' she says as they leave the stable. 'Just as you hoped.'

171

'And Jennifer's expecting, too. She told me. I'm going to be an auntie.'

Back in the wagon they change, bring out old dresses kept for best, that haven't seen the light of day since they've been on the road. Violet lends Rosie one of hers, in palest blue with a tulle skirt and a high collar. It fits like a glove, lights up her eyes, gives Rosie an ethereal, almost angelic look.

'Beautiful,' says Violet, and smoothes her hands down Rosie's tiny waist. 'But it's missing just one thing.'

She rummages in her packing case and produces a box. She opens it to reveal a brooch in the shape of a butterfly. It is brightest blue, glisters in the fading light, its wings boned with silver.

Rosie's hands rush to her mouth. 'Oh,' she says.

'Oh,' repeats Violet. 'A little gift for you. Picked it up in Aberdeen.'

Rosie lifts the brooch out of its box, turns it this way and that. 'It's the most beautiful thing I've ever seen. Can you put it on for me?'

Carefully, Violet unpins the brooch and affixes it at Rosie's throat where it seems to hover, as though it has merely landed for a second before taking off again in flight.

Lena feels a warmth towards these two young women, their deep and obvious affection for each other. She has never known Violet quite so benevolent and kind, so enthralled by a person other than herself. She has been wrong to worry. Perhaps they really are made for each other. And if they are happy, why can't she be too?

Her mind flits to Harry again. That lopsided smile, the fuss with the tickets, his earnest voice, telling them about his singing. Had he been nervous? Is it her he really wants to see tonight?

The Show Woman

Lena is wearing a long cream skirt, a white blouse edged with lace, and a waistcoat. She has done her hair carefully, pinning it to create height at the crown, and put large hoops in her ears. Her mammy's pendant lies on her chest, close to her heart.

'You look nice,' says Carmen, applying her favourite red rouge to her lips. She has chosen black and red, her favourite colours, she says, so different from her rainbow costume, and yet the outfit accentuates her dark eyes, her silky black hair.

'Are we ready?' asks Lena, and they trail out into the fading dusk of the evening. It has been a hot day, too hot for September, and the air feels thick and close. It prickles at their skin, even as the sky turns dark.

'Could be rain coming,' says Violet.

As they make their way towards the town, arms linked, laughing about the boy in the last show of the day who insisted on being ridden round the ring on Tommy Pony after the show then stood up on his back, promptly toppled over and had to be caught by Violet, they attract attention. A cart goes past with two lads on the back, barefoot and with bottles of beer in their hands, and they wolf-whistle at the four women and ask if they want a ride.

'Not where you're going,' says Violet and they laugh as the wagon disappears into the dark. They pass a flower bed, and on a whim Lena leans in and plucks a small white flower for Carmen's hair.

Further into town now and men in smart suits and bowler hats cast admiring glances their way, right up to the theatre door. There is a clamour to get in, through the grand foyer with its sweetie stand and refreshments stall, a huge electric light hanging from the ceiling with cascades of shimmering crystals, and down a narrow carpeted corridor into the auditorium.

Lena is taken aback at the size of it. The heavy curtain across the stage. The seats, covered in a rich, burgundy velvet. The fashionable ladies and be-suited gentlemen. Giggling, excited, as if they are doing something naughty – should not be caught in such polite company and in somewhere so strange – they find their seats, just four rows back from the stage. Lena thinks she hears one lady say behind a fan, 'Gypsies, I'll warrant, just look at the dark one,' but she ignores it. Nothing can prick her buoyant mood tonight. And besides. She has heard it all before.

The house lights go down. A hush passes over the auditorium. And then the curtain rises and there stands Harry, alone, a spotlight highlighting his golden head, wearing a kilt. A violin in the orchestra, unseen in the pit below, plays a single note. And then, in the silence, Harry opens his mouth to sing.

'O my love is like a red, red rose
That's newly sprung in June;
O my love is like a melody
That's sweetly played in tune.'

Lena is spellbound. She has never heard Harry sing before, had no idea his was such a good voice, deep and rich. It makes her want to cry and to smile, all at the same time, and when he intones the words '*I will love thee still, my dear, Till all the seas gang dry*,' she feels something in her chest fizz with excitement and longing and hope.

Afterwards they wait for Harry outside the stage door, the air sticky on their skin, Violet swatting at her face with a programme she pinched during the interval.

The Show Woman

'There he is,' she says as Harry emerges into the warm night, still wearing his kilt. 'Not bad,' she adds. 'Not bad at all.'

'Well?' he says. He is looking at Lena.

'You were wonderful,' she says. 'You really do have a good set of pipes on you.'

Violet clears her throat theatrically. 'Rosie, Carmen, I think we have some urgent business to attend to back at the showground.' And she links arms with both of them, flashes a smile at Lena and departs.

Harry is suddenly shy.

'Would you like to get a drink?' he asks.

They find a small pub by the river. It is dark and busy; men eye Lena as she threads her way through the lads crowded at the bar, and Harry gives her his hand to hold, just in case. It is warm and dry, reassuring. It is the first time she has ever been inside a public house, and she notes she is the only woman in the place.

They take their drinks outside, wander over to the riverbank. In front of them, a large swan is waddling back to her nest, three dirty brown cygnets following behind.

'So you liked the show, then?'

Lena nods. 'I didn't know you could sing like that. I remember you liked singing as a bairn – your mammy always said you should have been in the cathedral choir – but good male voices don't always come through when they break.'

She colours a little at this reference to puberty, to the other things that change when a boy's voice breaks, but Harry doesn't notice, nodding thoughtfully.

'Aye, I think my mammy thought I could do all sorts of things I didn't really want to do. And now my pa's gone she's been on at me to take on the travelling theatre. But it's not what I fancy. Proper theatres, places like that tonight, that's the place for me.'

Lena sips her whisky. It is rough and warm, and she enjoys the tingling sensation as it floods through her, fills her body with a simmering heat.

'There is something I've been meaning to tell you,' says Harry. 'Tommy. The hole that was cut in the tent. I've been hearing that it was the Linden woman.'

Lena is shocked. 'From Linden's Circus?' she says. 'What would she have against us?'

'Well, Violet crossed her, and I hear she's a bitter old crone. Nasty piece of work.'

Lena remembers something. 'At Blairgowrie. It was there that the hole was cut. And Linden's were in town. Everyone was talking about it, don't you remember?'

Harry nods. 'I do. You've got to watch her. She's up to no good. Just . . . be careful. I can't be around for the rest of the season to protect you.'

He grabs her hand and she lets him hold it, feels him stroke the side of her thumb.

'We'll be alright,' she says. 'We're show women. And Carmen's taught us how to look after ourselves. We won't let anyone get the better of us.'

He looks at her. His face is inches from hers now.

'I know you won't,' he says. 'I think you're . . . well, you're quite something, Lena Loveridge. And I'd like to see more of you. Would you fancy that? Us getting to know each other, I mean?'

He leans in, cups her chin in his hand. She feels his mouth brush against hers, soft as feathers, and nods.

It is late when they arrive back at the showground, a damp thick smell on the air, as though a storm is coming. Harry has walked her home, and leaves her at the gates before heading back to his digs in the town. 'Don't want to see Violet again, she'll only craik at me,' he says.

The Show Woman

He kisses Lena on her forehead, lets his hand linger round her waist.

'I'll see you back at Vinegarhill in a couple of weeks,' he says. 'When the season's over. Then we can start to make plans.'

Lena feels dizzy, her head spinning. She waves at his retreating form and begins picking her way through the detritus of a day at the fair. She can still taste him on her lips: whisky, tobacco and something else, salty, like the sea. On her skin she can feel the first spots of rain. The weather is beginning to break.

Back at the wagon Carmen, Violet and Rosie are still up. They have clearly been drinking and Violet's eyes are glassy. She is waving a bottle around and singing some tuneless number that might, or might not, be the hymn 'Onward, Christian Soldiers'.

'Lena,' she says, then starts singing 'Lena lo-oves Ha-a-a-rry-y' to the same tune.

'Well, clearly not all the Weavers are blessed with as good a voice as Harry,' says Lena. She feels a bit tipsy herself, takes the bottle from Violet and has a swig.

'And since when were you the authority on my family?' asks Violet. There is an edge to her voice.

'Ach, away with you,' says Lena. 'What have you been doing anyway?'

'Just having a little chat,' says Violet. She sits down heavily, slings an arm around Rosie, who is struggling to keep her eyes open, and reaches the other out to Lena for the bottle. 'The real question, Lena the ringmistress, is what were you doing with Harry?'

'Just having a little chat,' Lena retorts.

Violet watches her closely. 'I bet that's not all,' she says.

'And what if it isn't, eh?' says Lena. 'Does it matter?'

'Well, that depends,' says Violet.

She takes a swig of the bottle. There is a hardness in her eyes. A meanness. The rain is starting to come down now, thick droplets landing all around them. 'What do you have to say about it, Carmen?'

Carmen looks up, startled. She has been knitting, a long scarf in blues and purples, and the clack of her needles comes to an abrupt stop.

'About Harry and Lena,' says Violet.

'It is very nice,' says Carmen flatly.

'Nice,' says Violet. 'Nice,' she repeats, rolling the word around in her mouth. 'Is that what you thought about him? Harry, I mean. Was he nice with you?'

Carmen flushes, looks stricken, but says nothing.

'What are you talking about?' says Lena. Cold dread creeps up her arms.

'She went with him,' says Violet. 'Back in Glasgow. Before the circus. Ages ago. You didn't tell her, Carmen?'

Carmen has flung her knitting on the ground, put her head in her hands. Her whole body is convulsing. Lena is frozen to the spot. Violet must be lying. But one glance at Carmen and she knows it is true.

'I told you not to get worked up over Harry,' says Violet. 'You wouldn't listen. Do you really want to be with him now? *My love is like a red, red rose* indeed. I ask you. He's pathetic.'

Lena cannot speak. Her body thrums with fury and shame. Carmen is sobbing loudly now. Rosie has her head in between her knees, rocking back and forth.

'You bitch,' Lena says finally to Violet. She walks straight past her into the wagon so she does not see her tears. High above them, the heavens finally open.

Rosie tears across the ground after Carmen. The acrobat is running towards the gates, her battered suitcase hastily

The Show Woman

packed, hair slicked with rain. Rosie catches up to her, grabs her free arm, long and skinny, and clutches at her wrist.

'Carmen, please. Don't go.'

The Spaniard turns to look at her, her angular face washed with tears and rainwater, and shakes her head. 'How can I stay? After that? After what Violet did. It is no good. I must go.'

'Please. We can sort everything out. Perhaps if you and Lena just talked? It's all in the past, isn't it?'

Carmen gives her a sad smile. 'Yes, of course. It was a long time ago. It was nothing. That is why I have avoided him, Harry, as much as I could. But I should never have told Violet. It was a big mistake.' Carmen looks at Rosie. 'Did she tell you, too?'

Rosie shakes her head. 'Honestly, I didn't know. And I don't care either. And once Lena has calmed down, neither will she. I'm sure of it.'

Carmen lifts her hand to her friend's cheek. 'My sweet little shrub. You are so very good. But you are an innocent in these matters. It is not that simple.'

She leans in and gives Rosie a hug. It is pouring now, pitch black, and Rosie shivers.

'Can't you just stay for tonight?' she says into her chest. 'You could come and sleep in the stables.'

Carmen shakes her head. 'I do not know that I can control myself around Violet. I am very angry with her.' She steps back. 'Please look after Lena for me. She is a good woman. And so are you. And give Tommy Pony a pat from his Spanish friend.'

She picks up the suitcase and walks away, leaving Rosie alone at the gates of the ground.

Violet is pacing the floor of the stable, kicking furiously at the straw on the ground, when Rosie creeps in, soaked to the skin. Tommy Pony is unsettled and keeps one eye open at the commotion. He does not like his rest disturbed, even by his beloved Rosie.

'I've done it now,' says Violet. 'I've buggered it all up.'

Rosie sits down cross-legged in the corner of the stall, says nothing.

'Go on,' Violet continues. 'You can say it. I'm an evil witch, as bitter and twisted as my own mammy.'

Rosie shakes her head. 'You were angry. Jealous maybe. I know how much you love Harry. Lena, too. Perhaps you thought that if he and Lena started going around together, they wouldn't have any time for you.'

Violet looks at her and laughs, mirthlessly. 'You're far too clever for your own good, my lass.'

'Come here,' says Rosie, and Violet, weakening, collapses in a heap beside her.

'It's going to be alright,' says Rosie. 'We'll make good with Lena tomorrow. And then we'll find Carmen. We've come too far; we can't let it all slip through our fingers now.'

Violet flings her arms around her.

'I hope so, Rosie Posy. I really bloody hope so.'

Lena sits alone in the caravan, listening to the rain drumming the roof. She is shaking with fury and fear. One moment a new life, tantalising, possible, stretched out before her. The next it was snatched away by a snarling Violet, and Carmen along with it.

Why had she lied? Why had Harry? Had they been meeting up behind her back? Was Harry just being kind to her?

And what of the circus? With Carmen gone, they have lost not just her act, but her music, too. Will Violet and Rosie even turn up tomorrow?

The Show Woman

On the floor a single ribbon from Carmen's costume lies discarded by the door. It must have broken off in her haste to get out. Lena picks it up, trails the colourful fabric through her fingers, and lets herself weep. She has never felt more alone, or more lost, in all her life.

The rain drums harder on the roof of the caravan, echoing the staccato beats of her heart.

28

The fall, reprised

Showtime.

High above the tent Violet glistens like a sleekit fish. Stock-still, toes pointed, head bowed as though in prayer. Lena circles the ring, walking endless laps to quell her fury. She feels Violet's eyes upon her as she paces, a resting malevolence emanating from the rafters.

Carmen has not returned. Rosie and Violet did not come back to the wagon, and Lena suspects they slept in the stable. But they have, at least, turned up to do the show.

Lena's hands shake as she introduces Violet.

'Look up,' she says. 'Can you see her? Right at the top of the tent. Look up, ladies and gentlemen, because this young woman is about to fly.'

Grasping the bar, Violet pushes off the board, her body taut as piano wire. For a single, perfect moment she is flying. Soaring through the tent, light as the air that carries her.

Lena will not look up, will not give her the satisfaction of knowing she is watching her. But then, as if it were planned, as if it were the most graceful of movements, Violet's hands slip from the bar as though it were spun from silk. Or coated in grease. And just as Lena turns her head, she falls.

The tent glitters. Lena runs. But not even the tail-coated ringmistress can stop gravity.

Violet, heavy as the moon, lands on the sawdust with a toneless thud. The crowd begins to howl. The greatest trapeze artist who ever lived is lying flat on the floor of the tent. Her toes are still pointed. And it is Lena who is looking down, and screaming.

PART TWO

One Star Awake

Two months later

Vinegarhill Showground, Glasgow
November 1910

29

Clackity clack

Rosie wakes to pitch black. She dresses quickly, a long cotton dress, worn boots and a shawl, patched and threadbare, wrapped tightly around her shoulders. Frost has formed spindles on the window and, even fully clothed, she shivers in the cold. Creeping out of the door, she casts a glance at the other figure in the wagon, blankets piled up high, but there is no movement from the bed.

Across the showground and out on to the Gallowgate, already thrumming with early morning traffic. Milk carts on their rounds, glowering trams whose bells clang their arrival through the mist, warning all and sundry to get out of the way, or else. She wishes she could afford to board one.

Instead she follows the road down to Bridgeton, past the old market, and on to Glasgow Green. Her boots crunch on the stiff grass as she crosses the great park, her breath leaving gales of steam behind her as she walks.

As Rosie arrives at the gates of the factory, she looks up. She has been told it is meant to resemble the Doge's Palace in Venice, an Italian masterpiece, they say, but to her it looks forbidding and sinister, like the palace of an evil king in a story.

Round the back now to the weaving sheds, already filling up with weary-faced women clocking in for the day.

There is banter and laughter, stale breath and the smell of unwashed clothes. Rosie keeps her head down, steps forward, moves through the shed to her station.

It is only when she is seated, the methodical rhythm of the machine in front of her, that steady *clackity clack*, that she allows herself to think of Violet, and what might have been.

There had been a doctor at the fairground that day, the last of its kind. He had been fetched to the tent, elbowed his way through the crowds, bent tenderly over Violet's unmoving form. Lena stood, transfixed, looking down at her, as though she could not quite believe what she was seeing. Rosie was wailing, collapsed beside her, tried moving the head with its unseeing eyes on to her lap.

Then came men from the St John's Ambulance carrying a stretcher, and Violet had been borne away on it, Lena following behind, Rosie entrusting Tommy to Tam, racing to catch up. Lena grasped her hand.

'She must be alive,' she said, breathless, tears streaming. 'Otherwise they wouldn't have taken her. Oh, Rosie. Did you see what happened? She slipped from the bar. She's never done that. It can't have been an accident.'

Rosie shook her head. Normally she liked to watch Violet on the bar before her own entrance, marvel anew at the liquid movements, the way she turned her body to oil so high up off the ground. But Tommy had been fussing, unhappy with a new bridle, and her attention had been on him, not on what was happening above.

The next three days were interminable. Violet was taken to a hospital in the town, and the staff would not let them in to see her. They were told only that it was 'touch and go', and would they be able to pay? Lena had panicked, feared Violet would be tossed out on to the street, but when they'd arrived back at the showground that night they had discovered there had been a whip-round among the showmen and women with whom they had spent the season. People were shocked; they wanted to see Violet done right by. Both Lena and Rosie were overwhelmed.

It was Harry who, on that third day, came to tell them that Violet would live. Lena would not look him in the eye and Harry, baffled and hurt, had slunk away, said he would head back to Glasgow, tell his mother, get somewhere ready for Violet to be settled.

And then, one week later, Violet emerged from the hospital, pushed by a crisply dressed nurse in an old wooden wheelchair. Her bill had been settled, between the takings of the circus and the showground whip-round, and the chair was hers. They did not know if she would walk again. Her spine was damaged, and they could not tell yet if it would heal.

Rosie burst with joy to see her, ran to throw her arms around her love, but Violet shrugged her off, kept her hands flat in her lap, said nothing.

She seemed to have shrunk during her time on the ward. Her eyes were sunken, her lips thin; her hair hung greasily down her back. All the vigour had been drained from her. She was like a different person.

That had been two months ago. They had returned to Vinegarhill, to a wagon Mary Weaver kept aside for emergencies, made a sort of home there. Violet had told Rosie to leave, to go home to her ma and her sister, that she didn't want her to stay, but Rosie had been insistent. She loved Violet as much now as she always had. She wanted to care for her. Look after her. And so she had moved in.

Lena stayed in her own wagon. She came to visit regularly, brought card games, the odd nip of whisky.

Violet seemed to cheer slightly when she visited, which stung Rosie a little, but she tried not to mind. She believed that one day Violet would walk again. And if she could convince Violet, then maybe, one day, she would believe it too.

30

No travellers

Lena pounds her way down Union Street, past the daytime drunks and the veering vagrants, caps in hand, faces leering. She has always been intimidated by this grimy city's central maze of streets, its cobbled roads full of people and horses. She remembers her daddy bringing her here once, the year her mammy vanished. Despite it all, there had been a good season on the fairs and her daddy had pennies to spare, wanted to buy her a treat that might make up for it all, somehow.

And so they had walked out of the showground gates, something she had done rarely except for her sporadic visits to the local school, and down into the town, to a big toy shop with shiny tin soldiers in the window, ruby-red drums, running hoops with gaily coloured ribbons, and a collection of wooden farm animals arranged around a paddock of real grass. Lena was entranced.

The bell tinkled as they pushed their way in. A boy in a sky-blue sailor suit was holding a kite, swooshing it this way and that while his father, smart in a suit with a high collar, and the shopkeeper, who wore a clean brown apron and was sporting a trimmed moustache, watched on indulgently.

The shopkeeper's eyes narrowed when they landed on Lena and her daddy.

'Can't you read?' he said.

Her daddy, flustered, took his cap off, turned it round in his large, meaty hands. 'Sorry, sir,' he said, and Lena recognised the tone as one he used with non-show people, with flatties, when he was trying to be polite, deferential. 'I didn't see the sign. Just trying to get something for the wean here.' And he gestured towards Lena, who smiled her best impress-the-flatties grin.

'Well, I suggest you go back outside and read it,' said the man. 'Or get your *wean*,' and he sneered at the word, 'to read it for you.'

They shuffled back out the door, the bell tinkling all the time, while the man apologised in hushed tones to his customers.

Lena squinted at the sign on the door. NO IRISH, NO TRAVELLERS.

They turned back towards Vinegarhill, her daddy stopping at a sweetie stall on the Gallowgate to buy her a poke of striped humbugs instead, but the experience had humiliated them both. She saw the look in her daddy's eyes, felt his shame and his anger.

Yet here she is, flitting down Union Street as though the devil were on her back, because she wants to get something nice for Violet. Violet, her sort of sister, who lies immobile and miserable in a wagon in a showground, who might never walk again.

The guilt has made her heavy, borne down on her like a great sack of coal. She should never have kissed Harry. Should never have called Violet a bitch. Should never have started the circus. Should have checked the trapeze bar every day herself.

She knows now that Violet's fall was no accident. When they took her away, Lena had rushed to the tent, climbed the rigging to the trapeze. Never good with heights, she had wobbled there, arms outstretched, until she could grab the bar. It immediately slid away from her. She let it swing, then reached out to grasp it again, this time grabbing the ropes that secured it. Pulling it to her, she saw the bar glisten.

The Show Woman

It was covered in grease, slippery as an eel. Not even a trapeze artist of Violet's calibre could have clung on to that. Lena had flung it away in fury. Violet's fate had been set before she'd even climbed the rigging. She was descending to the floor when Harry appeared, eyes hooded, his face streaked with worry, to tell her that Violet was in hospital.

'How is she?' Lena wouldn't look at him.

'They think her back is broken.'

Lena exhaled slightly. It was the best, and worst news, she had ever received. Above them, the trapeze swung silently.

'They won't let anyone other than family in for now,' Harry said, 'so you won't be able to see her. But I'll keep you posted, I promise.'

'You can talk to Rosie,' said Lena. 'I'll hear all the news from her.'

Harry paced up and down the tent, his shoes kicking on the sawdust where Violet had fallen, the faintest outline of her body still visible.

'Can we talk?' he said.

'Why?' she replied coldly. 'I'd have thought you'd be running off after Carmen by now.'

He looked like a puppy that had been kicked. 'She told you, then,' he said softly, his cap limp in his hands.

'No, Violet told me. And I'm glad she did. I just don't understand why you lied. Why Carmen lied either.'

'It was a long time ago. I'm sorry. It's not something I'm proud of, but I didn't see the sense in bringing it up. Not when the circus was doing so well, and you women were all so close. Why rake up the past?'

'That's the problem with the past,' said Lena. 'It has a habit of turning up in the present.'

Harry was silent.

Lena looked at him briefly, saw regret and misery on his normally open, kind face, but could find nothing left in her heart for him. It was as though the sun had gone in. He turned to leave and she watched his retreating back, the sturdy shoulders, the way his hair curled over his shirt collar, vanish into the night.

She shakes away the thoughts that clatter into her head. The important thing now is to be there for Violet, to make her smile, help look after her. She thinks of Rosie, working hard now at Templeton's carpet factory to bring in a few pennies to pay for Violet's doctor, who comes to visit every three days with draughts for the pain. Lena worried that Rosie would blame her, direct her rage and fury at their ringmistress. Instead she has acquired a bleak, methodical calm.

Almost at the end of Union Street now, and she can see the dirty river ahead. It is running high after a long bout of rain, five days in a row, and the river bus heading in to moor bobs dangerously in the swell, tiny figures on deck holding on to precious hats, unsteady on their feet.

She stops outside the shopfront and checks for signs but sees none. She pushes the door, and enters a treasure trove of riotous colour. Bolts of fabric are piled up on every side, sheer organdie in pink and blush, opaque poplins in dove-grey and bold blue. There are silks, too, sheening in the late afternoon light, in ochre and emerald and palest lilac. Spindles of wool are stacked at the back of the shop, sensible navy and midnight black, with jaunty flashes of reds and sunshine-yellows.

'Can I help you?'

A woman emerges from behind the wools, looking intently at Lena, but not unkindly.

'Oh, yes, please,' says Lena, in her usual placate-the-flatties voice. 'I'd like to buy some wool. I'm knitting a friend a bedjacket.'

★

The Show Woman

'How are you today, then, hen?' asks Lena.

The figure on the bed flicks her head from side to side.

'Bloody glorious. I've pissed the bed three times, stuck so many pins into my legs to see if I can feel anything that I've made them bleed, and read exactly one page of *Pride and Prejudice*. Jane Austen is shite, I've concluded.'

'Well,' says Lena, settling down on the bed next to her, 'at least you've still got your health.'

Violet emits a low, gravelly chuckle. The air in the wagon is thick, foetid, and Lena wonders if Mary Weaver has been in to see her daughter today, brought her food or changed her bedding.

'You need clean sheets?' asks Lena.

'Nah,' says Violet. 'Belle came in earlier. Didn't thank me for making her, but she did it after I threatened to box her ears.'

Violet's little sister has shot up since they left Vinegarhill all those months ago, and is now taller than her mother. She is probably taller than Violet, too, not that they'd know. Lena's heart sinks again.

'I bought some wool,' says Lena, ripping off the brown paper of the parcel she is carrying to show Violet the thick balls in various shades of purple. 'I'm going to knit you a bedjacket for the cold nights. Violet for violet.'

Violet rolls her eyes. 'Aye, well, it'll keep you busy,' she says.

'There's something else I wanted to talk to you about,' says Lena.

'If it's Harry, then he wants to—'

'It's not Harry. It'll never be Harry. We've agreed on that. No more now.'

Violet flicks a hand to her hair, scratches vigorously at a spot at her temple. 'Go on, then,' she says.

'It's Serena Linden.'

Violet's eyes narrow dangerously.

'I want to go and see her. I think it was her that greased the bar, I really do. And if it was, I want to get it out of her.'

Violet snorts. 'Don't go,' she says. 'Lena, I'm serious. She's a vicious old crone. There's no telling what she might do.'

'But we might never know the truth if I don't,' says Lena.

Violet shrugs. 'So? It won't change anything. These legs won't work whether Serena coughs to putting me in that chair or not.' She gestures at the old wooden wheelchair that sits, malevolently, in the corner. 'Promise me you won't go,' she says. 'She's nothing but an auld bitch.'

They both flinch at the word.

'Actually, there's something I wanted to talk to you about, too,' says Violet. Her face has lost its previous animated quality. She looks serious, sad. But before she can say anything the door of the wagon swings open and Rosie walks in.

'Hello, you two,' she says, and she bustles around straightening Violet's sheets, opening the window to clear the air, and taking off her hat, seemingly all in one fluid motion.

'It'll keep,' says Violet. And she pats Lena's hand.

31

Fillings

That night, Lena dreams of the coal merchant's cart. Her father's body, little more than bones now, rattling viciously in the back while she sits up front with the horses, their breath heavy and forced. Before she can stop them they plunge into a river, and it is deep, too deep, and they are sinking into the rushing water, and Lena is gasping for air, and just as she disappears below the waves she can see her mother's blue shawl in the watery shadows beneath them.

She wakes, soaked in sweat. Outside there is only the faint rustle of the wind, blowing through the sparse leaves that remain on the trees. Winter is at the gate. Soon it will be dark by four o'clock and the city will take on a pale, sickly glow in daytime, the sky a pallid, effortful grey.

Lena has been restless since the moment they arrived back at Vinegarhill. Most of the shows were still on the road, the familiar clatter replaced by a deadening flatness. It was as though the showground herself had slept through summer, stirred only by the lazy time-keeping of the dandelion clocks that wound around her edges, the land waiting patiently for her occupants to return.

Lena did not want to be here, yet she could not, would not, go anywhere else. She had been born at Vinegarhill, in the same wagon she now lay in, and it was here, on this same bed, where her father had died. But even then, in those harsh, bright days after her daddy's death, she had still felt as though she was in perpetual motion, forever moving forward.

Lena thinks of the promise she made to her father. *Find her*, he said. But her daddy is dead and gone. For all she knows, her mammy might be too. Violet is here, weak and feeble, but alive. Several times in these past, dark, miserable weeks Lena has considered lashing up the wagon, heading for Galston, searching for the tree, just as she had decided. But then she will think of Violet, the way she spun downwards, the sickening thump as she hit the ground, her body crushed, the spine bent, and she knows she must stay here, for now.

Like Violet, albeit in a different way, Lena too had been grounded.

'Are you in there, hen?'

There is a loud thump on the side of the wagon. Lena has slept late, unusually for her, and her eyes feel sticky and sore as she hauls herself out of bed. Mary Weaver is at the door, as stout and implacable as she was the day after her daddy died.

Lena was not sure if Mary would blame her for Violet's accident, would be furious with the lassie who put her daughter in such danger. But Mary has instead laid the blame squarely at Violet's feet.

'It was bound to happen,' she said when Violet was eventually brought back from Ayr, strapped to the back of a cart, lifted gingerly into a wagon by Harry and her oldest brother, William, down for a brief visit. 'All that swinging around on the trapeze like a wild woman. I'm only amazed she didn't break her back long before this.'

Lena is astonished that Mary could be so detached from her own daughter's pain, particularly when she had been so attuned to Lena's. But Mary had always been something of an enigma. With old Billy dead, she preferred to stay at Vinegarhill with their youngest, Belle, now fourteen, rather

The Show Woman

than do the shows each summer. Her daddy had called her a 'sour' woman, which had confused Lena when she was younger because she was always so nice to them both, particularly in the years after her mammy was first gone, bringing them plates of leek and potato soup she'd made fresh, or offering to lend a hand with their washing.

'You need any clothes done?' asks Mary, and Lena shakes her head.

'I'm alright, Mary. It's just me now, don't forget. I can do my own washing easy enough.'

'Aye, well,' says Mary. She does not move.

'Do you want to come in?' Lena says eventually.

Mary steps in without another word and parks herself on the unmade bed while Lena unfurls herself into the old rocking chair. Mary's eyes flit around the caravan. Apart from the rumpled sheets the place is as neat as a pin. Clothes hung up and carefully folded, Lena's mammy's old silks hung on the wall, the window clean, surfaces scrubbed and polished until they are gleaming. It is one of the only benefits of no longer being on the road: the time to get the place straight, only one body in the wagon each night instead of four of them sharing the same tiny space. Lena's heart strains with sadness.

'It's about Violet,' says Mary. 'She's going to have to go. Harry and I had her away up at the hospital today and it's no good. Her back's gone. She'll never walk again.'

Lena says nothing. She feels a weight in the pit of her stomach.

'They're willing to take her at Stobhill. She'll be on a ward with the ones with broken spines. It's for the best. We just can't take care of her here. That wee lassie that sticks to her like a limpet isn't up to it.'

Lena is suddenly furious. They can't dump Violet in a hospital for the rest of her life, surely? Violet who loves the open road and the air, who used to fly on her trapeze? She'll wither and die in a place like that.

'Can you not keep her here? I can help look after her, and there's Rosie, and you. Even Belle's been helping her get dressed. Surely between the four of us we can work something out?'

Mary shakes her head. 'I'm not up to it any more. And Rosie can't afford those pain draughts that doctor's been giving her, not long-term. I'm afraid this is the only option. She will never walk again, the doctors confirmed it. The Corporation will pay for her, and she'll have a place for life.'

Life, thinks Lena grimly. What sort of a life would that be, hidden away in an institution?

'But she'll hate it. Surely you know that.'

Mary shrugs. 'She'll have to get used to it.'

Lena is panicking now. Surely the old woman wouldn't do that to her own flesh and blood? To her wee girl?

'Please, Mary. You can't do this. We'll sell a wagon, I'll get a job in the factory; we could sell the tent, come to think of it. I started a show by myself, didn't I? Surely we can give her something of a life?'

'Oh, come on, hen. You're talking nonsense. Are you going to give up everything you own to wheel Violet round in a spinal chair? Clean up her piss five times a day? You realise she wouldn't be able to live here at Vinegarhill at all, don't you? She'd need full-time care in a house or a flat somewhere. You think you can afford one of those on the money you'll get from that tent? No, the institution is the only answer. They'll give her more care than we can here. She'll be grateful one day. So will you.'

Lena slumps back, defeated. 'Does she know?'

Mary shakes her head. 'Not yet. The doctor told me privately. She'll only get all worked up about it. They'll give her a bed in the new year. It'll keep until then.'

She looks at Lena, sees her horror-stricken face.

'You can still visit her, hen.'

She smiles. Mary has a tooth missing, near the back. Lena has never noticed it before. Mary sees her looking.

'Fell out years ago,' she says, tapping at her gum with her finger. 'Never could find it. A right bugger. It had a wee filling in it, real gold. Could have sold it.'

She laughs, a deep guttural crack, and Lena smiles politely, wondering how she could ever have believed this coarse, uncaring woman to be a mother figure.

32

The rat pit

Glasgow, they say, is a warm place. Its people are friendly and kind. A little rough around the edges, but they'd rather take a drink with you than fight you. It has large parks plump with greenery, cool, clear lakes, sputtering fountains, a grand main square and turreted city chambers that befit this second city of the Empire. There are fine sandstone mansions, long, wide streets that traverse the west end, far from the belching smoke of the grinding factories that keep the town in the style to which it has become accustomed. But Glasgow has many cities inside it. It unfolds differently for each of its occupants, offering up a plethora of refined delights for its richest, jobs and public amenities for its working man. And for its desperate, its most downtrodden and its damned, Glasgow is a dark city with a cold heart.

Lena has always understood this. She had it drummed into her as a child by her father, who knew he would never be accepted there, would never truly look, sound or behave like a true Glaswegian. For Joe Loveridge, Vinegarhill was merely a stopping point. A place to hole up for the winter, keep warm, feed up your horses and wait for the first buds of spring. But it was never home. Not for her daddy, or his daddy before that, or his daddy before that. The Loveridges' home was on the road.

As Lena makes her way through the cramped, narrow streets of Cowcaddens, near the top of the town and away from the half-frozen river on a stinging December morning, she thinks about her father's ambivalent relationship with this city that took them in each winter, gave her a half-formed, vague education, played host to their wagons and rides. Had he ever strayed this far into Glasgow's underbelly? Into its darkly cavernous insides? Because the further she goes, the more it would seem that here, deep inside the gates of the city, might be what they meant in school when the minister talked about hell. The buildings have turned black from the endless smoke, panes of glass are broken, flimsy pieces of wood hammered up to keep out the cold. Urchins scurry across the cobbles, swerving to avoid broken bottles, horse shit, human shit. Most of them are barefoot. Occasionally what Lena takes for a pile of clothes moves, and she sees it is a human being, bundled into a doorway, resting its weary head.

She keeps her head down as she walks, a scarf wrapped tightly round her head. She has wheedled the address out of Mary, who knew a lassie who ended up here once, although what happened to her in the end, she could not recall. 'Filthy place,' she said, scribbling it down for Lena. 'You'll find all sorts in there, most of whom you wouldn't give the time of day to.'

After the way she has treated her own daughter, Lena would rather not give the time of day to her, either.

On Muse Lane she stops, counts the numbers up to thirty-five. The wind is biting now, howling down the alley, lashing at filthy curtains on glassless windows. The sign above the tenement close reads MODEL LODGING HOUSE. A curious name for a place everyone else calls 'the rat pit'.

Inside, it is chaos. In a cramped front room are at least ten women, and twice as many children, wailing and shouting and running around in the state they were born. The air is pungent. A small fire sparks in the grate and the women huddle round it, some of them in little more than rags. An older woman, stout, with no front teeth, looks up.

'You wantin' a bed?'

Lena shakes her head. 'I'm looking for someone. Carmen. She's Spanish.'

The older woman looks down again, says nothing, coughs. But a younger lassie, with a sickly, underfed-looking baby in her arms, says, 'Carmen's in the kitchen. You can go through, Mrs Pinnock won't mind.'

Lena walks through a doorway into a small, dark kitchen. Carmen is standing with her back to her, frying a grizzled piece of meat on the stove.

'Carmen,' she says. She is painfully thin. Her eyes are deep hollows and there is a faint bruise on her left cheek. Her dress hangs off her bony frame.

'Lena,' she says, shocked.

She fusses at the stove, makes to turn it off but Lena says: 'No, please. Finish cooking and eat. You look like you need it.'

Embarrassed, Carmen puts the leathery piece of meat on a plate, takes some dirty cutlery from the cracked sink and eats hungrily, stuffing forkfuls into her mouth, not stopping to swallow before shovelling in the next. Lena wonders how long it is since she last had a meal. Lena has known hunger like this, although thankfully not often. But she understands how it gnaws at you until it is painful, until you can focus on nothing but the next bite of food, when even the greyest, most pallid piece of tripe seems like a hearty dish, fit for a queen.

Finally, Carmen finishes. She wipes at her mouth, runs her tongue over her teeth, and there is something carnal about her sated appetite, as though she were an animal who has finally feasted on a kill it has stalked for days. She pushes the plate away.

'You have come to see me,' Carmen says eventually.

'Yes,' says Lena. Now she is here, she is unsure what to say to Carmen in this dank, sorrow-ridden place. She just knows she wants to take her away from here immediately, never to return.

'You want to know what it was like? With him? You want me to tell you everything?'

Lena shakes her head. 'No. No. God. Nothing like that. Harry and I are done. It's over. But I came because I wanted to see you. To see if you were alright. And ask if you wanted to come back.'

It is Carmen's turn to shake her head. 'I cannot face it. The shame. I cannot.' And she bursts into tears.

Lena does not know whether to comfort her, put an arm round her thin shoulder, just like she did that day back in Stirling. Something stops her. Instead she places her hands in her lap, waits for Carmen's sobs to subside.

'I ran away,' says Carmen. 'I am sorry for that. I should have explained. But Violet made it sound so bad. Worse than it was. As though I had met Harry on the streets.'

'You didn't?' says Lena. 'But I thought . . .'

'Harry was the acrobat. I lied to you, all the way back at the beginning. I told you I met an acrobat and then I was pregnant. But it was not an acrobat. It was Harry. He did a show near where our circus was, in Edinburgh, and I met him. He was very nice. A gentleman. He came to visit a few times. But then the circus moved on, and I did not see him again. And then when I was pregnant I ended up here, and I lost the baby. And Harry never knew.'

'Oh, Carmen,' says Lena. 'I'm so sorry.'

'For what?'

'For you. For the baby. For Harry too. It could all have been so different.'

The Show Woman

Carmen stands up, puts her dirty plate in the sink, shrugs. 'Could it? I did not love Harry. Not like you do.'

Lena flushes.

'He did not love me either. It was just an arrangement, and we were young and stupid. It is gone now. All in the past. This is my present.' She looks around the room.

'What can I do to help?' asks Lena.

'Nothing,' says Carmen. 'You do not understand. You cannot know, how it feels to do what I do.'

Lena shivers at her use of the present tense, wonders how she paid for that awful strip of meat she has just gorged herself on.

'This is just how it must be,' says Carmen.

'But surely not. You left once. You can do it again. Please, Carmen. Come back. Come back to Vinegarhill with me. Did you not hear about Violet?'

She tells Carmen about Violet's fall, that she has lost the use of her legs, may never walk again, but holds back on telling her the full, awful truth.

'I am sorry for her. I did not always like her but she does not deserve that. But with no Violet, and no me, it sounds as if your ladies' circus is over.'

Lena bridles at this. Nothing is over until she decides that it is. And even though she knows her dream, her show, lies scattered amid the burning embers of these past few, terrible weeks, she will not give in.

'Come back to Vinegarhill. At least for a couple of weeks. Get yourself settled and then we can talk about what happens next.'

But Carmen shakes her head. 'I need money. I am trying to save. To go home to Spain. If I come to Vinegarhill it will just slow me down. This . . .' she gestures round the miserable room '. . . is the right place for me now.'

Lena fumbles in her pockets, brings out a sixpence, offers it to Carmen. 'Please, take it,' she says.

But Carmen simply shakes her head. 'I have my pride, and you have yours,' she says.

'Are you still going to church?' Lena asks.

'I am. I go often.'

'Can I come and see you there some time, then? Come and pray with you like we did that time in Stirling?'

She sees Carmen soften, and Lena's heart leaps when she nods.

'Yes. Come and see me there some time, if you like. Then, at least, we can say goodbye before I return to Spain.'

Lena walks over to her, bends down and kisses Carmen's cheek. She smells of spoilt cooking oil, but her skin is soft as butter.

'You will always have a home with me,' she says to her.

She feels in her pocket, produces the rainbow ribbon Carmen dropped that awful night in the wagon, and hands it to her. The colours shimmer in the dank little kitchen, as though someone has let in the sun.

'Never forget that,' she says.

She leaves Carmen twirling the ribbon in her hands, letting the silk run through her fingers.

33

Trinkets

Rosie pulls her hat down over her ears as she walks home in the flickering gloom. It is cold today, a brisk wind blowing off the Clyde, and ahead of her as she turns on to the Gallowgate street sweepers are clearing out the last of the fallen autumn leaves, emptying them into huge sacks to be taken away and turned into mulch for the grand gardens up west.

Her fingers ache from the rough carpet material, the spindles on the thrumming machine she must operate each day, and her head is pounding from the relentless *clackity clack*. What she would give for a ride out into the fields with Tommy Pony, just the two of them. Or one of her mother's honey cakes, still warm from the range, home-churned butter pooling into the sponge. Sometimes she even aches for the old iron bed she shared with Jennifer, its softness so different from the hard little racks in the wagons, although the price for that comfort, the temporary warmth, was always too high.

She loves Violet. It is a fact, plain and shining, and Rosie has never once thought to question it. She loved Violet from the moment she came to her that night in the stable, when Tommy Pony was so ill, when she feared she might lose him forever. Violet made her feel safe. Protected. Violet had cupped her heart gently in her hands, and never let go.

Now, it is her turn. She does not resent her work at the factory, long, painful and numbing as the hours may be. It is a small price to pay for Violet to shrug off her agony, the terrible pains that sometimes keep her up at night, sobbing, biting her pillow. She cannot always afford the medicine, and sometimes the relief lasts only a few hours. But she will not stop. She will do her best to provide for them until Violet is up and about again. It is as simple as that.

Rosie feels in her pocket for the gift she has made for her love, a little project during her tea breaks at the factory, when she has no desire to join in the yakkering gossip that fills the frozen weaving shed. It is a tiny ring, fashioned from strains of carpet wool, each one a different colour. She has been saving them for weeks, winding them round each other, tightening the threads until they form a small, continuous loop. Blue wrapped with green, orange with red, gold with silver, and through the middle a skein of rose-pink, woven round a thread of deepest violet.

She turns into the showground and heads for the stables to visit Tommy Pony. He does not like it at Vinegarhill, in this dark, smoky landscape, and stamps his foot impatiently each time he sees her. She feeds him a sugar lump, saved from her tea break that morning, and strokes his long muzzle.

'I'll take you a good ride on Sunday,' she says into the white star on his forehead. 'We'll go for a long run and you can stretch those little legs of yours.'

The pony whickers softly.

'He's not happy, is he?'

The voice is young, girlish. Rosie turns around to see Belle, still in her school uniform, rake-thin and with two tight plaits in her hair, one trailing down each side of her sullen face.

'No, I don't think he is,' says Rosie. She has barely spoken to Belle since their return to Vinegarhill, finds Violet's younger sister awkward and unfriendly.

Belle takes a step towards her and there is a flash of movement at her feet, a flurry of oil-black feathers.

'Is that a crow?' Rosie asks. The bird has stopped directly in front of Belle, its beady eyes looking straight at her, and Belle leans down and strokes its long feathers.

'Oh, this is Morag,' she says. 'Of course, I don't actually know if Morag is a girl, but she's so pretty that I decided she must be.'

Belle holds out an arm and the crow hops up, turning round to regard Rosie with interest.

'Would you like to see what Morag brought me today?'

Rosie nods hesitantly. She has always thought of crows as mangy, unpleasant birds, best avoided if possible. Her father regarded them as a menace on the farm, had erected several scarecrows over the years which, to his eternal fury, never seemed to make a blind bit of difference.

Belle fumbles in her pocket and produces a tiny sliver of something smooth. She hands it to Rosie. It is green and cloudy, its edges soft and rounded.

'My brother says it's sea glass,' says Belle. 'Morag must have been down by the river and decided to bring me a present.'

Belle's talk of presents makes Rosie think of Violet, lying in the wagon, bored and alone. She must get back to her.

'You need to get back to Violet,' says Belle, as though reading her thoughts, and Rosie, giving Tommy Pony a last pat, stops in her tracks.

'I knew it was going to happen,' says Belle.

'What do you mean?'

'I knew Violet was going to fall.'

Rosie is suddenly furious. 'What? Why didn't you tell someone? What do you know? Who told you?'

Belle remains implacable, sturdy, the crow still rooted to her arm.

'Morag told me.'

She finds Violet propped up in the bed, looking peevish.

'You're late,' she says. 'Where have you been?'

Rosie takes her hat off. The wagon is chilly, has none of the cosiness that Lena's did in the summer. No brightly coloured silk panels or homely camaraderie, created, it now dawns on her, by the four of them simply being together.

'I went to the stables to visit Tommy Pony. And then I saw Belle.'

'I see,' says Violet. Her eyes are cold. 'So it was more important to see a horse and my irritating sister than to come and see me?'

Rosie says nothing. She has learnt to be wary of Violet when she is in this sort of mood. She counts back. It is two days since the doctor has been, and he will not be back again until the morning. Violet is in pain. Violet doesn't mean it. The words dance through her head like a mantra.

'I asked you a question,' says Violet. 'What have you got to say for yourself?'

Rosie sits down on the bed, takes her hand. 'I'm sorry,' she says. 'I won't do it again. From now on I'll come straight home.'

How will she be able to take Tommy out on Sunday now? Could Violet come in her chair? No. She'd be freezing and, what's more, she'd hate it.

She looks up at Violet and is surprised to see there are tears in her eyes.

'I'm sorry. I'm being an awful bitch. I'm just so . . .' She casts around for the right word. 'I'm just so miserable. And angry. And rotten. And sore. I'm no good any more, to anyone.'

Rosie catches her hand. 'You're good to me,' she says. 'And I love you.'

She fishes in her pocket for the little ring, wrapped in her favourite handkerchief, a gift from her ma for her tenth birthday.

'Here,' she says. 'This is for you.'

Violet unwraps the delicate cotton, frees the burst of colours. Rosie picks it out and gently slides it on to her ring finger. And for a brief, blistering moment, a soft smile flares across Violet's careworn face.

34

Regrets

She has made it to the big top. It is an effort now, to get trussed up in her finery, squeeze her bloated feet into dainty, too-small shoes, affix her gold and ruby brooch to her collar, her very own royal standard. Her chest crackles dangerously with every movement she makes. Her back aches as though she has carried a thousand circuses on it.

But she is here, gripping her cane, standing in the centre of the ring as the audience around her, a panoply of local dignitaries and townsfolk, stand to applaud her.

'Ladies and gentlemen,' says Bobo the clown, his garish smile alighting upon her, 'I give you Serena Linden, circus proprietor, founder of Linden's Circus and beloved by royalty, past and present.'

She has told him to say this, of course, hauled the sour, balding old coot in for a harsh word that very afternoon. He was not pleased. But then, Bobo has not been pleased with much since 1897, the year he lost Momo, the other half of his double act, to Pinders-Ord. She should retire him soon. Get some young blood in. If only he weren't so popular.

Serena waits for the applause to die down. She may not be so steady on her feet these days; her body may have turned to blubber, her face does not have the sparkle that was once so admired when she was a young lass. But she can still command a crowd.

'Thank you, ladies and gentlemen, boys and girls,' she says. Her voice is husky, weak, and she coughs briefly before continuing. 'I am greatly honoured to be here today, among you all. The Royal Linden's Circus has always striven to be the gold standard – the royal standard, you might say – in high-quality circus acts. We have brought you the very best, and we intend to continue to bring you the very best.

'When my father started this circus back in 1850 with just one acrobat, a horse, and two rather down-on-their-luck donkeys . . .' here, she pauses for the inevitable flurry of laughter '. . . he could never have imagined that, one day, we would be celebrating sixty years in the business. And yet here we are, stronger than ever.'

She stops. Coughs. Feels the bile rise in her throat, the blood slick down her windpipe. She turns away, forgetting, just briefly, that the audience are all around her, a perfect circle watching her from every angle.

She coughs so violently that the force pushes her to her knees. She gasps for air, clutches her chest. Bobo runs forward, huge shoes flapping, but she waves him away, eyes streaming.

There is blood now. She rocks back and forth, blood streaming from her mouth, is vaguely aware of the horrified wheel of faces that surround her.

'Well,' says Bobo in his best silly-clown voice, 'that's it from us tonight. Thank you, ladies and gentlemen, boys and girls, and enjoy the rest of your evening.'

There is a smattering of applause. Some members of the audience look appalled as the old woman remains on her knees, wheezing wildly, spitting globules of ruby-red blood from her throat. A young nurse, still in her uniform, runs forward, but she too is shooed away.

As the crowd disperses, muttering loudly, Serena slowly gets back to her feet, clasping her cane for support. She watches their retreating backs, pictures Bobo's sniggering, too-wide smile, and chokes again. Except this time, it is a sob.

The Show Woman

Time with the soothing bottle. For some reason she cannot seem to bend down far enough to remove her shoes, and so they remain on her feet, pointing out at a jaunty angle from underneath the covers as she lies prone, uncomfortable, half-seated, on the daybed.

She should go to a doctor. She has the money for it, could ask for one immediately in this refined city of Edinburgh, chock-full of surgeons and medical students who would no doubt be grateful, even honoured, to examine the extraordinary Serena Linden.

But the truth is that she cannot face it. She already has her suspicions about what ails her, and what good would a quack do when she already has one in her hand, in liquid form? She takes another swig. But the brandy does not do its job as well as it used to, cannot quite blot out the pain.

And there is another thing the brandy no longer obliterates. She thinks of Violet Weaver, her body broken, on the floor of a candy-striped tent. The Loveridge girl – a Loveridge; she still cannot quite believe it – stripped of her show in a mere second.

She pauses, taps the side of the bottle with her old pearl bracelet, the one Davey made for her so many years before. It makes a pleasing tinkling sound. All those pearls, so easily turned to dust.

Her thoughts flutter like birds. Guilt mingles with shame and something else, something deeper. Perhaps, she thinks, as she takes another swig, it is regret.

35

Carnival

December creeps on. Light retreats. The short days are blanketed by a thick, winter-white sky while the nights, long and interminable, stretch well outside the confines of the clock. Sometimes Lena is amazed when morning comes, as though the dark's vice-like grip might never be relinquished.

Ten days before Christmas, the carnival starts. A Glasgow tradition, held here at Vinegarhill, it is the summer fair's frosty cousin. Rides are sloughed of summer mud and cranked up, carousels whirl, the fortune-tellers and boxers and penny shies and menageries all set out their icy stalls. Gas lamps are erected for the occasion, giving the showground a pale, spectral glow, and the scent of roasted chestnuts and hot meat pies carries on the air.

One of the big attractions this year is the cinematographers, who are showing grainy, stop-start footage of the King's funeral. It brings in the ladies from up west, bundled in good wool coats and fur hats, gentlemen in bowlers and trimmed moustaches, all wishing to pay their respects to their dear departed monarch, watch the grand procession, bow their heads in solemn reverence.

Lena had started making plans for the winter carnival during those last, jewel-like days on the road. Imagined costumes in red and green for Violet and Rosie, a crown of holly leaves for Tommy. She had been dabbling with the idea of learning a skill herself, perhaps the fire hoop, notoriously dangerous but back then, when she dreamt of it, when the summer still reigned over them and hope was on the air, anything had seemed possible.

Now, as the carnival clatters around her, she spends her days shut up in the wagon. She knits bedjackets and hats, Christmas gifts for Violet and Rosie, or patches her old, worn dresses. Her tailcoat and top hat hang silently at the back of the caravan. One particularly grey day just before Christmas Eve, she darts out to a food stall, buys a bag of hot, roasted apples sprinkled with brown sugar.

She taps softly at the door of Violet's caravan but there is no answer. Inside she finds her friend asleep, her hair, the only part of her which has not dimmed since her fall, splayed out on the pillow like paint. Lena leaves the bag by her bed, but as she tiptoes out, Violet moves.

'Stay,' she says. 'I was only dreaming about the trapeze. Talk to me. What have you been doing lately?'

So Lena tells her about her recent visit to the rat pit, her suspicion that Carmen is back on the streets, how thin she looks and how miserable – broken, somehow.

'Like me,' says Violet. 'Except I'd rather be there than here.'

'Oh, trust me, you wouldn't,' says Lena. 'It was awful. You should have seen it. The noise. And the smell. Never mind what she does for money.'

'What did she say about Harry?'

Lena hesitates. Wonders how much Violet really knows. Decides to tell her anyway.

'Back in Stirling Carmen told me that an acrobat in her circus from Spain had got her pregnant while they were touring here, and that's how she ended up on the streets the first time. Turns out she lied about the acrobat. It was Harry. They met when he was doing a show near their circus, then they moved on. He never knew she was pregnant.'

Violet sits up. 'Really? She never told me that. Perhaps she thought I'd be cross because I'm his sister. She told me she'd been with him once a long time ago, and I just presumed they'd met when she was on the streets.' She pauses, thoughtful. 'Poor Harry. And poor Carmen. There could have been a wee bairn. Another Weaver. Instead she lost everything. You should give her another chance, you know.'

'I tried,' says Lena. 'She wouldn't have it. Insisted she was just saving up her pennies and going home to Spain.'

'Spain,' says Violet. 'How I'd have loved to visit Spain.'

'You never know,' says Lena. 'You might yet.'

But Violet shakes her head. 'I'm not going anywhere. I never will. I'm doomed to a life in this wagon, waited on hand and foot by Rosie. I'm a millstone round her neck. And yours. And my mammy's. Unless I can walk again.'

Lena remembers with a chill that Violet does not know of Mary's decision, has not heard the doctor's words. She does not yet know she is to be sent to the hospital, for life.

'You don't know what your future is yet, Vi,' she says quietly.

'Well, unless something happens with these rotten old legs soon, you might as well send me off to the rat pit too. Then at least I won't be a burden on anyone.' Her eyes are cold and bleak.

Lena takes her hand, traces her thumb over Violet's thin, bony fingers.

'I've been reading *Alice in Wonderland*,' says Violet. 'Belle brought me a copy. It's a damned sight better than Jane Austen, I can tell you. But there's a line in it: "It's no use going back to yesterday, because I was a different person then." That's me. A different person. I wish I could just disappear. Vanish. Like one of those magic acts.' She realises what she has just said. 'Not like your mammy. I mean, I wish I could just click my fingers whenever I wanted and be gone. For good.'

Lena holds her hand, says nothing. They sit like that in the faltering dusk for a long, long time.

Two nights later, a shooting star sails across Vinegarhill. Its tail sparkles with the fury of the sun, a burst of brightness across the inky black sky, before its shards explode, glitter, and scatter into nothingness. But it is only Violet, awake and in pain, her throbbing head resting against the bitter glass, who sees it.

Christmas is a muted affair. Lena visits Violet and Rosie, gives them the bedjacket and hat she has knitted them. Rosie in turn gives her a bracelet she has made from carpet wool in a deep vivid blue. Violet gives her a bag of sweets.

'Rosie took me down to see the sweetie wives,' she says. She has large purple shadows under her eyes, and Rosie says she has not been sleeping. Rosie looks worried, as though she can no longer reach Violet, as if something between them has snapped.

In the afternoon they go over to the Weaver wagon, where Mary has procured a cheap side of beef for the occasion. There are glasses of brandy, and potatoes roasted in the kettle over the fire, boiled carrots and a few neeps, which Belle refuses to eat, pronouncing them 'disgusting'.

Morag the crow makes an appearance and Mary shoos her away, only for the bird to retire to the branch of a nearby tree, emitting the occasional angry caw. When Mary isn't looking, Belle sneaks her a bit of potato.

Mary's eldest son, William, has decided to stay with his family in Edinburgh for the winter. Harry, who is doing a winter tour of music halls – 'He's been getting some grand reviews,' reports Mary proudly – stays away.

The Show Woman

Violet says little, simply sits in her hard wooden chair in morose silence. Occasionally she holds Rosie's hand, lets her mother fuss round her, but she barely touches her food.

'She'll be better once she's in the hospital,' Mary says quietly to Lena when they are dishing up the small plum pudding, its dark sponge giving off great gusts of steam. 'They'll look after her, keep her right. She's got a place confirmed now. Third of January.'

'When are you going to tell her?'

'In a few days,' says Mary, 'as soon as I can get rid of the limpet for a few minutes.'

When Lena returns to her wagon that night, her belly full, she climbs into her bed and weeps. She imagines how Violet, her bright and beautiful friend, confined to her chair for life, will react when she is told that she must leave the place she loves, the world she has always inhabited. That she will be shut up in an airless hospital room, kept in her bed, all alone. She will never swing on the trapeze again, never run or cartwheel or soar through the air.

Deep down, though, she knows fine well what it will do. It will kill her.

36

Auld Lang Syne

Hogmanay. The highest of all the holidays, for auld lang syne. The carnival is rammed, drunken youths starting the two-day break with pints of ale, ha'penn'ths of sweeties and a fine time watching the girls go by in their best dresses and bonnets.

The queues outside the fortune-teller snake all the way round to the big dipper, as hordes of Glaswegians wait patiently to hear their fate for 1911. Will Lady Luck favour them? Smile their way? Perhaps Miss Sibyl will know the answer. There is also a medium, from one of the spiritualist churches, holding court in a smart white tent near the gates. She holds her head between her spindly fingers, casts her eyes around the room, asks if there is an Annie or a Dennis or a man with only four toes on his left foot, and did he have a father called Stuart? Belle crams in at the back, leaves Morag outside, petulant and tarry-feathered, and gets a shock when the woman, conservatively dressed, spectacles on the end of her nose, singles her out.

'You have the second sight, my lass,' she tells her. 'You have the gift.'

Belle gazes back at her sullenly. This news is no surprise to her.

And here come three women now, one of them thin and whey-faced, her body crammed into a hard wooden chair. The other two take turns pushing her, trying to make sure the contraption does not bump over the cold, frosty ground, fussing with the old tartan blanket that cascades over her knees.

It was Rosie's idea that they come down to the carnival, as if trying to recapture some of that old magic, remind them all of the day they saw the golden light of the fair through glistening new eyes, when life felt expectant and shining and new. But Lena can see that it is not working. Violet says nothing. Her face is so thin now it is like a sunken mask, and at times she seems half-asleep. It is as though she has given up, simply stopped caring altogether, and nothing that Rosie can do will change her. Lena suspects Mary has finally told her about the hospital. But she has said nothing, simply shut up like a clam.

'Do you fancy a go on the Wurlitzer?' asks Rosie, hopeful, pleading.

Violet shakes her head.

'What about the big dipper? I'm sure we can carry you on – they won't mind, will they, Lena?'

'No, not at all. Are you sure, Violet? You don't fancy it?' They have stopped now and Rosie crouches down in front of Violet's chair, takes her hand. 'Isn't there anything you'd like to do?'

Violet looks up at her and suddenly, her eyes are sparkling. 'Yes. Yes, there is something. Something you could both do.'

She looks round at Lena, holds her other hand out to her.

'You can help me fly again.'

Jamaica Bridge, down by the river, wide and grand as the Clyde itself. Electric street lamps glimmer in the frost, casting shadows that are long and thin. They have walked here, slipping and sliding on the rime, Violet more animated than she has been in weeks, since long before Christmas, laughing in delight as the chair goes skating along the street.

'Look, Violet, you're flying now,' says Rosie as she pushes the chair ahead on the ice. Violet holds her arms out, birdlike and laughing. She clatters to a stop near the middle of the bridge.

'Here.' The sky is hard and black as coal, studded with distant stars. 'Lift me up,' she says. Her breath makes steamy clouds. 'I want to sit on the bridge.'

'Are you sure?' says Rosie. She looks at Lena.

Lena understands why Violet wants to get up there, to perch on this grand bridge's stone sides, feel the air between her ears, the rush of life in her broken body. She hears Mary Weaver's words ringing in her head. *She'll need to go to an institution. We can no longer afford her. It's for the best. You can still visit, hen.* She shivers, wraps her scarf tighter round her throat.

'Come on, then, madam,' she says, and between them Rosie and Lena lift Violet, weightless as one of Morag's feathers, on to the flat wide stone.

On the other side of the river revellers spill out from a nearby tavern, shouting and whooping. It is almost midnight, and they stand on the cusp of a brand new year. There is just enough time for fond farewells to the old one.

Rosie fusses at Violet, pulls the tartan blanket over her knees, but Violet strips it away.

'Leave me be now,' she says. 'Just let me sit here awhile.'

She throws her head back and gazes upwards.

'I saw the most beautiful star the other night,' she says, patting the cold stone for Lena and Rosie to join her. They hoist themselves up. 'It went streaking over me, so fast and beautiful, as though someone was painting the sky with fire. And then it shattered into thousands of little pieces and was gone. So bright, and then nothing. Nothing at all.'

'I look for my daddy up there sometimes,' says Lena. 'I know it sounds silly, but I like to think of him in the skies, twinkling down on me.'

'I love that idea,' says Violet. 'That we all become stars. Tiny bursts of light, sparkling into the dark.'

Rosie leans over, strokes Violet's hair. 'It's a bird's nest,' says Violet, but she does not push her away.

Rosie shakes her head, runs the long red strands through her fingers. 'You're perfect,' she says. 'Just as you are.'

One minute to midnight. Across the river they hear voices counting down the seconds. Lena sneaks a look at Violet. She has stiffened, her body rigid. She pulls Rosie's hands from her hair, moves a palm to Rosie's soft, cold cheek.

'You have always been perfect to me, too,' she says. She stretches her other hand to Lena. 'You listened to me, even when I wasn't ready to talk. Thank you for being my sort of sister.'

Violet's eyes are blazing now, wide and fierce. Light streams from her. She pulls her arms away, raises them up towards unblinking stars.

'I love you both,' she says.

Nine. Eight. Seven.

'But I won't let them do this to me. I can't.'

Six. Five. Four.

'Not to the greatest trapeze artist who ever lived.'

Three. Two. One.

Violet rocks backwards and the sky explodes. The stars burst open and the heavens flame gold and before they can do anything to stop her, before they can scream her name, grab helplessly at her graceful limbs, spread out now as if she were on the trapeze, her greatest performance, Violet takes her final flight.

Down, down she goes, her skirts fanned out like the wings of a swan, past breath and flesh and blood and bone, while all around the fireworks erupt and people are cheering and the new year awakes, trembling and wide-eyed. Violet hits the rushing, darkening river, and is gone.

The Glasgow Herald
5 January 1911

RIVER TRAGEDY OF TRAPEZE GIRL

On Saturday evening Violet Weaver, the famous trapeze artist who once performed with Royal Linden's Circus, threw herself off Jamaica Bridge in Glasgow.

Miss Weaver, aged 22, of Vinegarhill Showground, on the Gallowgate, had recently broken her back after a fall on the trapeze, and was shortly to be committed to Stobhill Hospital for the Sick. She went with two friends, Lena Loveridge and Rosie Carluke, to the bridge to see in the New Year, but once on the bridge she flung herself off the side and could not be saved.

The following day, dragging operations were instituted, with the result that the body was found near the banks of the Clyde by Glasgow Green.

A verdict of suicide while of unsound mind was returned.

37

Stars

Rosie cannot breathe. It is as though a great stone has been lowered on to her chest, compressing her, squeezing her insides. She lies on the bed in her wagon, their wagon, and thinks that she will never be able to breathe right again.

Her mind drifts to that night in the stable, the night she fell for Violet, the way her hand rested over her heart, how she had promised to breathe for her, until her raggedy gasps slowed.

She does not, cannot, believe that Violet would leave her. Not even when Lena explained about the hospital: that Violet would have been shut away, institutionalised, left to wither by her unfeeling mother.

'I could have cared for her,' Rosie exclaimed, red-faced and snotty, her cheeks still wet.

But Lena shook her head, stroked her hair. 'You know you couldn't have, not long-term, not on the pennies you were making.'

Rosie hates that Lena is right. Worry about money has nagged at her for weeks, snapping at her ankles like an angry little dog. The factory pays a pittance. She is a woman, an unskilled one at that, and she will only ever get the minimum. They had been living, largely, off Mary Weaver's watery cooking, whatever Mary could spare, and there were times when she could not afford the doctor, let Violet suffer because she could not pay for his draughts of medicine. Could it have gone on? She did not know. And now, she never will.

A great, bleak calm washes over her as she feels her breathing slow, her heart quieten. She thinks of Violet, her small, damaged body, that last effortful show of power as she hurled herself over the side. She had screamed her name, and Lena had pulled her back from going over the side too, following her in, saving her. Violet. Her love. All gone.

Outside, night is already dropping across the city like a cloak. It is barely five o'clock and for once the showground is quiet. The carnival has finished, its rides silenced, Vinegarhill's occupants taking a well-earned break from the short Christmas season.

With enormous effort she pulls herself out of bed. She has not eaten in days and Mary has not thought to feed her. She has not been to the factory since that terrible day either, has likely been struck off the shift. She scarcely cares. Only Carmen's absence, the disappearance of her tall, beautiful friend, penetrates her grief. She wonders why she has not come, reminds herself that she surely does not know, because otherwise she would not have left Rosie alone.

But Rosie still has one soul who depends on her. And so she pulls on her coat and her boots, and walks over to the stables to see Tommy. The little horse gives a whinny of pleasure when he sees her. It has been days, and although the stable boys have fed him – more money for her to find – he looks thin. She can see ribs sticking out of his side, although he nuzzles into her neck with all his usual devoted affection. She presses her cold forehead to his white star. At least, she thinks, I have him.

38

Funeral

The day of the funeral is hard and bright, the sky sheened to brilliant white. Lena dresses quickly in the cold as the first flakes of snow pitter-patter across the caravan window. Violet would have liked that. The drama of it: winter's chilly majesty.

She gathers up Rosie from her wagon, crumpled and tearstained in black, her butterfly brooch a brilliant blue at her throat, and together they walk arm in arm through the snow. There is a heaving turnout at the cemetery. Despite the nature of Violet's death – about which nobody says a word, at least not to Lena – every show person in the ground without a wean or a winter city job has come to pay their respects. They have known Violet since she was a tiny bairn, fleeing around the ground, always up to some scheme or asking impertinent questions, and, as she grew older, begging a free go on a ride or a borrow of someone else's trapeze. Violet was a daughter of Vinegarhill, of the shows, and the fairs. They will see her safely onwards, into the next life.

Mary Weaver, trussed up in a stiff mourning dress and veil, looks like an overfed crow as she perches on a stool by the graveside. Lena's stomach churns as she recalls her casual cruelty. Had it not been for her, Violet might still be here. William's face is lined and haggard. For the first time Lena realises he looks old, a showman past his prime, weeping for his dead sister.

And next to him is Harry. Cap in hand, his face etched with grim sadness. Lena feels a sudden, surprising surge of affection for him. He loved his sister, and she him.

As the minister drones about returning Violet to God, back into the arms of Jesus Christ our Saviour, Rosie grips Lena's arm.

'Look,' she says. 'Up there. In the tree. It's a magpie.'

The bird buries its beak in its feathers.

'She's OK,' Rosie says. 'She's telling me she's OK. She's free now. No longer in her cage.'

The minister has finished. Earth is tossed on the coffin and Rosie darts forward, flings a small rose she has made from carpet wool, its thick petals glistening in the cold clear air, down into the grave.

A wake then, held among the Weaver wagons, booze flowing as fast as the falling snow. Lena cannot face it but knows she must, finds herself a quiet corner where she sits with Belle, who is stricken and pale, her eyes drooping with tiredness. Somewhere a fiddle has struck up, a sad, melancholic tune.

'I never told her I loved her, you know,' says Belle. 'But I did. She was always so glamorous, so much older, sophisticated. I even had a surprise for her, for when you came back after the summer. I've been learning on the trapeze, I've got quite good, and I wanted her to see it. But then she came back all broken and sad and I was scared to. And now she never will see me.'

She chokes back a small sob.

Lena pats her hand, but she is barely listening. Her eyes are fixed on Harry, on the other side of the wagon, which is stuffed to the gunwales with show folk. She can see only the top of his strawberry-blond head, the way it bobs and weaves as he talks, nods, listens. I've touched that hair, she thinks. Run my fingers through it. Oh, for the comfort of touching that bonny head of hair again. Because what Lena craves right now, more than anything

The Show Woman

else, is comfort. To lay her head on someone's shoulder, to weep for all that she has lost: her mammy, her daddy, and now Violet. Here, in this crowded wagon, among a sea of familiar faces, she feels entirely alone.

She takes a nip of whisky, decides that now is as good a time as any.

'I'm just away for a word with someone,' she says to Belle, who is now staring morosely out at the snow. But as she stands up, a man accosts her.

'You're Lena, yes?' He has a heavy accent, a long, twirling moustache, and a five o'clock shadow so blue it reminds her of the fronds of a thistle.

'Aye, who's asking?'

The strawberry-blond head turns, almost imperceptibly, in her direction.

'I am Gianni. I was at Linden's with Violet. I am sorry. She was a wonderful trapeze artist. Magnificent. The best. And she was a friend of mine. Can we sit?'

Lena sits back down again. Belle has disappeared, threading her way through the crowd and out the caravan door, letting a great gust of snow in. Away to bed, away to cry tears into her pillow, just like Rosie.

'Are you still at Linden's, then?' asks Lena. Just thinking of that woman makes her heart harden, a kernel of fury burst open in her chest.

Gianni shakes his head, takes a drink of something concealed in a brown paper bag. 'I have joined another troupe now. Linden's, they had a great reputation but now they are trading on the past. The woman, Serena, she lives in the past too.'

'I'm not so sure,' says Lena. 'It's that woman who rigged Violet's trapeze, I just know it.'

'You think this was *Serena's* doing?' Gianni looks shocked. 'As revenge for some . . . indiscretions?'

'Who else could it be? Violet told me not to speak to her, told me to leave it, said she was dangerous, but I don't care now. I need to speak to her. Hear the truth.'

'She's not far from here now, if you want to see her,' he says. 'Linden's were in Edinburgh for Christmas but they're down in Falkirk now for a winter run.'

Lena puts her hands in her lap. 'Don't you think she should pay? For what she's done? It's all her fault.'

Harry materialises out of the crowd. He is holding a tin mug and Lena can smell the fumes from it, the heady tang of a decent dram. 'Want a sip?' he says to Lena.

'Aye,' she says, and takes it from him. It is warm and bitter and burns her throat.

Gianni stretches out a hand. 'I am so sorry about your sister. I am Gianni. I worked with her at Linden's.'

'I thought I recognised you,' says Harry. 'You're an acrobat, is that right?'

'*Si, si*,' says Gianni. 'But not with Linden's any more. Too . . . spicy, you might say, even for my tastes.'

'Gianni here was just saying that Linden's is in Falkirk,' says Lena. 'And I was thinking that I might go to Falkirk, pay the great Miss Linden a visit.'

'Well, I wouldn't do that,' says Harry.

Lena's eyes flash.

'I will leave you to your discussions,' says Gianni. He looks awkward, as though he has overstepped the mark somehow. 'It was nice to meet you both.'

Lena glances at Harry. The anger she felt kindling inside her has ignited.

'Who are you to tell me what to do? Where to go? Do you not care about your sister?'

As soon as the words leave her mouth she knows it is a low blow. Harry bows his head, puts his hand on Lena's wrist.

The Show Woman

'Of course I care about my sister. But I care about you too. And Linden's is dangerous. Serena has thugs working for her, always did. And she's got a reputation for revenge. Loves nothing more than to run another show out of town the rough way. And, well, look at you. A young show woman, your own circus, you're exactly the type she'd set the dogs on.'

Lena stands up, pushes past him. She will hear no more of this. All summer she was trying to get to Galston, to find out what happened to her mother. Then Violet fell, and she has tried to do her best by her. But now she has gone, and she must set out, first for Falkirk to see the Linden woman, and then for Ayrshire. There is nothing left for her here in Vinegarhill. She doesn't care about Serena's thugs, or whether the old woman will wreak her revenge; she just wants the truth. Now. It is time to go.

She flings open the door of the wagon and runs down the steps, her long black mourning dress catching on the steps. The snow is heavy now, flitters into her eyes, and she can barely see in front of her.

An arm grabs her from behind. 'Lena,' says Harry. 'Stop. Please.'

She turns round. Her face is wet, but whether it is from tears, or from the snow, she neither knows nor cares.

'I want to find out who sent Violet to her death as much as you do,' he says. 'That's what I was trying to tell you. I'll come with you. I'll come with you to Falkirk, meet Serena Linden. If you'll have me.'

His eyes are bright, blue, sincere. A snowflake lands on his bottom lip, and Lena resists the urge to wipe it away.

'Alright,' she says finally. 'If that's what you want. We'll go together.'

39

Feathers

Rosie is lying in Violet's bed. It still has a whiff of her, that spiced, woody scent, and when she buries her face in the pillow she sometimes catches it. Or perhaps it is simply the memory of her.

Violet flying on the trapeze, utterly, resolutely herself. Violet gripping her hand as they whirled through sun-soaked afternoons at the fair. Her soft, rose-petal mouth. The smooth skin, creamy as milk, at the delicate tops of her thighs. The way she sighed with pleasure when Rosie kissed the nape of her neck.

Before Violet died Rosie made a matching carpet wool ring for herself, and now, she twists and turns it on her finger. The material is rough, and scratchy. Violet had been buried wearing hers. Rosie would be put in her grave with hers now too. She would never take it off.

Lena has not been by today. Rosie thought she might have looked in the day after the funeral to see to her, check on how she was doing, tell her tales of the drunken night. Perhaps Lena is in her bed too. It's not as if there is much to get up for.

The door to the wagon opens, and Rosie sits up.

'Hello,' says Belle. She is wearing a hat and coat, and Morag perches on her shoulder. Beyond her Rosie can see that the ground is carpeted with thick, gleaming snow. 'I brought you a piece.'

Belle approaches the bed with her offering, thick slices of ham sandwiched between hunks of good bread, and

Rosie realises that she is hungry. She has not eaten for days, has not been able to face it, but now she is ravenous.

'Thanks,' she says, taking the piece, ramming it into her mouth. Both Belle and Morag eye her with interest.

'I expect you're missing your sister,' says Rosie, between mouthfuls.

Belle nods, but says nothing.

'I had a sister. Still do, I suppose. Jennifer, her name is. Sometimes I miss her too.'

'Why don't you see her?' asks Belle. 'Is it because she's away on the road?'

Rosie gives a small laugh. 'Jennifer? No fear. She's married. Lives in Ayrshire. Husband works down the mines. And she'll be busy making babies now.'

'Violet never wanted babies,' says Belle. 'She told me. Said she'd leave that to me. The other girl in the family.'

'And do you want babies?'

Belle shrugs. 'There's other things I want to do.'

Rosie finishes her piece and, seeing there are a few crumbs left, offers them to Morag. Daintily, with her beady eyes never leaving Rosie's, she pecks at them.

'She'll like you now,' says Belle. 'No one around here ever offers her food.' She points at the little wool ring on Rosie's finger. 'Violet had one like that too, didn't she?'

'I made it for her,' says Rosie. 'They matched.'

'You must have been really good friends.'

'We were.'

Belle stokes Morag's feathers thoughtfully. 'Can we be friends, then? Since you were such good friends with Violet? Only, I'd like to show you something, and Lena's away now, so I can't show her.'

Rosie sits up. 'Lena's away? Where to? She didn't say anything.'

The Show Woman

'I don't know,' says Belle. 'She and Harry left first thing. Seems a daft thing to do with all the snow, but my mammy says they wouldn't be telt.'

Rosie wonders where on earth Lena could have gone. To Galston, finally? But with Harry? It seems unlikely.

'Will you get dressed now?' asks Belle. 'I'd like you to see me on the trapeze.'

40

Flurries

It is slow going on the road out of Glasgow. The snow has stopped but it is thick and soft, and the horses' hooves kick up flurries at every step, ploughing through relentless banks and drifts. They have taken Harry's wagon and two of the smaller Weaver horses. On a good day they might have made it to Falkirk by nightfall, but in this weather it will be tomorrow at the earliest.

Lena sits up front on the box beside Harry, her body taut, back straight. Her heart pounds with the strangeness of being so close to him, his gloved hands holding the reins, his bunnet pulled down close over his eyes. She would rather have done this alone. Confronted Serena Linden unannounced, with no fuss, and no man to protect her. But Harry is right: it could be dangerous. And she'd rather have him to keep an eye on her than anyone else.

Serena has become, in her eyes, a monster. A vicious, careworn battleaxe with nothing but vengeance in her cold black heart. Nobody knew better than Lena how difficult Violet could be. But she will never understand the woman's desire for revenge. She had plenty of acts to pick from. Why was Violet so special?

Except that Violet *was* special, always had been. Lena had known it as a child, when Violet darted round Vinegarhill, her hair an orange cloud, always the loudest, the fastest, the most infuriating. An image occurs to her now of Violet on the bridge, the way she had fallen, the serene smile that played on her lips as she leant into the black night and vanished. She had lived life on her terms. She had ended it on her terms, too. No stale hospital ward for her. Beneath the deadening weight of her grief, Lena almost admires her for it.

'Whoa,' says Harry, and pulls the horses to a stop. On the road ahead a cart has fallen on its side, two lads on the box hanging on for dear life, the horse on the ground half-submerged in snow, eyes bulging with slackening fear, chest heaving.

'Stay here,' he says, and hands Lena the reins. He jumps down, runs on to the cart, helps pull the boys down one by one. They are shaken, animated, shouting to him about how the horse skidded, must be a patch of black ice, their father was going to give them so much trouble if the horse was dead.

Harry helps them detach the cart from the harness and set it upright, crouches down and strokes the mare's head and scratches behind her ears. 'It's alright, girl,' he says, tender, attentive. 'You're going to be alright.' He feels down the horse's flanks and over her legs. 'Nothing broken,' he says. 'I think she's just winded.'

They wait and watch until, slowly, the horse's breathing slows and she clambers on to her knees and finally back on to the road.

'Thank bloody God,' says the older boy. 'Thank you, sir. Thank you.'

'I think you'll find it's your horse that did the hard work. Now drive safe out here.'

Harry climbs back on the wagon as the cart disappears into the grey. Lena can feel the chill off him. It has started snowing again, tiny flurries. He would have made a good father, even if Carmen and he had not made a go of it. She is unsettled, carrying this secret with her. But it would do no one any good to tell him now.

The Show Woman

It is not long before they stop again.

'I think we'll call it a night,' says Harry. 'No point pushing on just to come a cropper like those lads.'

They pull off the road, park the wagon by a small field, and Harry turns the horses into a nearby paddock and fills their feed bags. Inside the wagon Lena feels awkward and uncertain of herself. She lights candles, bustles around with cheese, bread and ham, all they managed to gather together before their early morning departure. Finally they sit huddled in the wagon, the snowy wind whistling round the tiny cracks in the woodwork.

'We probably shouldn't have rushed off like this,' says Lena. 'We should have waited for the weather to clear. It was stupid.'

Harry smiles. 'Aye, but you're impulsive, just like my sister was. I quite admire it.'

Lena feels her colour rise.

'Carmen was a mistake,' he says now. He has stopped eating, is looking straight at her. 'I met her when she was with the Spanish circus and I was trying my luck in a music hall. She was friendly. And I was awful lonely. I know it's no excuse, but it's the truth. It didn't really mean much. Just two lonely souls. But I need you to know that I didn't meet her on the streets, in case that's what Violet told you.'

Lena looks down at her plate. It is old, made of tin, and flecks of rust coat the rim.

'I know. I went to see Carmen. She told me. She's back in the rat pit now. It was just awful. But I couldn't persuade her to come back. Violet was just messing with me. Honestly I think she was a wee bit jealous. She'd be jealous of anyone stealing her big brother away.'

'Stealing him away?' Harry cocks an eyebrow. 'Is that what you were doing that night in Ayr?'

Lena laughs. It might be the first time she has done so since Violet's death. There is a relief in it.

'I still can't believe she's gone, you know,' she says. 'She was just so present somehow. So full of life.'

'She was full of something,' says Harry and this time they both laugh, knowing that if Violet were here she'd be laughing too, coming out with a cutting retort to put Harry in his place.

'What do you want from this Linden woman?' he says. 'Are you expecting her to confess? Because I'm not sure she will. She's cunning and sly, from what I've heard. And she's not going to allow us to have her dragged off to the jail, not without proof.'

'I want to look her in the eye,' says Lena. The humour has drained from her, and she feels suddenly exhausted. 'I'll know. No matter what she tells me, I'll know if she's telling the truth, trust me.'

'I do,' says Harry. 'I always have.'

Outside the wagon the snow has stopped. Lena bundles herself up in a bunk, wrapped in blankets. She hears Harry pottering about the caravan, tidying up, blowing out candles and, finally, getting into the opposite bunk. Before long he has started a light snore. But Lena lies awake until long into the night, thinking of Violet, and Serena, and the desire for the truth that fizzes through her.

She wakes to a glimmering white so bright, it is as though torches are being shone into the wagon. It is Harry, opening the door, bringing with him a small pail of milk, a loaf of bread and the crisp scent of a winter's day.

'Got these from the farm down the road,' he says. 'There's been no more snow overnight so if we look lively we might get there before nightfall.'

The Show Woman

Lena pulls herself out of bed. She is still wearing last night's clothes. Her mouth feels sour, her bladder full. She goes outside, finds a tree and squats behind it, watching the hot liquid melt the blanket of white beneath. She wanders further into the thicket, fishes a small cloth out of her pocket, dips it in the snow, then washes herself.

She tries to imagine what she will say to Serena. Will she scream? Cry? Beg her for the truth? No. She must be calm. Measured. She will keep her hands still, her eyes fixed on the woman before her. But she will not leave until she has found out just how evil and depraved Serena Linden is. She must do. For Violet.

41

Outcasts

Serena is spinning. Round and round she goes, toes pointed, calves taut, spine arched like an alley cat. Her body is the shape of a star. It is weightless. Suspended in the air, she spins and she spins and she spins, while, far below, a shadow watches from the wings. She does not care. This is where she is supposed to be. This is her purest self. Her truest form. Her innate, unchanging essence.

And then, without warning, she falls. She is no longer spinning but tumbling down, down, until the ground is so close she could touch it.

She wakes with a shuddering jolt, her breath coming in brittle wheezes. The wagon has a milky glow. A snowy dusk, smearing the windows.

She has been dreaming of the ribbon again, one of her acts as a young girl, and always her favourite. Suspended from the top of the tent by great swathes of silk wrapped tightly round her middle, another clutched in her hand that she would swish and sway. By sixteen years old she was outperforming the adult acrobats in her pa's circus, could pull in the punters all by herself.

Well, almost by herself. She recalls that shadowy figure in the wings, the one who appeared from nowhere and then was suddenly, always there. She had a habit of ruining things, that one. Taking the spotlight away from Serena. And now, it looked as though she had done it again.

Oh, how she misses the spinning. This leaden, lumpy body, whose lungs feel they are on fire with every breath, whose legs no longer operate under her command, has become useless to her. It is little more than a living coffin.

Serena feels under the covers for her pipe, loads up the cherry-wood bowl, strikes a match. Perhaps it will help soothe her aching chest, that smooth, seductive tobacco. She takes a puff, and for a fleeting moment feels a serenity, a satisfaction. And then, of course, she coughs. Hacks. Spits. Takes another suck. Repeats the process.

Serena misses her old pa. Now *there* was a showman. He had the circus running through his blood, the open road too. Thought nothing of picking up and heading to a new town, just because he heard another circus was planning on going there in a week or two, so he could undercut their profits. He could spot a good horseman a mile away, lick him into shape in the ring, turn him into a real act. And the way he commanded the crowds . . . *Roll up! Roll up!* he'd cry. *It's time for the greatest circus of them all.* He'd have been proud of her. Of how she'd built the place up, brought in the money, performed for royalty, made stars of them all.

But, as she takes another suck on her pipe and coughs again, she knows this isn't quite true. For, after he'd gone, carried away by the TB one bleak winter more than thirty years ago, Serena had betrayed him.

Why must the past seep into the present? Wrap its icy tendrils around her thoughts, when she wants nothing more than to leave it where it belongs? She is amazed to find her face is wet with tears. Pa would have been devastated, of course. How could she have done that? To her own family? But he hadn't understood. He'd never been able to reconcile why Serena and that woman did not get on, just as he couldn't comprehend Serena's guilt over the death of her mammy.

The Show Woman

'It wasnae your fault,' he soothed when she was old enough to ask how her mammy had died. 'You were just being born. And we wanted you.'

All she'd ever had of her mammy was a lock of her hair, thick and dark. As a child she would search it out among her father's belongings, old silver-backed combs, an elegant matchbook, and sit with it on her lap, stroking the thin strands, trying to conjure up her mammy's face. Had she looked like her? She would stand in front of the looking glass inspecting her features. Was this long, slightly crooked nose hers? Her father bore no sign of one. What about her hooded eyes, her thin lips?

And then one day, after *she* arrived, and a new baby was born, had grown loud and rambunctious, tearing around the cabin, getting bigger and chubbier, the lock of hair was gone. Vanished. When she'd asked, politely, nobody had owned up to it. But she knew that woman had taken it. Thrown it away in a fit of jealousy. It made Serena wonder if she wanted to throw her away too. And she had never forgotten it.

She never forgot how the bairn was treated, either. The finest dresses, the plumpest feather bedding in her corner of the wagon. Serena had always made do, when it was just her and Pa. But this wean was to be handled like a princess, and it made Serena's blood boil.

It wasn't the wean she hated. She was pretty, sweet. She adored Serena, followed her around the big top, asked questions, gazed up at her thoughtfully, as though she were the most beautiful and interesting person she had ever seen in her life.

But *her*. The mother. Her father's new woman. Not even a wife, because he said he could never marry again. Serena never liked her, not least because they were near enough the same age. And the woman always seemed annoyed that her pa came along with a daughter, would have preferred it if she hadn't been born. What pained her most was that at night, secretly, when everyone else was asleep, this thought troubled her too. Surely her own mother would have preferred her not to have been born, had she been given a say in the matter?

And so Serena became an outcast in her own family. She wowed the crowds on the ribbons and on horseback – was, her pa said, the greatest performer in the whole show. But back at the wagon, after the circus finished for the night, she was ignored, spoken down to, her father seemingly oblivious to the way the woman treated her.

Her pa was so busy, any free time he could spare was given to *her*, or the bairn. It was as though he had simply forgotten that Serena existed outside the big top.

She was twenty-three years old when he died. Still the star performer, still the biggest draw. She was courting Davey, thinking of marrying him. Serena thought she was unbreakable. And so it proved. Because, when her pa went, she'd found that the circus had been left to her, Serena; that the woman had got nothing.

And so she had cast them out. The mean, angry woman and the wean, who was becoming a dab hand on the rings. She left them on a quiet road in Perthshire after a winter performance, told them it was time they made their own way in life. Her pa would have hated her for it. But, well, he should have changed his will. As it was, they got nothing. And even though she knew it was a betrayal, she felt she was doing right by Linden's. And herself.

The past is restless tonight. She takes a long, slow sook on her pipe. A life on the road, she thinks, yet my troubles follow me wherever I go. She coughs. Her chest feels hard and tight. There is a long way to go until morning, and there will be no show tonight. The snow has been coming down thick and hard for two days and the punters are hunkering down in their warm, toasty homes. She might as well head down to the big top, take a look at the acrobats' latest rehearsal. Her memories may be bubbling up, but she is Serena Linden. Broken, but unbowed. And still the proprietor of this great circus.

42

Secrets

Lena is trembling as she steps through the high arch of the big top. Harry is behind her, tall, reassuring, but still. She cannot quite believe the moment is finally here.

The space is huge, cavernous. She is amazed that they have been able to walk straight in; they left the wagon at the side of the road, crept silently into a showground as still and silent as the falling snow, and towards the gleaming tent.

Above them, a troupe of acrobats are swinging effortlessly from a complex set of ropes and hoops suspended on the ceiling. They weave and soar, interlocking legs and arms, and despite her nerves Lena lifts her head, spellbound at the sight.

'Again!' shouts a loud voice from below. 'Terrible. No rhythm. You're a disgrace to this circus.'

Even from this distance, Lena can see that Serena is a formidable presence. Swathed in silk scarves, an imposing cane in her hand, she is an immovable point at the very heart of the tent. The acrobats strike up their formation again, swirling overhead like a flock of graceful birds, and this time Lena keeps her eyes on Serena, sees how she watches them with a critical eye, the practised air of a true show woman, a pro.

'You're the Loveridge lass,' a deep voice says in her ear. Lena jumps and turns. A dark-haired man is leering at her, his sharp teeth bared. 'What the fuck are you doing here?'

Harry steps forward, but Lena rests a hand on his arm.

'I'm here to see Miss Linden,' she says with more confidence than she feels.

The man laughs nastily. 'And what makes you think she'll talk to a wee trollop like you?'

On the far side of the tent Lena senses the old woman's head turning.

'Dougie? Who is that? What's going on?'

The man's neck stiffens, and Lena sees an unease pass over his face. 'Don't you move a muscle,' he says to her. She tries not to flinch.

'He's one of the chaps who was sniffing round your wagon that night back in Stirling,' Harry says as the man walks towards Serena.

Fear trickles through Lena's veins. So that was Serena Linden's doing as well. She thinks of poor Tommy Pony, the deadly nightshade, the hole cut in the tent. Had Serena been behind all these cruel acts?

And yet something like envy pricks at her, too. This great tent, Serena's magisterial presence – is this not what she has dreamt of? That one day her ladies' circus might also command such showmanship, and talent?

On the far side of the big top Serena is conferring with Dougie. He shakes his head but she raps her cane violently on the ground, forces him into silence. And then slowly, unhurriedly, as if she possessed all the time in this dark, snow-covered world, she makes her way towards them.

'Miss Linden,' Lena says, and is astonished to find herself bobbing slightly, as if curtseying.

'I see you've got some manners, at least,' says Serena. 'Come away back to my quarters.'

The wagon, when they reach it, is dim. An acrid smell hits Lena's nostrils. Despite an array of pretty furniture – a day bed in burgundy velvet, swathes of silk strung across the ceiling, carvings in ivory adorning the windowsill, a jewel box studded with gems – the caravan has an air of decay about it. As though something in it has been left to rot.

Serena sits on the bed, hunched over. There are smears of blood on the blanket, and more round her mouth. Now Lena is up close to her, Harry at her heels, she notices that the face is grey, the eyes sunken. She sees immediately that Serena has a sickness, and feels an unfamiliar pang of sympathy. Then she thinks of Violet, of the look on her face as she lay there on the floor of the tent, eyes gazing upwards, unmoving, and she clears her throat.

'I'm Lena Loveridge,' she says. 'I'd like to ask you some questions.'

The figure on the bed flinches, coughs nastily into a handkerchief.

'Ach, I know who you are,' she says. 'Do you think I'd have let a stranger come marching in here if I didn't?'

Her answer unnerves Lena. 'Well, I am a stranger, aren't I? Or have we met before?'

Serena laughs. It is more of a cackle. 'In a manner of speaking,' she says. 'Who's your man?'

'This is Harry. He's Violet Weaver's brother. He wants answers as much as I do.'

'Out, lad,' says Serena. 'This is between us two show women, no more. We don't need you earwigging on our business.'

Lena turns, looks at Harry. He shrugs. 'I'll be right outside the door,' he says softly. 'The first sign of trouble and you just shout my name. I'll be in here as quick as Jack Flash.'

'Sit, sit,' says Serena, once he has gone, waving the cane she clutches in one hand.

Lena perches on the day bed. It is hard, overstuffed, and she wonders how the old woman can possibly find it comfortable.

'As you can see, I'm not well. Some damned winter cold has got into me. Can't seem to shake it.' Serena hawks a globule of spit into her handkerchief, raps her cane on the floor. 'So, what questions have you for me?'

Lena looks at her. Her breathing is steady now, her nerves calmed. She feels completely in control.

'Did you know Violet Weaver is dead?'

'Aye,' says Serena. 'Shame, that. She was awfully talented on the trapeze. Threw herself off a bridge, I hear?'

'But it was you!' Lena exclaims. 'You greased her bar! You made her fall! She broke her back, she was never going to walk again, so she killed herself. This is all your fault.'

Serena is shaking her head.

'No, no. I never greased the bar. I didn't even know the bar had been greased. Thought she'd just taken a tumble. It's always a risk. You should know that, being a circus proprietor like myself.'

Lena is stunned. 'It wasn't you?'

She looks at the woman, her pallid skin, the rheumy eyes, the yellowing whites. But Serena is gazing at her steadily, her expression unflinching. This is the truth, Lena thinks. She is telling me the truth.

'Listen, hen, I won't deny I had a bit of fun with you and Violet. I was sore that she hit me. She gave me a right old shiner. I hoped she might disappear. But no, there she was bold as brass, joined up with a new show, a ladies' circus of all things, and pulling in the flatties. So I got my boys to mess with your horse, cut a hole in your tent. Violet needed to learn a lesson. And you, lassie, need to learn that running a show is hard. You don't get to be me overnight with . . .' she waves her cane around at her various glittering trinkets '. . . all this. But as soon as I found out it was you that was running the lassies' circus, I decided we'd had enough fun.'

The Show Woman

Lena swallows hard. 'Why me?' she asks.

Serena says nothing.

'You poisoned Tommy Pony, then. And the tent was you as well. But who could have done that to Violet?'

Serena emits another cackle. 'Have you tried asking her own mother? She was always a wrong 'un, Mary. I tried telling Violet before she left but she wouldn't have it. Didn't want to hear a word. The sainted Mary Weaver. That's a lie if ever there was one.'

Lena's head is spinning. An image of Mary, matter-of-fact, discussing Violet being locked away in the hospital, floats into her mind.

'What did Mary do?' she asks.

'You'll have to find that one out on your own, lassie. And you will. I can see you're a bright thing. Smart as your mother, in fact.'

Lena's voice is almost a whisper. 'You knew my mother?'

Serena has produced a pipe, an old, battered-looking thing with a dark, cherry wood bowl. She puts tobacco into it, lights a match and takes a slow puff.

'Aye, I knew your mother, and better than most. She loved me, your mother. Wee Maggie was always following me around. She had a kind nature. She was spoiled, but sweet. But you know how people talk about two peas in a pod?'

Lena thinks of Violet, nods.

'Well, your mammy and I were the opposite. Two different pods altogether. That was the problem.'

'But how did you know her? Did you grow up together?'

'I'm getting to that, hen. When my mammy died, my pa was lonely. I wasn't enough for him, even though I was the star of the show. But he needed a woman's touch. Most men do, as I'm sure you're discovering. And so he took in this woman, a bidey-in, not even his wife. A waif she was, turned up at the circus one day havering about horses and wanting a go as a bareback rider, not that she was a patch on me.'

Serena pauses, makes sure Lena is still following her.

'But my pa took a shine to her, and the next thing I knew she's got a great round belly and they're having their own bairn together.'

'But what has this got to do with my mammy?' asks Lena. 'I don't understand.'

'No,' says Serena, 'you won't. Your mammy made sure of that. Never spoke about it to anyone once I told them they had to get out. She forgot all about us. And I forgot about her, too. Mostly. Until that day she turned up at Linden's with you in tow. You were a wee slip of a thing then, a tiny wee bairn, and your mammy thought I didn't spot you in the crowd but I did. I wasn't sore about it either. I was pleased she'd had a family of her own. Thought maybe she'd got away from her mother, too.'

'You're speaking in riddles,' says Lena. She is frustrated now, desolate because this ancient, bitter woman does not, after all this, know what happened to Violet, and seems to be full of secrets that Lena did not know she needed to hear.

Serena clears her throat, a great rasp that fills the dimly lit wagon.

'Here's what I'm trying to tell you, lassie,' she says. 'Your mammy was my half-sister. And you're my niece.'

43

Doubts

Lena sits ramrod-straight on the box next to Harry. She has said little. Not when he asked her what happened after she emerged, struck silent, from Serena's wagon into the cold night. Not when they got back to the caravan and she went, mute and blank-faced, straight to bed, fully dressed. And not now as they travel the long road back to Glasgow on a chilly January morning. The snow is melting, turning to a dark, dirty slush, while above them a weak sun attempts to break through the clouds.

She can feel Harry's impatience. In the way he holds the reins, speaks harshly to the horses, and gives her the occasional irritated side glance. But she simply does not know where to begin. With the sinister words about his mother? The revelation about her own mammy, and the implication that the bent-over crone in that strange wagon was an aunt, of sorts? But she owes him the truth about Violet. He was her brother. He deserves to know.

'She says she didn't kill Violet,' she says quickly, blurting it out.

Harry looks at her sharply.

'I mean, she didn't do anything to her bar. She says it wasn't her.'

'And you believe her? Just like that?'

'I do. She admitted that it was her who tried to poison Tommy, or one of her goons at any rate. Says it was them who cut the hole in the tent too, back at Blairgowrie. But she was genuinely shocked when she heard about the bar. She honestly had no idea. She thought Violet just had a fall.'

'Well, in that case, I think it's about time we called the police,' says Harry. 'Perhaps this is a matter for them.'

'Are you kidding?' says Lena. 'You know what they think of us. Who we are. They think we're all the stinking, thieving type. They'll say it's nothing to do with them. That we should sort it out ourselves and not bring our troubles to them. Believe me, I know.'

'What do you mean, you know?' Harry is staring at the road ahead, watching a cart that is coming towards them laden with bales of dried hay, but there is a muscle twitching, right by his ear.

'That's what happened when my daddy went to them when my mammy disappeared,' she says. 'The man practically laughed in his face. Told us she'd probably shacked up with a man whose house wasn't on wheels. I wonder now if he also told them about the tree, what you'd seen, and they just dismissed it.'

She shivers at the memory, the policeman's bored, uninterested face, the way he'd wrinkled his nose at her daddy, as though he was scum on the sole of his shoe.

'Aye, that'd make sense,' says Harry. 'There's no doubt your pa took me seriously, might even have taken a look himself. But the coppers are . . . well, when it comes to us, they're bastards.'

Lena nods, thoughtfully. 'If we had real proof about who might have greased the bar it might be different. But we don't. Nobody saw anything. And Carmen wasn't even there.'

A sickening, treacherous thought occurs to her. Carmen. She had been furious with Violet the night before for spilling her secret, angry and hurt, fizzing with the injustice. She could not even show her face. They'd thought she

The Show Woman

had packed up and left that night, but what if she hadn't? What if it was her who had crept into the tent, covered the bar in oil or petroleum jelly or whatever it was that caused Violet's hands to slip? She shivers.

Harry stiffens at the mention of Carmen's name, but, when he opens his mouth, Lena holds her hand up.

'Whatever it is, I don't want to hear it.'

He closes his mouth, jaw set.

'But you have to believe me, Harry. It really wasn't Serena Linden. She's an evil, nasty woman, she almost killed Tommy Pony and she tried to ruin our act. But she didn't do anything to Violet.'

'Why are you so sure?'

She hesitates, stumbles over whether or not to tell him something she hasn't even begun to get to grips with.

'She told me something else,' she says. 'She says she found something out not long before Violet had her fall, and, when she did, she decided not to mess with us any more. Anyone would think there was actually a fractured little soul in the old crone after all.'

'Really?' says Harry. He is interested now, waiting for more.

'She told me she knew my mammy. That she grew up with her. Serena and my mammy shared a father. Serena's mammy died when she was born, and her daddy took up with a woman. That was my grandmother. She and Serena's daddy had a baby together: Maggie, my mammy. Serena Linden is my aunt.'

'My God,' says Harry. 'And you never knew? Never guessed?'

'Never. My mammy didn't talk much about her people. I knew that her mammy had raised her alone from when she was about seven, after her daddy had died. She didn't talk about him much, just said that he was a nice man, kind, quite old, and that they had been on the roads with a show. But after he died they were on their own and then her mammy was hard up. She never said it but I think she might have worked the streets. Then Mammy met my daddy and I think her mother died not long after that. I'm not sure what happened to her. She may have ended up in the poor house. She didn't talk about it much. Just said that me and Daddy were her family.'

Her mother's face rises, unbidden, into her mind. Those high, rounded cheeks. The shock of blonde hair. Her lavender scent. She was always graceful; even when she walked down the street her body would sway, as though she moved to her own internal music, a constant rhythm that thrummed in her head and only she could hear. As a child Lena had thought her mammy the most beautiful and glamorous creature she had ever seen, with long, elegant fingers and what her father always called 'a well-turned ankle'. She could make even the plainest, dowdiest dress look as if it came from a tailor in Paris, her tiny waist sloping in and out in exactly the right places. Sometimes she would ask Lena to help dress her and Lena would stand on her tiptoes, reaching upwards to fasten the many buttons of her frock.

Oh, she thinks, as she looks out on the grubby winter landscape, the barren trees, the silent paddocks, like empty battlefields, what she would give for just one more day in her mammy's company. One hour. One minute. She tries to remember if anything in Serena's face reminded her of Maggie. But that greyish, yellow complexion, like a waxing moon on a dreich spring night, held no clues. Serena remained a stranger. Perhaps that meant none of it was true.

She knew it had to be, though. It would be a ridiculous story to make up. Pointless. The old woman was a nasty,

The Show Woman

callous bitch, but she was in her right mind. Lena wonders what else she might have done to them had she not found out that Lena was her niece. Perhaps Violet had been doomed anyway.

Harry briefly rests his hand on Lena's knee. It is cold, even through his woollen mittens, but somehow, it warms her.

'I'm sorry,' he says. 'That's an awful lot to take in.'

He fumbles in his jacket pocket and produces a hip flask. Lena wonders why he has not brought it out before and realises he probably didn't want to frighten her with drink. The last time they'd sipped whisky together alone, that magical night in Ayr, things had been so different. There had been promise on the air. The show was going well. She was starting to see a future. And Violet was still alive.

'Thank you,' she says, and takes a long, lingering sip. She hands it back and he too takes a nip.

'So how are we going to find out who killed Violet?' he says.

But Lena simply shakes her head, and gazes out on to the endless, slush-filled world.

44

Soakings

To Rosie's amazement, when she finally turns up and begs for shifts, the carpet factory takes her back.

'It's all hands on deck,' says the foreman, a rabbit-faced man with splayed front teeth and a vaguely comical bunnet that sags, inexplicably, down both sides of his face. 'Had a big order come in from London. All very secretive but I've an idea these carpets are going straight to one of the big hooses. Maybe even the biggest hoose of all.'

As she sits at her machine, pedalling furiously, hearing the familiar *clackity clack,* Rosie wonders if one day royal shoes will grace this thick material, whether a regal hand might brush its fibres, perhaps leaning down to tie a shoelace, or pick up a dropped fan. Probably not. The royals likely had people around to do their every bidding, no matter how tiny or inconsequential. It seems unimaginable to her, to have so many servants to help you wash your face, or cook a meal, unbutton your stays. She remembers Violet talking about the showgirl who met the King once, how he was so fat his belly looked like it was the size of Ireland. She chokes back the tiniest of sobs.

Before Rosie was born, her ma had worked as a domestic servant at one of the grand Ayrshire houses. She had to wear a long white pinny and a white cotton cap, get up at the crack of dawn each day to set the fires and scrub the ancient stone floors with pails of water heated on the range.

'It wasn't for me,' she told Rosie and Jennifer. 'All that running around after others, and nothing to show for it at the end of the day but a few pennies and a roof over your head. That's when I decided to marry your father. On the farm, if I scrub a floor, at least I know it's my tiles I'm washing.'

Thoughts of her ma and Jennifer come often now. Rosie is deeply lonely in this cold, unfeeling city, is lost without Violet, desperately missing Carmen. Belle has been her only ballast, and it turns out that this strange little girl is a wizard on the trapeze, can do flips and jumps that remind her, painfully, of Violet.

Morag had perched daintily on Rosie's shoulder as they watched Belle perform, her talons digging lightly into her tender flesh. There was something comforting about that curious bird. Rosie had rarely allowed herself to be touched since Violet died, had shrunk from the comforting hugs, the consoling pats on the arm, yet she enjoyed the feel of the bird's claws. Morag was simply there, softly nudging her beak into her neck when she wanted a few crumbs, a new friend that demanded little.

'She likes you,' said Belle when she had finished her performance and the bird had hopped to the ground. 'So what did you think? Was I any good?'

Rosie had nodded approvingly. 'You've got real talent. Your sister would have been proud.'

'Thanks,' said Belle. 'My mammy doesn't want me doing it any more. Says she's not going to have another daughter ruin her life by whizzing round in the air, but I don't care. Violet would have loved that I'm doing this now. I bet she would.'

Rosie suspects that in reality Violet would have been irritated initially by Belle's talent on the trapeze, but would eventually have tolerated it, perhaps even taught her a few tricks. Her heart aches to think of it, and what might have been. A double act, perhaps. Two flying sisters.

The Show Woman

As she walks back to Vinegarhill from the factory this evening the rain beats down, turning the rest of the slush into rivulets of water that pour down the streets, make her heavy skirts leaden as she slops down the Gallowgate. The showground is quiet, shuttered, but as she picks her way across the mud she hears a wagon turning in behind her. Lena and Harry rush past her towards the stables, Lena's face stricken. Rosie plods on towards her own caravan. If there is news, she will know it soon enough. Sure enough, she has only been there for five minutes, is just unwinding her woollen scarf and unbuttoning her boots, when there is a loud, anxious rap at the door.

She opens it, expecting Lena. But it is her sister Jennifer who stands there, soaked to the skin, and trembling from the cold.

45

Jennifer

Jennifer stoats into the caravan, heavily pregnant, belly blooming like a hot air balloon.

'Dear God,' says Rosie, as Jennifer flings her arms round her sister. They are both wet, hair clinging to their scalps like damp leaves. Jennifer. Her lovely, kind, innocent sister. And a mother now, almost.

'Come in, come in,' she says, making room on the bed for Jennifer to sit down.

'This is where you've been living? Oh, Rosie.'

'It's not so bad. You get used to it. And in the summer it can be fun when you're on the road all the time. Well . . . it was fun.' She smiles weakly. 'It's a very long story. But how did you find me?'

'I heard about your friend Violet,' says Jennifer, smoothing her palm over her belly. 'After we came to see you. It was the next night, wasn't it? Everyone in the town was talking about it, how this beautiful girl had gone flying off the trapeze and broken her back and that someone had greased her bar and done it deliberately. People were shocked. I realised it had to be Violet.

'Ma and I wanted to come and find you but by then Pa was wise to us and he wouldn't let Ma go, and told her that if I went he'd give her a beating, and me too. So I decided I couldn't. Not with the babby inside me.'

She cradles her stomach and Rosie, unable to help herself, leans forward, touches the soft, rounded bump.

'Can you feel a wee kick?' asks Jennifer, and Rosie nods, marvelling at the sensation, at the tiny new life growing in her sister's belly. A daughter or a son. Her niece or her nephew. How different things might have been had she stayed home, instead of running away. Perhaps she could have moved in with Jennifer and her man, helped them keep house, seen them raise the bairn. Perhaps she could still.

'But I asked around, wondered where you'd have gone, if the show wasn't on the road any more, and someone said you'd likely have come back here. To Vinegarhill. You're a long way from home here, lass, you really are.' She pulls her sodden shawl tighter round her shoulders, casts an eye at the dark, grubby caravan, untouched almost, since Violet's death.

'But that was months ago,' says Rosie. 'Why come now?'

'Don't start,' says Jennifer, and an unfamiliar fire flares in her eyes. 'Have you any idea the trouble I had getting here? I had to walk to the town, take a train, then a tram, packed in like a sardine. It's no journey for a woman in my condition. And you're the one who ran away, remember? Left me on my own, a bride with no bridesmaid, Ma weeping, Pa drinking more than ever. You just walked away and left us.'

Rosie hangs her head. Over these past sunlit months, and the grey, bare winter ones, she has done her best to block out thoughts of her family. She is used to trying to forget about her father, about his great ham-like hands, his sour breath. But until she left them, Rosie's entire world had revolved around Jennifer and their ma. Thoughts of them have snuck in, entirely uninvited. The first time she kissed Violet there was a part of her still hovering in the corner of the milking parlour, waiting for her ma to bring in the pails. Performing on Tommy Pony, soaking up the applause, she was still cantering round the empty fields of the farm, Jennifer watching on from the stables. And,

The Show Woman

holding Violet's thin hands in those days after she came home from the hospital, the memory of her father's fat fingers had risen, unbidden.

'Do you want to know why?'

'I know why,' says Jennifer. 'I always knew more than you think. But I wanted you to be the one to say it. I never knew how to talk to you about what he was doing.'

From nowhere, a great, thundering sob begins inside Rosie. It billows and swells and bursts forth until she is shrieking with pain and sadness, for all she has lost, all she has left behind. Jennifer holds her, soft and safe, lets her weep.

Finally she brings out a hanky, gives it to Rosie to dab at her eyes. Rosie feels a bleak release, as though something she has been holding in for too long has finally been let go, returned to the air.

'There is another reason I came,' she says. 'It's about Pa.'

Rosie tenses, every hair on her skin prickling. 'He doesn't know where I am, does he? Is he coming here?'

'I don't know,' she says. 'That's why I need to tell you.'

And so she does. About how one day last week Jennifer had visited their ma and found a tin of petroleum jelly hidden away behind some of this year's crop of freshly made jam, great handfuls scooped out of it. She had never seen such a thing in the house before. Asked her mother about it, but she said she'd never seen it before either, barely knew what it was. Then her father had exploded in a rage. Told her she was nosy and a good-for-nothing, that she should stop asking questions.

'And that's when I realised,' says Jennifer. 'It was him. He was the one who'd greased the bar and hurt your friend. I confronted him, asked him why, and he said he knew about you both.' She pauses, swallows, looks away. 'Said that you were doing *unnatural things*. And that no daughter of his would be allowed to do that, and the other lassie didn't deserve to live.'

Rosie clasps her hands to her mouth in horror.

'No, no, no,' she says. Her heart feels as though it has shattered into tiny fragments, scattered across the floor. How could her own pa have done this to Violet? To her?

But she knows, deep down, that he could. He had always carried a thick jealousy about him when it came to Rosie. He'd treated her as though she were a possession, a trinket, a toy he could do what he pleased with. He would not have been able to bear the thought of another's hands touching her. Particularly those of a delicate, beautiful woman.

'We think he had been following you,' says Jennifer. She is holding Rosie's hand now, stroking her palm in soothing, circular motions. 'He went away in June, said he had to go and see about some grain, but we had a sense it was something else. I always said to Ma that he'd go and find you if he could.'

Rosie shivers, feels trickles of ice slip down her back. The idea that her father was stalking her, his own daughter, like prey, spying on her, plotting against her, makes her feel sick.

'So what happened?' she asks. 'After you confronted him?'

'I thought he was going to kick me, right in the stomach. I've never seen him so furious. He looked as though he was going to thump me, or Ma. But then he got ahold of himself. He went to the stable, saddled Scout, and rode out on to the road. That was a week ago. He hasn't been back. I came to warn you, Rosie. He might come after you still. He'll have the devil in him now.'

He has always had the devil in him, thinks Rosie. It's just that I saw more of him than you.

'Will you stay the night, at least?'

'Aye,' says Jennifer. 'It's been a long journey. My feet are squealing in these boots.'

But just as she starts to unbutton them, there is another knock on the door and Lena and Harry walk in, clothes sodden. Misery clings to them like wet hair.

'Lena,' says Rosie brightly, flicking a glance to Jennifer, who has risen, unsteadily, to her feet.

'You're Jennifer,' says Lena. 'I remember you from Ayr. Please, sit down for goodness' sake. When are you due?'

'Soon, I hope,' says Jennifer. 'Can't take much more of this back pain. I'm so sorry to hear about Violet.'

'Thank you,' says Harry, who is standing by the door, cap in hand. 'She was my sister. We all miss her.'

Rosie looks at her sister again. Jennifer gives her a slight nod.

'Jennifer's come with news. Bad news. The worst, the most terrible . . .' She breaks into heaving sobs again, and Lena's face collapses.

'Oh, no, Rosie, is it your mother?'

'It's our father,' says Jennifer. Her voice is calm and even. 'He greased the bar. He killed your . . .' She breaks off, looks around the wagon at the three horrified faces staring at her. 'He killed your Violet.'

The silence is punctured only by Rosie's heaving sobs. Jennifer continues, looking at Lena.

'He found out about Violet and Rosie and he was furious. He's an evil man, and, now he knows that my mother and I understand the truth, he's gone, left the farm. We haven't seen him in a week.'

'Jesus Christ,' says Harry softly. 'The bastard. The complete and utter bastard.'

Lena looks at him. 'So it really wasn't Serena,' she says. She looks pale, tired. Defeated. 'Now do you believe me?'

Harry nods. 'I do. I just – I despair. It's so cruel. To Violet – to you, Rosie; to all of us. And I don't even know the bloody man's name. Jennifer, do you think your father would come here? Will he come after Rosie?'

'He might,' says Jennifer. 'There's no telling what he'll do in a rage. And this was about the worst rage I've ever seen him in. His name is James Carluke, by the way.'

Rosie recalls a night when she was around ten years old. It was before her father started interfering with her, before she could even begin to conceive of such horrors. And yet she had never truly felt comfortable around her pa, had always shrunk at his touch, and his temper. She and Jennifer were in bed when she heard her father crashing about down below, swearing at her mother, calling her a *stupid old cow* because she'd let one of the sheepdogs into the parlour to have her puppies instead of leaving them in the barn. They had been born earlier that cold, rain-lashed night, four tiny, squiggling balls, pink and blind, the littlest one, the runt, struggling to find his mammy's teat in order to feed.

Rosie, pitying him, had wanted to bring him to bed with her. But her ma said she should stay with the mother, it was cruel to rip them away so young, and anyway, she wanted him to grow big and strong, didn't she? Rosie had reluctantly agreed, giving the tiny puppy a soft stroke with the nail of her pinkie finger. And now there was her father, raging at the puppies' mere existence.

The next morning she was relieved when she went down to the parlour to see the collie, Meg, still there, her puppies asleep beside her by the dying embers of the fire. But then she looked closer, and saw that the runt – whom she had already christened Patch on account of the little black splodge on his left eye – was missing.

The Show Woman

She had run around the parlour, shouting his name, searching frantically, but there was no sign. Then she opened the back door and found the little puppy lying lifeless on the doorstep. He had been strangled. His tiny eyes had never opened. Rosie had been inconsolable.

'When my father gets a thirst for revenge he's terrifying,' she says now. 'There's no saying what he might do.'

She feels a hideous powerlessness. When she had left the farm that night last spring, cantered away on Tommy Pony and into a new life, it was the first time she had ever felt any real control. She was holding the reins of her own destiny and it made her feel giddy and free. She might have known that that evil man would find a way to ruin it for her. She had been foolish to think it could ever have been otherwise.

'So you saw Serena Linden?' Rosie asks Lena finally, wiping her eyes. 'What did she tell you?'

Lena shakes her head and looks away. 'Not much. Except that she had been messing with us. It was her who sent those men round the wagon, and poisoned Tommy Pony, and cut the tent.'

Rosie winces.

'It's a fine set-up she has there with the circus, but she's not a woman you want to stay chatting to for very long. We couldn't get out of there fast enough.'

Lena and Harry turn to leave, Harry promising to speak to some of the other showmen in the ground, ask them to keep an eye out for any strange men.

'Or we could move you to another showground if you like?' he says. 'There's Garngad, a bit further out. You might be safer there.'

But Rosie shakes her head. She cannot face leaving Vinegarhill, its memories of Violet, just yet. And she can't afford the tram fare from Garngad that would be the only way to get her to the factory each morning.

After they've gone, she makes up the bunk for her and Jennifer and they both pile in, Rosie pulling Violet's pillow with its woody scent, fainter each night, over to her side.

'This is like old times, isn't it?' says Jennifer, and gives her hand a small squeeze.

'It is,' says Rosie into the dark. And squeezes back.

46

Locket

The hard earth begins to soften, snowdrops peeking through the gloom. Lena is down to her last few pennies, counts them every night, wonders if she too should take a job at the factory with Rosie, drown her grief in the clatter of the machines, the steady methodical work.

She sees little of Harry, who has got himself a few shows at one of the Glasgow music halls. He invites her along one night, but she cannot face it. Instead she sits alone in the dark, searching the sky for single stars. Proof that somewhere out there, far beyond her understanding, someone who loved her is still awake.

She worries about Rosie, who is terrified and on edge now that Jennifer has returned home, and sometimes comes to her wagon to sleep, bringing an old battered pillow filled with straw. They are long, fearful nights, and they bolt the door, just in case. But Rosie's pa has made no appearance.

Lena thinks of Serena, trapped in a body that will no longer do her bidding, surrounded by memories she would rather not have. How could this woman be her flesh and blood? Her own aunt? She had been four when her grandaddy on her father's side died, a big man who even into his fifties had the sinewy physique of a boxer who'd made his living punching other men for show. That she had another grandfather had rarely occurred to her. That it could be Serena's own father seemed inconceivable.

One night she looks out her mammy's old box, searching for clues to this strange new family. The picture, her mother's face sad and serene. The buds of lavender and the old Linden's ticket stub. The letter. And her pendant. Lena picks it up, runs the thin chain through her fingers, rubs her thumb over its smooth oval shape.

To her surprise, she finds a tiny catch on the side. All these years, and she had never realised that it wasn't a pendant, but a locket. She flips it open, hoping to find another picture of her mammy, or perhaps her daddy, gazing up at her. But when she sees the face staring back, she drops the box in shock.

The floor of Glasgow Central Station is hard and smooth, but Lena feels as though she is adrift on shifting sands. She blunders past men in smart suits and ladies in frilled coats and elegant hats, scrunching her eyes up at the clinking departures board, the high glass ceiling.

Queuing in the ticket office, a group of ladies eye her shabby dress, elbow each other, mouth 'traveller' with their painted lips.

'Where to?' The man behind the counter is wearing a smart navy-blue cap with gold brocade.

'Galston,' says Lena.

'Return or one-way?'

'What's the difference?'

'Well,' he says with exaggerated slowness, 'return means you want to return, today of course; one-way means you're thinking about moving all your worldly goods to Galston and planning never to come back.' His eyes shift up and down her body. 'Got some friends down the mines, have you?'

She hears the titters of ladies' laughter behind her.

'Return,' she says.

'Third class, I presume?'

She nods, handing over her pennies.

He shoves the ticket at her and she pockets it, avoiding the gaze of the women behind her. She will not give them the satisfaction of seeing her smarting eyes.

She heads towards the platform, thoughts swirling. She was ten when her mother disappeared, thought she could do no wrong, but now, nothing seems the same any more. Perhaps her whole life is a lie. Perhaps she should never have been born.

Into the carriage now and she finds a window seat, is soon joined by a mother and her crying baby. As the train chugs out of the city, across the bridge and over the river – oh, Violet, she thinks, as its darkening tide rushes towards the sea – she makes faces at the bairn until, entranced, he laughs, reaches out one chubby hand to touch her cheek.

'Sorry,' says the mother. She looks exhausted, great sooty rings under her eyes.

'It's no bother,' says Lena.

'What's his name?'

'Harry,' says the woman, and Lena falls silent again.

At Galston she hurries over the bridge and into the town. She would never have thought of the train had it not been for Jennifer. It seems miraculous to her now that she can get here so quickly, when it would have taken days by horse, or wagon. It's a year or two now since she was last here but she knows where the showground is. Down the main street, past the miners' cottages, into the wide expanse of park.

It is empty and silent as the grave. A lone building – the stables, she realises – stands in a corner. Beside it a single tree, bare of leaves. And, past that, a winding stream, its water levels high after the recent rain. She makes for the tree, crying now, sobbing out loud, louder and louder, because who will hear her in this barren place where her mammy once came, where she vanished all those years ago during the thrum and the noise of the fair, amid the smell of toffee apples and the fizz of excitement, the place Lena always considered her home.

A tree, that was what Harry had said all those months ago. As Lena reaches it, a single magpie watches her from a high branch. She scrabbles at the hard bark, its jagged edges cutting her fingers, slicing at them. There is blood. A strange smell rises from the tree, as though it were waking up from a long sleep, emitting an ancient earthy breath into the cold air.

There is nothing here. She has felt all round the bark, along its branches, down by the thick, twisting roots. But then, deep inside the tree's heart, she finds a little hole, just big enough for her fingers to squeeze in. They clasp something hard, metallic. No wonder her father never found anything. His large, showman's hands would never have been able to reach in this far.

Lena brings the object out into the fading light. It is another locket. And she knows, without even looking, whose picture will be inside.

PART THREE

Long Love

Crieff Market Park
February 1911

47

Milky pearls

It is done now. For good or for ill. Mr McClaverty has made light work of a difficult subject. And now, she must try to do the same.

Serena has always liked Crieff, nestling in the bosomy swell of the Ochil hills, with its well-heeled flatties who come for the restorative waters and the dry bar at the Hydro hotel, then sneak out after sundown to take in the circus show, and a quick dram on the fly.

'It's the invisible border between the Highlands and the Lowlands,' her pa once said. 'That's why the drovers brought their cattle here for market, raked so much money in. Did a roaring trade.'

The drovers are mostly gone, but it is a place with a brisk, professional air. That was why her pa chose a man here to deal with his legal affairs. And she has done the same, sending the youngest McCracken out to fetch the now ageing, wizened McClaverty, bending her stiff back, so sore now, to dictate her orders, sign her 'X' mark, handkerchief at the ready to stop up the blood that threatens to run from her throat each time she coughed.

Now she lies on her bed, a red velvet throw pulled up to her doughy chin, a shroud almost, although one fit for a queen. What will the Loveridge girl do now? Serena had searched for a flicker of familiarity in that young, frightened face, and thought that, right enough, her mouth turned up at the corners a bit the way her pa's had. Something about the eyes, too. That piercing quality. As though they could see right through you. A bit like hers were, once.

And she can see Maggie, too. The upturned nose, the staunch defiance, a trim elegance. Maggie Linden was a talented girl, already learning the ropes on the rings when Serena cast them out. It wasn't the girl she had loathed, her little half-sister, who thought Serena as magnificent as the crowds did, who followed her everywhere like a puppy, gathering her lavender buds and crushing them into her pillow at night because she had heard from a gypsy girl on a showground once that lavender gave the sweetest of dreams.

But her pa had left the circus in her hands, to do with as she wished, and Maggie's mother, that woman, had to go. She was lazy, always on the beg, sloppy, drank too much, there was often more in her pipe than just tobacco. She had seduced her father when he was weak and vulnerable and already on the decline, always had her eye on the big prize. And, most importantly of all, she wasn't a Linden. At least Maggie was. And so was the Loveridge girl.

Serena closes her weary eyes, shuts out the weakening daylight. There will be a performance tonight. She can hear the clank of the big top outside as the final flags are adorned, the stage set, but she will not be there to see it. Her charges will not know, until later. As it should be. The show must always go on.

The Loveridge girl must surely have realised, by now, what happened to her mammy. That *she,* that woman, was to blame, as she was for so much that became rotten and ugly in the lives of others. If she didn't now, she would soon.

The Show Woman

Serena thinks of her own mammy, the one she never knew, of the lock of hair she once treasured that was now, surely, gone forever. If only her mother could have held her, just once. Pulled Serena into her, told her she loved her, kept her warm and safe as only a mammy could. Instead she had been nothing but bones, right from the very start.

Her chest is heavy, her breathing laboured and slow. It is coming now. She can feel it. Soon the darkness will close over her, as if she has never been. She spins, spins, down into the blackness, towards oblivion, and release.

And as she takes this perilous final journey, it is not to the royal brooch at her throat that her hand moves, but to the milky pearls at her wrist, her tiny lost loves, gleaming in the dusk like miniature rays of light.

48

The stream

Lena is on the train back to Glasgow, swaying from side to side, barely listening as two drunks further down the carriage start up a brawl. In her pocket she feels the cool metal of the two lockets warming gently in her hand. The one she found in Galston, tucked away inside the old oak tree, has corroded from years of rain and winds, covered in rust and mud, but the picture inside is remarkably untouched. It is of her mother.

She is younger, yes, not much more than a girl really, but it is the same face that graces the postcard taken when Lena was a bairn. It is unmistakably her. The high cheekbones, the Cupid's bow mouth. Her hair parted down the middle and pulled back in the old Victorian style. If her mother had hidden this locket all those years ago, she must have been trying to keep it from someone. Her daddy? Surely not. It could only be the person whose picture is contained in the other locket.

She can hardly wait to get off the train at Glasgow, past passengers fussing with trunks and luggage, past the policemen on the platform now fighting their way on to the carriage to deal with the drunks, batons raised, past the tobacco stands and newspaper sellers and out into the sodden city. It is raining here too, a persistent grey drizzle, but she does not care as she skites down Union Street, past the bridge where she will not look, she must not look – oh, Violet; she cannot think of her now – across Glasgow Green and past the High Court where a judge, still wearing his wig, holds a newspaper over his head as he waits for his carriage, then up the High Street, on to Gallowgate and back, back to Vinegarhill.

She bursts into the wagon, finds her sitting on a stool, knitting a long, intricate shawl.

'Why is there a picture of you in my mother's locket?'

Mary Weaver looks up. Her face is old and ragged, weatherbeaten from years on the road. But, looking into Lena's eyes, it softens.

'Have you got it, hen? Have you got the locket?'

Lena says nothing.

'The one in Galston, I mean. I know you've got the other one, the one of me. I put it there. In among your mammy's things. Just in case your daddy went searching. He always thought it was just a pendant, you see.

'No, the other one I never could find, although I did look. Every year when we went to Galston I'd scrabble about, see if she'd buried it somewhere, hidden it in a copse or down by the stream. But I never had any joy. Well, you always were a smart one. Just like your mammy. Let me see.'

Lena, trembling, brings the old, battered necklace out of her pocket and hands it to her. Mary unfastens the little catch.

'Ah, there she is,' she says, admiring the tiny image of Lena's mother. 'We got those pictures done at the same time. Studio away over on Union Street, got all tarted up for it. It was my idea. I thought we could wear each other's lockets, a wee keepsake, a reminder of the past, but then I was so taken with my own likeness that I kept mine, and your mammy kept hers.'

She gives a thin laugh.

'And of course, Maggie said she wanted to give it to her daughter one day. Sit down, love, you look soaked to the skin.'

The Show Woman

Lena sits on the edge of the bed. Rainwater is trickling down the back of her neck.

'I don't understand,' she says.

'No,' says Mary. 'You wouldn't. We worked very hard on that. Well, your mammy did. It would have made no difference to me – to have folk know she was my daughter, I mean. But she wouldn't have it. Fresh start. Wanted to get away from me, I think, but then, I wouldn't have that.'

'She was your daughter,' Lena repeats. 'So that means I'm your . . .' she stumbles on the word '. . . granddaughter.'

'It does, aye. Although it was hard to think of you like that, what with you and Violet being almost the same age. Just like me and Serena.'

'Serena,' says Lena slowly. 'My aunt.'

'Ah, so you've been to see the auld witch, then, have you? Harry did mention it. I didn't think she'd come clean, though. She must be up to something.'

Lena looks at a spot of damp on the roof of the caravan, single drops of water plopping down on to the floor below. Her mind is racing. Mary her grandmother. Violet a sort of sister, but really a sort of aunt. Did that mean she and Harry were related as well? The thought made her feel ill.

'William and Harry aren't mine,' says Mary, as if she is reading her thoughts. 'Auld Billy was a widower when he married me, two weans already. We just carried on as if we were all one big happy family, didn't feel the need to tell people our business. That's one of the good things about the shows. It's so easy to . . .' She stops, relishes the word. 'Disappear.'

Lena leaps to her feet. 'What did you do to my mother? Tell me!'

Mary gives her a calm, maddening smile. Her knitting needles continue to click. 'All in good time, lass. Don't you want to hear about your grandfather first? And me?'

And so Lena sits back down in the little caravan, the hushed drizzle pattering down outside, and listens to Mary talk. An orphan, she'd been, a city girl from Glasgow cast out alone at just sixteen years old and desperate to avoid the poorhouse, when she'd come across the great Benjamin Linden, circus proprietor, widower, and spotted an opportunity to make a good life for herself. He'd been easy to seduce, an old man like that, and his daughter, only a year younger than Mary, helpless to do anything about it.

Mary laughs. 'Oh she hated me from the off, did Serena. Couldn't stand to look at me. Spent all her time on horseback or on the ropes, just to get away from me. And then the babby came along – that's your mammy, Lena – and she was just fizzing with rage. Thought she was going to be replaced.

'And she would have been too, if I'd persuaded old Benjamin to marry me and change his will. Then that circus would have been mine. A proper show woman I'd have been then, hobnobbing with the royals, my picture in the newspaper. But the TB carried Benjamin off far too quick, and I never managed to get him to change the documents. And before he'd even been buried, your dear Auntie Serena kicked wee Maggie and me out. That was when things got difficult.'

On and on she goes. They'd ended up in Glasgow, Mary trying to look up old relatives, falling on hard times, Maggie still a bairn. Mary had taken a liking for the drink, had a fall one night on the hard cobbles and been given laudanum.

'It wasnae my fault,' she says. 'I just liked the stuff. Life was hard. And it made things softer around the edges.'

The Show Woman

She had taken to working the streets, living hand to mouth, the occasional rich benefactor making life easy for a few days or even a few weeks.

'That's when we got the lockets,' says Mary. 'Rich old man from the west end, liked a bit of the rough stuff but he paid well. He bought them for me, real silver they were, and paid for Maggie and me to have our pictures taken, too. Looking back, I think he had his eye on Maggie.'

At sixteen years old it was Maggie's turn to run away. Said she was going to join a circus, just like the one her daddy had run. Wouldn't live the life her mammy was living.

'I knew she'd come to Vinegarhill. We'd visited the winter fairs here; she always loved it. So when I came to find her, discovered she'd already shacked up with Joe Loveridge, I wondered why I hadn't done the same thing myself.'

And so Mary had hung around the shows, taken up with and eventually married Billy Weaver, an old pal of Joe Loveridge, and the two women's lives had remained inextricably linked.

'She didn't want anyone to know our past,' says Mary, baring her rotten, yellowing teeth. 'Joe must have thought she'd been conjured up in a puff of smoke. And so of course, I thought I could use that to my advantage. Every week she'd have to give some of their takings to me, or I'd blab the whole story to Joe. You could call it blackmail, I suppose, although I preferred to think of it as a business transaction.'

For years the two families had trundled round the fairs circuit, sometimes together, sometimes apart.

'I knew Maggie was itching to get away for good, particularly as you got older,' says Mary. 'She'd talk about going down to England, joining the fairs in Yorkshire or

Cumbria, but Joe wasn't keen. Scotsman through and through, that one.'

Mary stops knitting and stands up, goes to the door and opens it. 'All quiet out there,' she says, as a smattering of rain lands on her skirts. She shuts the door again and this time Lena can see she has locked it, put the key down her stout cleavage.

'Ach, well, the truth of the matter is, hen, I got greedy. Started asking for more and more money. Joe couldn't understand it. Where their takings were going. He was never good with the pennies but even he could see that he and Maggie were struggling. Caused a fair few rows.

'I was old when I had Belle, too old to be having more bairns really, and the pain afterwards was unbearable. So I went back on the laudanum. It was easy really. Billy was away all summer with the fairs and the older weans while I stayed back with the babby, so I could do what I liked. Only, Violet got canny to it. Asked me why I always looked like I was about to fall asleep.'

An old memory swims into Lena's mind. An autumn evening, fires crackling across the showground just weeks after the end of the season, the last full one with her mother. Lena tucked up in the Weavers' wagon with Violet, and Mary standing over them, havering about ghosties and ghouls, tiny flecks of spittle landing on the blankets. At the time they had giggled, thought it was funny, Violet's mammy having a silly turn. Now Lena sees that she must have been out of her mind.

'Your mammy found me that day in Galston in their wagon, rooting through their things. I had decided to come out on the road with Billy that year; it was an awful mistake, and I had the jitters bad. I was desperate, hen. You have to understand that. I'd heard there was someone in Galston could help me out, a doctor, and I needed

The Show Woman

something to sell. I had her locket in my hand when she found me.'

She pauses, looks down at her knitting. The needles have stopped.

'It's funny. Couldn't bring myself to sell my own. It was a wee reminder of the good life. So I thought I'd sell hers instead. But no, she wasn't having it. Said that was enough now. She didn't care any more who knew I was her mother, just wanted the world to know I was a wrong 'un. A thief. That I'd been on the streets to get by. She would tell Billy, and Joe, and Harry and all the weans. Even you. And she wasn't going to let me have that locket. Wanted to leave it to you. So she snatched it out of my hands and went haring off towards the stables.'

Lena swallows hard. 'So what did you do?' It comes out as a hoarse whisper.

'We got into a little tussle, when I found her. Fell into the stream, the pair of us. Soaking wet, we were. And then there was nothing for it but to hold her under until she stopped wriggling. I took her away into the woods after that, left her under a big pile of leaves and sticks. She was heavier than she looked, I can tell you. But I knew the police wouldn't look for her for long, if they even looked for her at all. People like us, the law doesn't pay much attention.'

Lena holds in a sob, thinks of her mammy bidding her goodbye that bright, sparkling day all those years ago. The pat on her cheek. The beautiful blue shawl. She had only been going for apples, she said. Lena finds herself wondering if she had already bought them when she went to meet Mary, was thinking about how they would share them that night, back in their cosy wagon. Her hand flies to her mouth.

'Of course your daddy wouldn't let it lie. I was always telling him he had to forget about Maggie, move on, find someone new. That's why I sent the letter. He'd been poking his nose in at Galston, and I felt I had to put a stop to it. It was only years later I remembered that Maggie didn't read or write, what with being a circus bairn, rather than a city girl like me. And I realised you'd never told him, that you'd kept quiet. Otherwise he'd have kicked up hell. That's why I know you won't be telling anyone this time either. You'll keep your counsel, won't you? You always have. And after all, who would listen to a wee show woman with no family and no show, eh, love?'

Lena springs to her feet. 'Don't you "love" me!' she says. 'You ended everything. You killed my mammy. My poor, lovely mammy. Your own daughter!'

'Except she wasn't really, by then,' says Mary. 'She'd disowned me a long time before. Ashamed of me, she was. Of us. Of all of it. There's a lesson in there for you, hen.'

Lena flings her arms out towards Mary but the old woman, surprisingly spry, is too quick for her. She is on her feet in a flash, brandishing the knitting needles.

'Come one step closer and I'll stick these in your eye,' she says, and she bares her teeth. There is a granite hardness in her voice. 'You're too much like your mammy, I can see that now. Too concerned with what's right and what's wrong. I might have known she'd produce a poor specimen like you.'

Lena kicks at Mary's heels and the woman doubles over, her hands still grasping the needles.

'Oh, you're a vicious wee bitch, are you? Your mammy fought too, you know. But I was too strong for her. I always was. She was never going to get the best of me.'

She lashes out with the knitting needle, catches Lena on the arm. Lena pulls it away, sees it is bleeding, looks round blindly for a weapon and snatches up an old cooking pot.

The Show Woman

For the first time she feels a visceral fear. This woman has killed before. She could easily kill again.

'Stay away from me,' she shouts.

Which is when the hammering on the door starts up.

'Mum? Mum, is that you? Are you alright? What's happening in there?'

It is Harry. Both women freeze. The blood is running from Lena's arm now, pooling into her palm.

'Aye I'm alright, son,' says Mary. But her voice is wavering, weak. She is breathing heavily. The fight has taken it out of her.

There is a crash at the door and it bulges dangerously. Another bang, a click, and Harry falls through it and into the wagon. He looks first at his mother, still brandishing the knitting needles, and then at Lena, cowering in the corner, saucepan in hand, berry-red blood rushing from her open wound.

'Jesus Christ!' says Harry. 'What the hell has been happening here?'

'I don't know, son,' says Mary quickly, her breath recovering. 'Lena here just came barging in, made all sorts of accusations. Then she cut herself.'

Lena is on her knees now, shaking violently. She drops the saucepan, shakes her head.

'No,' she whispers. 'No, no, no.'

Harry comes to her, bends down. 'Let me see that arm.'

She holds it out, and he feels in his pocket for a handkerchief and ties it round the wound in a makeshift tourniquet.

'There,' he says. 'That ought to stop the bleeding for now.'

'She's mad,' Mary is saying behind him. 'Doolally. Gone round the twist.'

Lena shakes her head, sobbing now, willing Harry to believe her. 'She killed my mother,' she says in a low voice, and she grips on to Harry's shoulder. 'She killed her. Please believe me, Harry. She killed her. She just told me. She drowned her in the stream, that day back in Galston.'

'Don't listen to her, Harry,' says Mary. Her voice is hard now, dangerous. 'She's away with the fairies.'

Harry stands up, turns towards his stepmother.

'Where have you been, any road?' she says. 'Three days you've been away, not a word. What have you been up to, eh, son?'

Harry's clothes are rumpled and dirty. He looks as though he hasn't slept in a couple of nights. There is a cut under his left eye.

'Never you mind. I think you need to tell me everything,' he says, and in one graceful movement he swipes the knitting needles out of his stepmother's pudgy, grasping hand.

Glasgow Evening Times
15 February 1911

GLASGOW SHOW WOMAN ARRESTED ON CHARGE OF KILLING OWN DAUGHTER

At Vinegarhill Showground yesterday, show woman Mary Linden Weaver was arrested on suspicion of the murder of her daughter, Maggie Loveridge, née Linden, twelve years previously.

The circumstances are somewhat peculiar, the show woman having allegedly confessed all to the victim's daughter, her own granddaughter, before stabbing her with a knitting needle, but causing only minor injuries.

The victim's daughter confronted Mary Weaver, who told her that she had, at a fairground in Galston, in Ayrshire, drowned the victim in a stream, before burying her body in nearby woods, in a row over money.

Police in Galston are said to be investigating. Mary Weaver was charged at today's court, and remanded pending an inquiry.

49

The mystery of faith

Each day the light lingers a little bit longer, as if reluctant to drain the darkening skies. Lena finds she no longer needs the woollen coat that once belonged to her mother to battle through the cold days but she wears it still, fingering the frayed cuffs, cherishing its thin warmth around her shoulders.

Mary's arrest is the talk of the steamie. A steady line of showmen and women beat a path to the door of Lena's wagon, ostensibly to pay their respects but mostly to hear the gossip. One old woman she has never seen before says Mary was never off the bad stuff, oh, the stories she could tell about that woman, she should have been in the asylum and no mistake.

Old Billy Weaver's brother Donald comes to see her, cap in hand, and says that Billy was always a nice lad, but never too bright, and he wasn't surprised he couldn't see what was so clearly under his nose. Had he seen it, then? Lena asks. And he turns his cap in his hand like the wheel on a motor car and says no, miss, he hadn't.

Esmeralda the fortune-teller materialises on the doorstep trailing chiffon and a deep, musky scent, informing Lena she'd always known Mary Weaver was a murderer, and had she considered there might be a second victim?

Lena endures their visits, pours tea, listens, nods. She tells them she is shocked, that she could never have imagined Mary capable of such a thing, or, indeed, that the woman was her grandmother. It is true, to a point.

But what she really feels is numb. Cold. As though her heart has been replaced by one of the chips of sea glass that Morag brings for Belle, sharp edges worn away by the swells of the ocean, blurred into un-being.

At night her dreams are of running rivers and coal carts. Her mother's face, contorted in fear under the water, cherry-red blood pluming beneath the current.

To her amazement the policeman who came that day after Harry heard the whole sorry tale from his stepmother, her hiccupping and asking forgiveness at every step, had been kind, and interested. His own mother had been a show woman, it turned out, born right here in Vinegarhill. But his daddy died and they'd taken a flat in a tenement and well, he said, that was the end of that.

He and another copper had taken Mary away to the police station, and then to court. It seemed unlikely she would be coming back. That, at least, was a relief.

Lena expected that Belle would take it the hardest, would weep for the loss of her mammy, no matter what it was she had done, but in fact the young girl is silent, blank-faced. She seems more interested in her trapeze than ever now, and Rosie tells her she has talent. Lena promises herself she will go and see her practise some time, when she is up to it.

One afternoon as she sits in the caravan counting her dwindling number of pennies – so few now, it frightens her – she hears someone outside calling her name.

'Miss Loveridge? Are you there?'

She opens the door to find the policeman, Sergeant Cooper, standing in front of the caravan in his uniform, brass buttons glinting in the late winter sun.

'I've come with some news, miss,' he says. He takes his hat off, and with a lurch of dread, Lena realises what he is about to tell her.

The Show Woman

'You've found her, haven't you.' It isn't a question.

He nods.

'Yesterday, miss. She was – well, she was where the Weaver woman said she would be. I'm very sorry.'

'Thank you,' says Lena. Her hand strays to her throat where her mother's locket rests. 'Will I get her back?'

'Yes, miss. Not immediately, but you will. Then you can make arrangements.'

'Thank you,' she says.

After he has gone she sits on the caravan steps, a hollow emptiness surging through her bones. Bones, that's all her mother will be now. Even after Mary's confession, she had still nursed a kernel of hope. All those years she had spent believing her mother was still alive, thinking the letter stood as some sort of proof. Even now, it is hard to let go.

And the secrets. The secret her mother kept about who her own mother was. The secret Lena had kept from her father about the letter. What if her mammy had spoken up? What if she had? Now, the silence and the subterfuge all seem so pointless.

One morning, head bent against the wind, ignoring the curious stares, Lena sets out for Miss Sibyl's caravan, on the far corner of the ground.

The fortune-teller is sitting outside drinking a cup of tea, shorn of her usual headdress of golden coins, her face spidered with lines in the harsh daylight. She looks up as Lena approaches, says nothing.

'Can we talk?' asks Lena.

To her surprise the woman smiles at her. 'I always hoped you'd come back,' she says. 'Come away in.'

Inside, her wagon is painted ruby-red and emerald-green, like a Christmas tree. Her crystal ball sits on the windowsill, its contents clouded and perfectly still.

'Take a seat,' she says. 'I won't be charging you.'

Lena sits down on the small day bed, plump with feather-stuffed cushions. Miss Sibyl clearly does well enough at the shows to make a nice home for herself. Lena admires it. Her taste. Her independence. It's what she had vaguely imagined for herself once, in those heady days of the previous summer.

'What did you know, that day I came to see you?' she asks. 'What did you see? I mean, I take it you know what's happened. About Mary Weaver. About my mother.'

The last word comes out as a small, constrained sob.

'I do,' says Sibyl. Her eyes are kind. 'I heard about it all. It's a terrible business and I must tell you I am so very sorry about your mammy. She was a lovely lady. We used to travel the same routes when you were a wee bairn, and she always had a kind word for me. She even came to see me once for a reading.'

Lena stiffens. 'And did you see anything? Did you see what might happen to her?'

Sibyl straightens her skirts, stands up, and brings her crystal ball over to the small table in front of them.

'What you have to understand is that this gift I have, the second sight, it's not always clear. It's not like watching a cinematograph, or playing a memory in your head. Sometimes I get a fragment. A single image. And sometimes it's just a feeling.'

Lena nods. Tries to understand.

'When your mammy came to me I knew she was carrying secrets. She didn't want to tell me what they were, but I knew she had them. And then, as we were talking, I felt cold all over. As though I was freezing, and I couldn't breathe. As though my heart was doing its best to pump blood, keep my fingers and toes moving, but the rest of me had given up. Gone numb. I've only ever had that feeling

The Show Woman

once before, and, well, the lad died. Thrown from a horse three days later.'

Lena sits, spellbound, gazing at a spot of red paint on the green wall ahead of her.

'So when it happened with your mammy, I said nothing. I was scared for her, and I didn't want her to live her life in fear. And anyway, whatever it was, it could have been years away. We all die some time, don't we? Who was I to put the fear of God or—' she waves her hands towards the ceiling '—whoever is up there, into her?'

'When was this?' asks Lena. 'When did she come to see you?'

Sibyl swallows hard, looks down at the still glass of her ball.

'It was in Galston,' she says. 'The day before she went missing.'

Lena feels a chill spread through her own bones, wonders if that is what Sibyl had felt that day. What her own mammy felt down there in the water, under the rushing current.

'After that, after I heard about your mammy disappearing, I decided that no matter what I felt, or saw, when people came to see me, I had to tell them. Even if it upset them. That's why I warned you last summer, in Aberdeen. I could see danger was coming for you; I had an image in my mind of a woman holding something sharp. So I tried to tell you. But you did what many people did. You ran away. That's the thing about these predictions. People don't want to hear them.'

She reaches over and pats Lena's arm with a warm, dry hand.

'I'm glad you tried,' says Lena. 'Maybe it made me a wee bit wary. Thank you.'

Sibyl smiles sadly. 'I just wish I'd been able to do more for your mammy.'

★

The church, when she comes upon it, is of a cheerful red sandstone. She had not meant to walk so far, past the scorching wail of the Gorbals, through the city centre and into a wide, hushed square of tall grand houses, where motor cars sit idle on cobbled streets, maids scurry about in smart white aprons and caps and a man in a three-piece suit bends down to brush an immaculate front step. Down a hill past Sauchiehall Street, busy with carts and trams, businessmen hurrying home from work, and up another hill to this peculiar building, a steep stair that takes her on to a wide sweeping terrace.

She stands for a moment, unsure of herself in the looming dusk. A lady touches her arm. 'Are you here for Mass, dear?'

The woman is elderly, with a puckered face and soft, rheumy eyes. She is wearing an enormous hat covered in lilac flowers. And, for reasons that Lena cannot quite answer, she nods, and follows her inside.

The church is cool and quiet. Candles flicker on the long altar, sheeted in white. A vast golden sun with three letters in the middle sprawls across a high wall, while above it a dome opens up, revealing eight high arches of coloured glass. On sunny days it must look as though God himself is sending shards of light down on to the cross that sits, impassive, on the altar below.

Lena follows the old lady down the long aisle, hears her own steps echoing, before darting into a pew. And there in front of her, next to a pillar of sea-green marble, is Carmen.

She is deep in prayer, kneeling on the hard wooden bench before her, rosary beads clasped between her fingers, silently mouthing words that Lena would not be able to understand, even if she could hear them.

Throughout that strange, beautiful Mass, where a priest, sheathed in angelic white, sings the liturgy and reads from gospels, commands his altar boys to swing burning,

The Show Woman

fragrant pots of incense, a peace descends over Lena. She does not comprehend what is being said, and does not try to, and yet it soothes her aching, battered soul. When the priest holds up a goblet and sings haunting words in Latin, she swallows a small sob.

At the end, Lena waits in her pew until Carmen rises, turns and makes her way down the aisle. When she sees her she freezes, then tries to hurry past, but the lady in the lilac hat is having a long conversation with the priest and a queue has formed.

'Carmen,' says Lena, and grasps her gently by the arm. 'Please talk to me.'

They walk down Sauchiehall Street together. It is dark now, and the shadows are narrow and long. Lena tells Carmen about Rosie's father, and Mary Weaver, and how it was she all along who had killed her mother.

'So you and Violet were sisters?' she asks. 'That makes so much sense. You looked after each other. Cared for each other. Fought with each other. Hated each other, at times. You always seemed like sisters to me.'

'Not actually sisters; but yes, we were family. Who is caring for you now, Carmen?' Lena asks.

Carmen stops. 'Don't,' she says. 'I will be just fine.'

'What would you have done if you'd had the baby? Would you have tried to find Harry?'

Carmen shrugs. 'Perhaps. I don't know. I doubt it would have been a good marriage, though. He is not . . .' she hesitates '. . . my type. That is how you say it, yes?'

They sit down on a bench. Opposite them, a drunk in a battered brown coat is snoring gently, an empty bottle clutched in his hand.

'But I know he is yours. And it sounds as if he has been good to you. You should go back to him. Make something

good from all this sadness. All this death. Oh, but wait . . .'
She frowns.

'Mary was his stepmother; we're not related,' says Lena, smiling. 'You're good at advice, you know that?'

Carmen laughs, shrugs. 'I like to tell people what to do.'

'Can I give you some advice, then, just for a change?'

Carmen furrows her eyebrows. 'Alright.'

'Come back to the circus. I've been thinking about it. There's a new season starting and Rosie's still at Vinegarhill with Tommy Pony. And I've got my eye on a new trapeze artist. But we need you, Carmen. With your flute, and your costumes. The crowds loved you. I know it won't be the same without Violet but it's just like you said. We need to make something good from all this sadness. All this death. You can't stay at the rat pit forever.'

Carmen nods slowly, gives her a small smile.

'I'll think about it,' she says, and from her pocket she produces the rainbow ribbon Lena gave her in the rat pit, and winds it round her finger. 'I never stopped thinking about it.'

Opposite them the drunk wakes with a start, and the bottle drops with a great crash to the ground.

*The Stage 24
February 1911*

FROM OUR SCOTLAND CORRESPONDENT

The circus world is in mourning in the far north this week after the death was announced of Miss Serena Linden, Scots show woman and proprietor of Royal Linden's Circus.

Miss Linden, who was a favourite of the late Queen Victoria and whose circus performed several times at Balmoral Castle, where Her Majesty gifted her with a jewellery box and exquisite brooches as a mark of her affection, died in the town of Crieff, in Perthshire, after an illness.

Linden's Circus was particularly famous for its 'Bobo the clown' act, its elephants, its magnificent lions, and for Violet Weaver, 'the greatest trapeze artist who ever lived', who came to a sad end in the River Clyde earlier this year.

It is believed that the circus will continue under the proprietorship of Miss Linden's son Benjamin, currently touring with Saffo's Circus in the south of England.

50

Plumes

Rosie is knitting a baby's hat. A letter has arrived. Jennifer has been safely delivered of a little girl. She and Richard are still deciding upon a name.

Several times she has been on the verge of packing up, leaving this place for good, and returning to her sister. She is still in one of the old Weaver wagons, and, although Harry has assured her that it is hers for as long as she wants it, she feels awkward here, out of place. This was never her world, after all. Sometimes she wonders what on earth she was doing, trying to make it her own.

The knitting needles click in the silence. How could Mary Weaver be capable of such cruelty? Lena has shown her the picture of her mother, and she cannot imagine the evil that must have coursed through Mary's veins, to make her take that life away.

Every day she fears a knock on the door from her father. But it has not come. Harry has told her not to worry, that he would have been by now, so why worry about something that's probably not going to happen? But still, she keeps up a fearful watch.

She lays down her needles and goes to the window. It has stopped raining. Time to feed Tommy Pony. She has spent more time with him recently, even taken him down the Gallowgate on quiet mornings before she is due at the factory. He has never done well with the cold, or being shut up. If only Lena were to bring the circus back together. Get out on the road for the summer. Would it be possible? Belle is coming along well on the trapeze, and would surely enjoy getting out of this dark, miserable place after everything that has happened with her mother.

Rosie wonders what little Belle went through with Mary during those long stretches when it was just the two of them in that wagon. Her sullen, blank face, her curious habits, her endearing friendship with Morag, her gift of the second sight – they all seem to make a little more sense now.

And perhaps Violet, too, makes a little more sense. The way she could lash out. Her sharp tongue and quick temper. Rosie was one of the few who saw her soft underbelly, the quietness that stilled in her heart, but even she knew how harsh Violet could be. Perhaps it was all her mother's fault. A woman who could murder her own daughter must surely have instilled fear in the hearts of her remaining children, even if they didn't know the true nature of the evil that squatted inside her.

She pictures the show again, tries to imagine it without Violet, or Carmen. They would need new acts, posters to advertise for them. Would Lena want that? After all that has happened?

She heads across the showground to the stables. The grass is soft and wet underfoot, and camp fires have started up, plumes of woodsmoke rising lazily into the sky.

'Rosie?'

She turns around in fear. But it is not her father's voice.

'Carmen?'

Her beautiful Spanish friend is standing in front of her, carrying a small suitcase, a red flower in her hair.

'What do you say, little Rosie?' she says. 'Will you have me back?'

51

Blooms

March arrives, dewy and brisk. It will soon be a full year since Lena's father died and once more the showground is stirring into life, its occupants becoming restless, ready to break free of the invisible tethers that tie them to the city in winter.

Lena knows she must make a decision, and soon. Either it is time to create a new ladies' circus, try out Belle on the trapeze, engage Rosie and Carmen – who has already moved into Rosie's wagon – for another season, or move on. To where, she does not know, for thoughts of the future seem so clouded and uncertain that they have paralysed her.

The nice policeman has returned, once more, and informed her that her mother's remains will be brought back to her in a few days' time. She has spoken to William Weaver, Mary's eldest stepson, who has insisted on paying for the funeral, and organising it too.

'I'm sorry,' he keeps saying to Lena, as though all of it, any of it, were his fault. 'Harry and I always struggled with Mary. She wasn't our real mother and she never really bothered with us. But then she was so harsh with Violet that we were quite grateful, just kept out of her way. Particularly when she'd been drinking.'

It is a long speech for a man whom Lena has never really known, and who always kept his counsel. She is grateful. And weary.

Three days before the funeral Harry catches her at the showground gates as she is coming in with fresh carrots and mutton, ingredients for a simple stew. He looks smart, a suit in tweed and a dark bunnet on his head, the cut on his eye now healed. He has a horse with him she has never seen before.

'Hello, girl,' she says, giving the chestnut mare a pat. 'Where did Harry get you from, eh?'

'She was going cheap at a market. You can never have too many horses. I'm just about to put her in the stables and then I have to head up town.'

'Going somewhere nice?' she asks.

He smiles shyly. 'Maybe,' he says. 'It depends if you'll come with me.'

The tram is noisy, windows steaming up on the inside as they approach the city centre and mothers and children pile on, bags of messages with them, the occasional gentleman hopping from one important meeting to the next. But the crowd thins out as they head up Great Western Road, a wide, long street with grand sandstone mansions on either side.

They are up west now, where the houses have double-fronted doors and the ladies wear elegant French lace. They walk slowly down clean streets with parasols and small dogs, while maids with necks bent scuttle guardedly behind them.

'Here,' says Harry, pulling the bell. They jump off the tram. Ahead of them is a busy junction, and on one side there are two curious red brick buildings on either side of a smart iron gate. At first Lena thinks it must be a gentleman's estate. She has seen plenty of them on the road over the years, towering gateposts guarding long, tree-lined drives, but, as she looks closer, people are strolling into the grounds. A lady with her maid, a nanny with a baby carriage, behind them, a flock of stately young women.

The Show Woman

'Come on,' says Harry, as they walk through the gateposts and into a park. The grass is neatly cut and slopes down a gentle hill, and here and there townspeople sit perched on rugs, or, for the less fancy, old newspapers. There are oak trees flushed with new leaves, and vast bushels of daffodils nodding in the spring sunshine.

'That's our destination,' says Harry, pointing to a glasshouse, its dome veined in white, at the top of the hill.

'What is it?'

'It's a palace. But the kind that opens its doors to everyone. Even the likes of us.'

He opens the door to a wall of heat. Stepping in, Lena is amazed. It is like high summer in here, one of those endless days when the air feels like liquid. And the silence – the sort she has only ever heard in the country, deep and rich. She could melt into it. There are flowers everywhere. A little fountain of trickling water, huge orange fish moving languidly beneath the ripples at its base.

They move through the glasshouse, Harry holding his good tweed cap in his hands. They marvel at the tall, exotic palms, the violently pink and purple orchids, flowers all the colours of a rainbow. Bright bursts of blue, smatterings of orange and yellow. Lena stops at an orchid of pale violet, examines its delicate oval petals, each one flecked with tiny smatters of gold, a fragile stamen at its heart. She has never seen anything so exquisitely formed in her life.

'It's beautiful,' she says. 'How did you find this place?'

'Ah, that would be telling. My little secret. But I wanted to share it with you. These flowers – they're not quite a red, red rose, but . . .' He tails off.

Lena looks back at the flower. She is desperate to touch it, to see if it feels as she thinks it will, soft and velvety. Instead she settles for its scent, breathes long and deep, inhaling its rich sweetness.

Harry is watching her intently.

'I know you've had a terrible time,' he says. 'And I'm sorry.'

'Everyone keeps saying that to me.'

'But I am. I'm sorry I didn't keep a closer eye on Violet. I'm sorry about Carmen. I'm sorry about my awful excuse for a stepmother. And I'm sorry about us.'

Lena turns to him.

'Was there ever really an us?' she asks.

'Well, I thought there could have been. I was thinking about it. That it could be a possibility, you and me. And I think there could be now.'

He turns to face her, lifts his hand to her cheek.

'I'd really love there to be an us,' he says quietly.

And perhaps it is the heat, and the softness it infuses into her bones. Or perhaps it is that she is weary of carrying her heart alone, wants to hand it over to this earnest, kind, flawed man to cherish and take care of. Or perhaps it is that she has always known that it was Harry. Only Harry.

But there, in the glasshouse, on a cold afternoon three days before her mother's funeral, Lena kisses him. And everything else melts away.

Ayrshire Advertiser
12 March 1911

AYR FARMER FOUND DEAD

Police were called last week after an Ayrshire farmer, James Carluke, was found dead near a country lane around three miles from his farm at Mainholm. The man had sustained injuries after being thrown from his horse, which is presumed to have bolted.

The farmer, well known in the area and in the drinking dens of the nearby town, was said to have left his family two months earlier, and has not been seen since. His wife said she assumed he had gone drinking, and had perhaps fallen in the river. His horse has not been found.

James Carluke is survived by his wife Mabel, his daughters Rose and Jennifer, and a granddaughter, Rose Violet Wright, born two weeks ago.

52

Long love

And so they come. The showmen come, and the show women come, and the fortune-tellers and the sweetie wives and the acrobats and the horse-riders and the carousel-operators and the menagerie-owners and the jugglers and the hawkers and the boxers and the cinematographers and the whole, bristling multitude.

Down Gallowgate streams the procession, thick with mourning, showmen in black bearing the coffin aloft, heads down, until the traffic stops and a deep, reverent hush falls across the city, the only sound to be heard the creak of worn leather shoes on the cobbles.

And on a sunlit morning in March, as wild primroses creep from the earth and the blackbirds strike up a tender chorus, Lena buries her mother.

Maggie will lie next to her husband in this quiet corner of the showground, two lovers reunited in death, brought together by the daughter they adored. A final, chosen resting place.

The crowd grows still as Lena scatters earth on the coffin, lays a bloom of lavender on its lid, turns to let the gravedigger do his duty.

There are three empty chambers in Lena's heart now. One for her father, one for her mother, and one for Violet. She will keep them that way. For it is in those hollow spaces that her love for them blossoms, untouched by time, unbruised by its turbulence, lengthening with the days. She will find them again, her three lost loves, back out on the road. For her father can always be found in the long, curving bend of a country track, in the redolence of a summer's morning after rainfall. Her mother in the swaying of a lavender crop in a soundless field, in the scent of a ripe apple at a fair stall on a hot day.

And Violet, her daring, beautiful sort of sister, will be there in the air above her. For in leaving the earth Violet has become one with the sky, its every rippling breeze, its squally nights and its stillness, soaring eternally upwards.

Lena stands for a moment in the swell of the crowd, an immovable point of light amid the whirl and the clatter, a single sprig of lavender clutched to her heart. Time for the road now. Time to go home.

THE LAST WILL AND TESTAMENT OF SERENA ELIZABETH LINDEN
11 February 1911

I, Serena Elizabeth Linden, Circus Proprietor of no fixed abode, currently residing in Crieff, in order to prevent disputes after my death, do hereby make over to and in favour of my niece, Miss Lena Loveridge, of Vinegarhill Showground, 917 Gallowgate, Glasgow, my whole estates heritable, including the entirety of Linden's Circus and all businesses therein.

Signed:
Serena Elizabeth Linden
X

Arthur Steven McClaverty, witness
Arthur Steven McClaverty

Acknowledgements

This book would not exist without my Mum, Vivienne. Over long conversations about the incredible women in our family who worked in Scotland's fairgrounds, she encouraged me to start weaving stories around the known fragments of their lives, many of them gleaned from her own childhood memories. For a long time my first and only reader, she knew before I did that there was, in fact, a book in it. Thank you for everything, Mum.

To my brilliant agent Amanda Harris, who believed in this novel from day one and loves its characters with as much ferocity as I do, who always has the right advice and the best words of guidance. Thank you for changing my life.

To my exceptional editor Jo Dickinson, who saw something special in my sparkly Edwardian women's circus, and whose deft hand brought out the best in my characters, and my writing. To Katie Espiner, Vicky Palmer and the whole team at Hodder & Stoughton for your passion, creativity and championing of this book. To Alainna Hadjigeorgiou and Kallie Townsend – the publicity dream team! To Ella Young and Emily Harrison for marketing magic. To Saffron Stocker for art direction on the glorious cover design, and Frieda Ruh for such beautiful illustration and lettering. My gratitude also to Kate Norman and copy editor Linda McQueen. To Samara MacLaren for bringing my ladies' circus thrillingly to life in the audiobook.

To Sara Cox and the Cheshire Novel Prize, without whom I'd still be on Chapter 10. Thank you for all your encouragement and advice, and for creating something unique that lifts up so many aspiring writers in the process. To Caroline Ambrose and the Bath Novel Award for seeing this novel's early potential and for continued support, and to the Blue Pencil First Novel Award for the precious longlisting.

To my dear Cheshire Cats, this past two years down the rabbit hole with you all has been such an adventure. It's a privilege to be part of such an incredible and supportive group of writers who are there for both the ups, and the downs.

To Kate Foster, for encouraging me to enter a competition for unpublished writers, patient advice and giving me that much-needed 'wee nudge'.

To David Mitchell who, at my first, nerve-wracking event as an author, generously took the time to reassure this trembling debut she wasn't an imposter, even if she felt like it.

To my former colleagues at the Scottish Daily Mail for your support, and the greatest send off a journalist could imagine.

To Anna, Kate and Kerry for being my steadfast, lifelong coven.

To Karen. How I miss our chats about books, and life. I wish you could have read this.

To Gordon and Alison for advice, encouragement, and all the hospital visits.

To Averil and Glyn for your love, kindness and enthusiasm, and for lending me your dining room table during that frenetic week of edits.

To Nick, Alex, Rebecca and Louis for support that stretches far beyond the confines of writing this book, and to Sienna and Henry for reminding me what really matters.

To Moses the cat for fluffy cuddles and only sitting on the keyboard 673 times during the writing of this book.

To my Great Aunt Violet, whose extraordinary early life as a bareback horse rider and trapeze artist inspired this novel and who just might, if she were around today, wonder what all the fuss was about.

To my beloved and much-missed Dad, Ian, who always encouraged my writing and my dreams, and made me the person I am today.

And finally to my husband, Jonathan, who always believed I should write a novel, and in the end, practically insisted on it. Who kept me accountable throughout the writing process, read an early draft of this book and offered wise, clear advice. I could not have done this without your love and support. Thank you for being by my side, in writing, and in life.

My name is Emerald, like the stone.
Turn me towards the light and I glitter.

I am one of the good girls. That's what they say in the papers. Emerald Vane, the Gaiety Theatre's brightest new star. Emerald Vane, she outshines them all. They don't know the half of it.

For there are secrets inside this island castle's walls of pink stone. It is a place where untold things happen behind locked doors, where servants are not who they seem, where waves roil and the heavens darken and tonight, I am expected to die.

They are coming for me now, and despite my trembling hands, the muffled scream trapped in my throat, I urge them forward. Go on, I think. Turn me towards the light. Watch what happens.

The Pleasure Palace
PUBLISHING SPRING 2026